Withdrawn

Praise for

Butterfly Bayou

"Lila's strength and vulnerability are balanced by Armie's intelligence and humor, making them an easy couple to root for. Blake captures the flavor of her colorful Southern town with a vividly drawn cast. . . . This charming series opener hits all the right notes." —*Publishers Weekly*

Praise for

Lexi Blake

"Lexi Blake is a master!"
—*New York Times* bestselling author Jennifer Probst

"I love Lexi Blake."
—*New York Times* bestselling author Lee Child

"Smart, savvy, clever, and always entertaining."
—*New York Times* bestselling author Steve Berry

"Lexi Blake has set up shop on the intersection of suspenseful and sexy, and I never want to leave."
—*New York Times* bestselling author Laurelin Paige

Titles by Lexi Blake

THE BUTTERFLY BAYOU NOVELS

Butterfly Bayou
Bayou Baby

THE COURTING JUSTICE NOVELS

Order of Protection
Evidence of Desire

THE LAWLESS NOVELS

Ruthless
Satisfaction
Revenge

THE PERFECT GENTLEMEN NOVELS
(with Shayla Black)

Scandal Never Sleeps
Seduction in Session
Big Easy Temptation

Bayou Baby

Lexi Blake

JOVE
New York

A JOVE BOOK
Published by Berkley
An imprint of Penguin Random House LLC
penguinrandomhouse.com

ISBN: 9781984806581

First Edition: August 2020

Printed in the United States of America
1   3   5   7   9   10   8   6   4   2

Cover image of home © Image Professionals GmbH / Alamy Stock Photo
Cover design by Vikki Chu
Book design by Alison Cnockaert

This book is about babies, so I lovingly
dedicate it to my own babies.
For Dylan and Lindsey and Zoey.

chapter one

❧

"Have you seen the new guy?"

Seraphina Guidry glanced over at her best friend. Hallie Rayburn had slid in next to her a few moments before, and she was practically vibrating with excitement. Gossip. The whole town ran on it. The good news was Sera loved some juicy gossip. "New guy?"

She kept her voice down in deference to the crowd around them.

"I got a look at him last night at the Piggly Wiggly," Hallie explained in a hushed voice. "I had to go buy diapers because Johnny said he would pick them up but then he forgot and blamed it all on breathing in fumes from the rig. He knows I'm scared of that. Anyway, he was napping with Gracie despite the fact that child smelled to high heaven. I think the oil rig has permanently ruined the man's sense of smell."

If Sera didn't get Hallie back on track, her bestie would end up giving a speech about how Johnny wasn't paid enough to work on a rig since it would give him every kind of cancer and there really probably were crazy sea creatures that would eat him one day. She should never have let

Hallie watch that mutant shark movie. "You were talking about the new guy."

If houses were towns, Papillon, Louisiana, would be one of those tiny houses where the bedroom was also the kitchen. And in a super-small town, anyone new was the focus of immediate gossip. The town had really buzzed when Gene Boudreaux's eighty-two-year-old friend from Facebook had come for a visit.

Hallie nodded and glanced around as if looking to see whether anyone was listening. "So I was in the baby section of the Piggly Wiggly and I decided to take a walk, you know, look at the expensive vegetables I can never get Johnny to eat. I kind of fondle them, to be honest. But then I looked up and there he was in that weird section where they keep the kids' toys and the tools. According to what I've heard, he's some kind of contractor and the hardware store had closed and he needed a hammer or something. I don't know. I needed a cold shower after I saw him."

"Hallie, you're married." Sera felt the need to point that out because she knew quite well everyone was listening. Well, everyone who could hear them, which was hopefully not a lot of people.

"I'm married but I can still appreciate a work of art," Hallie replied in a whisper. "That man glows. He has all those muscles Hollywood stars have, and when he smiled at me, I actually stammered. Me. I was the most popular cheerleader at Armstrong High and I couldn't talk to the man. I nodded and ran away with my diapers and a bunch of asparagus I'll have to eat myself. He's beautiful."

"Are you talking about that Harrison fellow?" Sera's mother leaned in. Delphine Dellacourt Guidry was in her late sixties, but there were days Sera thought she couldn't keep up with her momma's never-ending energy and zest for life. "Because Sylvie told Marcelle that he was the prettiest man she'd ever seen. Zep is up in arms because, let's face facts, his looks are all he has."

"Momma," she replied in a hushed whisper because Zep was her brother and he could be sensitive.

Zep leaned in from behind her. "Nah, that's fair. Look, there's always a trade-off. I couldn't be both stunningly handsome and super smart. That wouldn't be right. But I did get a look at the man and he wasn't all that pretty. Definitely not prettier than me. He's got a prominent forehead. I think that means he's close to our Neanderthal ancestors."

"You understand neither human evolution nor what women want. He's so much prettier than you," Hallie argued.

"He is." Her sister-in-law, Lisa, sat behind them as well. "He came into Guidry's last night and I swear women gawked. Not kidding. I thought Merrilee Jenkins was going to have a heart attack. I have to admit, I gawked a little, too. Remy says the new guy was in the Army and he was decorated and everything because he lost a leg."

"He was decorated for bravery in battle and he happened to lose a leg," her older brother chimed in. "And can we remember where we are and what we're supposed to be doing?"

"It's all right. I'm not starting the service for a few minutes." Father Franklin leaned against the church pews. "Your great-aunt wouldn't mind. She was late for everything. Are we talking about Harrison? He seems like a fine young man, Seraphina. He's here to rebuild the grand gazebo at Beaumont House before the big wedding. He's Celeste's sister's son, though they've never visited before. I like that she's finding some family again. It's been a hard few years for her."

Because Celeste Beaumont had lost her youngest son, Wesley.

Wesley, who had been Sera's best friend growing up. Wesley, who had fathered her child. Wesley, who had died hating her.

Sometimes she could still see him and the way he'd looked at her that day. Sometimes she could barely remember what he looked like. She couldn't decide which was worse.

She forced the dark thoughts from her head. At least she tried to. It was hard because being at a funeral always made her think of Wes, and hearing the word *Army* did, too. Wes had gone into the service to get away from her.

She was the reason he'd died.

"See, he's got a good job," her mother was saying. "A carpenter always has work."

"I don't know," Hallie replied in a way that made Sera think she'd missed something. While she'd been lost in the guilt well, the conversation had gone down a whole other path. "It's been months since she's been on a date. I think this guy might be like diving into the deep end of the pool when she's forgotten how to swim."

"Nah, Sera can handle him," Zep said. "But she might not want to because she's an independent woman and I've been told they don't like to be set up on dates. Apparently they like to troll bars and find men all by themselves."

"She was having a beer," Lisa shot back like this was a well-worn argument. "She wasn't trolling for a date. And you should keep your nose out of Roxie's business. She hasn't arrested you in a while. I think it's a great idea to set up Sera and the new guy. Hallie's right. She hasn't been dating and she needs to get back out there."

Whoa. She had definitely missed something. "I am not getting set up."

"Of course not, dear." Her mother patted her hand.

"Don't think of it as a setup. You're showing the new guy around town, and if he happens to take you to a nice dinner where you put on a pretty dress and follow up dinner with some dancing, that's a plus."

"I am not going out with the new guy." The thought was horrifying. Hallie was right. She hadn't been on a single date in almost eight months. She'd put it all on hold after the Jackson Lane debacle. She'd concentrated on her son and finishing up cosmetology school and starting her business.

Turned out she pretty much hated being a hairdresser and she wasn't all that great at it, but wasn't that the story of her life? The last thing she needed was to throw a guy into the mix. She had a man in her life, and he was currently in the church's day care center probably stuffing something he shouldn't into his mouth.

Father Franklin gave her a shake of his head. He'd been the parish priest for most of her life, and the man could make her feel like she was eight years old again getting caught sneaking cookies before lunch. "God wants us to try new things, Seraphina."

"I don't think he wants me to try the new guy on for size. I'm fairly certain he's opposed to that," Sera shot back.

"Kindness is what God wants for us always," the priest said, straightening up. "Your great-aunt Irene would have told you that."

"My great-aunt Irene used to scare small children by taking out her dentures and hissing at them. She was a terrible person." The only things Irene liked in this world were her cats, and Sera was fairly certain she'd trained them to attack.

"And yet the church is filled with love for her today," the father pointed out.

"Nah." Zep waved the thought off. "They're here because Remy made a big old pot of gumbo. Guidry's is catering and these cheap bastards want a free meal."

The priest sighed as though he knew Zep wasn't salvageable. "I think you should take the passing of your dearly beloved aunt as a sign that it's time to start living. After all, Irene waited too long to find love and she died alone."

"I thought she was loved by all." Sera thought Father Franklin needed to stick to one story. "Which one is it?"

He shrugged. "Whichever will get you to keep an open mind. Though I think maybe you should wait a bit."

Her mother pointed the priest's way. "Only because your nephew is coming into town next month."

"Archie is a wonderful boy. He's going to be looking to settle down." Father Franklin backed away. "We should get together, Delphine. You know there's nothing wrong with arranged marriages. They get a bad rap."

"You are not dating that Archie boy." Her mother sat back and fanned herself with the schedule. "I heard he ran through an entire sorority at that university he went to."

"I'm not dating anyone," Sera insisted. She certainly wasn't about to get set up at her great-aunt's funeral. She didn't want to get set up at all. The last few months had been hard enough. She'd watched as her great-aunt had gotten more and more frail. And bitter. It had all fallen to her because for some reason she was the only one in the family who got along with Aunt Irene.

She'd been the one who'd dealt with the funeral home, selected the coffin, and picked out Aunt Irene's best muumuu for the funeral. She was also the one who'd found homes for sixteen cats.

Was she going to end up with sixteen cats, a closet full of housedresses, and video tapes of every episode of *Mur-*

der, She Wrote? She glanced down at the bio she'd written. It was nothing more than a list of dates. When her aunt was born. When she died. Where she graduated from high school and how long she'd worked at the DMV. A single paragraph to sum up a whole life.

Would she even need a paragraph?

"It's probably for the best," Hallie whispered because the church choir was starting to hum. "I heard that Kellie Boyce bet Jenny Halstrom that she would have Harrison Jefferys eating out of the palm of her hand within a week. You know she's been on the prowl ever since she got back into town. I also heard he won't be staying long. The rumor is he's kind of a drifter."

Her mother shook her head. "Men like that only drift until they find a reason to settle down."

"Or until the police catch up to them because they use their good looks to facilitate their murder sprees." Sera might have been watching too much *Dateline*, but she wasn't about to become a cautionary tale. Not again. She was the example every mother in town used to steer their daughters away from premarital sex. *Don't let your boyfriend go too far or you'll end up like that poor Seraphina Guidry*. She wasn't about to add being murdered to her résumé of bad choices.

"Delphine, Remy." A cool voice had Sera's head turning. Celeste Beaumont stood at the end of the pew. She was roughly her mother's age but looked younger due to regularly scheduled trips to a plastic surgeon in New Orleans. The woman was still gorgeous and still as cold as ice. "Please accept my condolences on the loss of Irene."

Her mother held her head high. "Thank you. She will be missed."

"By who?" Zep asked, earning him a hearty smack to the back of his head from Remy. "Well, she used to turn the sprinklers on kids who tried to trick or treat her house. Sorry."

"A little respect goes a long way," Celeste said, settling her Chanel bag on her arm. "That's a lesson your mother should have taught you. You'll excuse me but I should go and join my family. Again, our condolences."

Her mother shook her head as Celeste walked away. "I will show that woman respect. I will shove it right up that tight—"

"Momma," Remy interrupted. "Church."

Her mother settled back. "That woman."

Yes, that woman. Celeste Beaumont had never liked her friendship with Wes. She'd tried to keep them apart, wanting more suitable friends for her baby boy.

What would she do if she knew Luc was Wes's child? Angela was the only Beaumont who knew, and Wes's sister had been adamant about keeping the secret. Angela had been the one to save her from making the worst decision of her life. Angela was probably the reason she still had custody of her son.

Sera turned toward the pulpit as Father Franklin stepped up.

"Still, you should look at him," Hallie whispered. "Because he really is gorgeous. Is it wrong that I think it's kind of sexy that he has a fake leg? Like he's a bionic man."

"Yes. It's wrong." It was wrong to think of anything but her son and getting them to a good place.

She didn't have time to date. She needed to build a life.

She might even need to build that life somewhere else.

The priest began to speak and Zep began to snore.

Some things never changed. She needed to make sure she wasn't one of them.

*   *   *

Celeste Beaumont sank into her place on the pew beside her older son.

Her only living son.

It hadn't been so long since she'd been in this very church for Wes's funeral. Her husband's funeral had been even more recent, but it was Wes's service that haunted her. Ralph's death had been . . . she hated to call it a relief, but it was an honest word. Thirty years she'd spent with that man and not once had he told her he loved her.

But Wes, oh, her Wesley had said it all the time. Her sweet boy had loved her with an open heart.

That same heart was the reason he was dead.

It was odd since she'd had so many nightmares about burying Wes young. Ever since that moment she'd been bathing him and found a lump under his armpit. That had started years of worry, treatment, certainty she would need a small coffin for her baby boy.

The worry had never gone away, even after he'd been cancer-free for years.

And he'd still ended up here.

"You managed to talk to Seraphina Guidry and the church didn't explode." Calvin looked perfectly respectable in his thousand-dollar tailored suit. He knew how to dress his best. Her older child was heartbreakingly handsome, but there was a devil-may-care glint to his eyes that always worried her.

She stared forward. She could see the back of Seraphina Guidry's light blond hair. She truly did have the look of an angel, but she had been poorly named. An angel wouldn't have led her baby boy into hell.

"I wasn't talking to her," she replied quietly. "I was giving my condolences to Delphine."

"I thought you hated Delphine, too."

"I don't hate anyone." Hate wasn't ladylike. Disdain was

acceptable as long as it was for moral or societal reasons and not based on emotion. It was a lesson she'd learned well from her husband and mother-in-law. "Delphine and I don't run in the same circles or see eye to eye on many important things. That's all. You know I never approved of the way her daughter kept trying to force her way into our family. She took advantage of your brother."

"She didn't take advantage of my brother, and that was the problem," Cal said under his breath.

She turned and gave her son a look she'd perfected over her thirty years as a Beaumont.

It was enough to make Cal sit back. "Sorry, Momma. Hey, is there a reason I'm the only one forced to come to this thing today? And honestly, why are we here? You might not hate the Guidrys but you sure don't like them."

Her son needed to understand that they had a duty to the community around them. She'd been lax in the last decade. Since her mother-in-law had gone on to her reward—the fiery depths of hell if there was any justice in the universe—she'd relaxed many of the normal rules and the motherly lectures. And then Wes had died three years ago and she hadn't found the will to do anything but go through the motions. "It's our duty to be here, to be seen. You're a Beaumont. We're one of the most important families in Papillon. Beaumont Oil employs much of this town, and being good stewards means showing our faces at events like this. We give comfort to the families."

At least that was how she saw it. Her husband had put it differently. He'd believed they had to show their faces so no one forgot how important they were. In Ralph Beaumont's mind, they had always been the royal family and no one should question their place.

"I don't know that Sera gets a whole lot of comfort from

you," Cal said wryly. "Do they need comfort? It wasn't like Irene was all soft and cuddly. That woman was mean."

"She was family so I assure you they feel the loss."

Cal's hand came out and covered hers. "You're right. You always miss family."

He was such an irritating boy, and then he would be sweet as pie and prove that he understood her. She squeezed his hand. "And Angie has an appointment. Weddings trump funerals. Everything has to be perfect for your sister's big day."

The wedding of her daughter to a lovely man who would make her the best husband was the first thing to brighten her life in what felt like the longest time. She was turning a corner. Her daughter was getting married, Cal was settling into his place at the head of Beaumont Oil, and she was making a connection with her nephew. It had only taken her years, but she might be able to find some small piece of herself again.

Being around Harry had proven that girl she'd been was still there deep down. Her sister was stamped all over that beautiful young man's face. And her sister's kindness was there, too. So many years had been wasted and now Janelle was gone. So much of her family gone. So much time lost.

She felt old and she wanted very badly to find one thing that could make her feel young again.

"Who do you think will inherit Guidry Place?" she heard herself asking. She kept her voice low because the last thing she needed was someone to overhear. It wasn't proper to talk about inheritance at a funeral, though often it was the only thought that went through people's heads. She was cynical enough to know that. "Didn't I hear something about Irene leaving it to the cats? Can you leave property to felines?"

Cal snorted, an inelegant sound she should correct, but she let it pass. "I believe the rumor is she's leaving the whole place to a cat shelter."

The idea made her shudder. Guidry Place was half a mile from her own house and had some of the most spectacular views of what the locals called Butterfly Bayou.

Wouldn't it make a beautiful wedding present to Angela? She didn't like the thought of her baby girl being so far away. One day Beaumont House would be Cal's. Shouldn't Angie's family have something, too?

Her husband will take care of her. All she has to do is take care of her family, and her husband will provide. Ralph's words came back to her. It was what he'd said the first time she'd mentioned setting up a trust for Angela. He'd been willing to do it for Wesley but only because Wes had agreed to go to business school and set himself up to become CEO for the company Ralph's grandfather had built.

Beaumont women were to be pretty, obedient, and well trained. A bit like a show dog.

The only reason Celeste herself had been provided for at all had been her husband's laziness when it came to rewriting his will. He'd intended to leave everything to Calvin. He'd told her it was family tradition, and it would be up to Cal to take care of her and his siblings the way he saw fit.

And she'd accepted it. She hadn't even argued with him. Being the "queen" hadn't turned out to be so great in the end. Not in a world where only kings were acknowledged.

She wasn't going to leave her daughter dependent.

"We should find that shelter," she said.

Cal leaned in. "You want to buy it? Why? We don't need any extra space, Momma. Hell, we have ten bedrooms as it is."

"I have my reasons." She settled back, satisfied for the moment. "Just find out that information for me. And look for your cousin after the ceremony. Helena called him out here earlier on some kind of lighting emergency. I don't like the fact that the townspeople are already taking advantage of Harry."

She had to watch out for her nephew. The women here tended to pounce on new men in town like tigers looking for prey. Every woman with an unattached daughter, grand-daughter, or niece would lick their chops the minute they saw her sweet, kindhearted nephew.

He reminded her so much of her Wesley.

"I'll look into who owns Guidry Place now," Cal promised. "And I'll look after Harry. Hell, I would do that anyway. You know how many women are going to be after him? I'll be drowning in the women he doesn't choose."

Again, she sent him that withering look.

He straightened. "I mean perhaps I can help him make good decisions."

She shook her head as the choir started up. He was such a scamp. "I think that will be the other way around. Remember we have to go to work on Monday, and don't spend the whole weekend trying to prove what a bad boy you are."

Cal breathed deep, a sure sign he was holding back on her. "Of course."

He hated work but someone had to take over Beaumont Oil and it wouldn't be Wes, couldn't ever be Wes.

She focused on the service in front of her. Duty. She understood that. She'd been doing her duty for thirty years and only once had she really failed.

She would not fail again.

Harrison Jefferys screwed the wall plate in and flicked on the now functioning light. The priest's office was illuminated once more. "Let there be light."

Helena Antoine clapped her hands together. "And you're funny, too. I would not have suspected anyone from Celeste Beaumont's family to be so warm and funny." The woman stopped and grimaced. "Sorry. That wasn't very charitable of me."

No, but it was a pretty accurate assessment of his aunt. He slipped the flathead screwdriver back into his toolbox. He hadn't needed to carry the whole thing in. It turned out to be frayed wiring that had done the deed. The mystery of the flickering lights was solved by handiwork once again. That was him. Harrison of House Jefferys, first of his name, single of leg, and the king of all things handy. "It's all right. I'm pretty sure my aunt Celeste lives to be feared."

Unlike his sweet mother. His mother had known how to love in a way he wasn't sure his aunt had figured out. His mother had loved his father despite poverty, despite illness, despite bad luck. They'd been the unluckiest family in the world, and god how he missed them now.

"Well, we were all surprised to hear you were coming for a visit," Helena said, straightening the papers on her boss's desk. She was the church secretary, and she'd been nearly hysterical on the phone. Apparently the good father wasn't used to working in the dark. Harry rather thought she'd believed there were supernatural forces at work.

"That's because it's not so much a visit as a command performance. I'm here to work. I think Aunt Celeste likes the idea of having family on this particular project." Or all the other contractors knew how picky his aunt could be and managed to find themselves too busy to do the job. His cousin Angela was turning into a bit of a bridezilla, too.

"Celeste never talks about the family she came from."

That's because Aunt Celeste was the grand dame of Papillon and she liked to forget that she came from a working-class community outside Dallas. She liked to pretend her mother hadn't cleaned houses and her father hadn't worked on cars for a living. "Well, you know how it goes. She moved away and started a family here."

It was only because Celeste hadn't abandoned her younger sister in her time of need that Harry had come when she'd called. Celeste had visited occasionally, always staying at some ritzy hotel in Dallas and inviting them out for lunch. She'd never come to the home he'd grown up in, the tiny two-bedroom apartment in a lower-class neighborhood. But when his father had passed, Celeste had been the one to sit beside his mom and promise her everything would be all right. Celeste had covered the funeral expenses and made sure they had food on the table.

His aunt had a heart, though sometimes it was hard to see through all the designer wear.

"Well, I knew Ralph's mother, and anyone who could survive living with that mean old lady would have to develop some thick skin," Helena said.

He was rapidly coming to realize that everyone knew everyone else here in Papillon and they liked to talk. It was interesting to try to figure out this family of his. "I never met my aunt's husband. He was obviously a successful man."

"His family was successful," Helena corrected. "Ralph's father was an oilman back in the day. His family once owned a big ranch in Texas, but back in the thirties they found oil underground, and that's where the wealth came from. He married a woman from New Orleans and settled here. I think they liked it here because they could rule the town. Still do. Not a lot gets done here without either Celeste Beaumont or Rene Darois having a say. The Beaumont and Darois families have run this town for a long time. The rich always seem to get their way."

"I don't think having her son die was my aunt's way. Or

Uncle Ralph having a heart attack a year later." His aunt wasn't the warmest person in the world, but she'd been through a lot.

"Of course." Helena had gone a nice shade of red. "I'm sorry. I didn't mean to offend."

"Takes a lot to offend me, but it's good to remember we all have pain. Money can't fix everything." It was one of the lessons he'd learned. His cousin Wes had everything going for him. He'd had money and connections and a bright future he'd traded for a deadly accident in the desert half a world away from home. Harry hadn't had anything material growing up but he'd managed to survive. Death, he'd learned, was the great equalizer.

"Yes, it is good to remember," Helena agreed. "How long are you going to be in town? I heard you're working on that beautiful old gazebo."

It would be beautiful once he'd torn most of it down and replaced it with not-rotting wood. His cousin Angela wanted the gazebo as the focal point of what she called her "rustic elegance" theme for the reception. It was a rich people problem, but then he was good at solving those. "I'll be here for about six weeks. I'll stay for the wedding."

And then he would roam for a while. It was what he'd done since he'd gotten out of the Army. His mother had passed and he'd found himself without a home to return to. He couldn't seem to stay in one place for long, so he moved around, doing odd jobs, visiting with old friends. At first he'd told himself it was only until he'd gotten his head straight, but he was going on two years now and it was beginning to be normal to sleep on a friend's sofa, and he knew every cheap motel in the Western United States.

Lately he'd started to think it might be nice to settle down somewhere, to find a job, to start his life. He just wasn't sure how.

Helena started to lead him down the hallway. A heavenly smell hit his nose and his stomach growled, reminding him that he'd skipped lunch to work on this project at the church. His aunt kept strict mealtimes. He would need to hit a restaurant if he wanted to eat before the six p.m. supper.

"Well, if you need anything at all, you call me. If you need someone to show you around, I've got a granddaughter who knows the town very well. She would be thrilled to familiarize you with our Papillon. She works at the courthouse, knows all the best places to eat." Helena had her keys in hand, but it looked like someone had left the door to the parking lot open. "I guess the reception's started. We had a service for poor Irene Guidry today."

His aunt had mentioned she was going to a funeral.

The door opened and a familiar face walked through. His cousin Calvin strode his way, adjusting his tie. "Hey, Harry, the funeral's over and the drinking can start . . . I mean eating. Cajuns know how to throw a reception. There's gumbo. If there's one thing Guidrys do right, it's gumbo. Mom left, but I get to stay and represent the family, if you know what I mean."

"Don't you dare spike the punch, Calvin Beaumont." Helena pointed a finger his cousin's way.

Calvin shrugged. "I don't have to. Zep brought it. It's probably eighty percent hooch. Don't worry. Lisa made sure he didn't get close to the lemonade. Besides, Harry can give me a ride home, so I don't have to bum one off someone here. Naturally my mother took the Benz."

"You behave," Helena said with a wave of her hand. "Don't listen to your cousin, Harry. He's a rascal of the highest order. Now you let me know when you want to go out with . . . when Debra can show you around."

"He will," Cal said with a smirk. "I'll make sure of it."

He put a hand on Harry's arm to lead him toward the reception hall. "This is going to be fun. They'll stop bugging me about getting married and start in on the new guy. Ever since Angie got engaged, my mother has been asking me when I'm going to settle down and give her grandkids. Every momma in town with a single daughter parades her past me like I'm some kind of prize to catch. Now that part is true. I'm very much marriage material. The trouble is I don't want to get married. I want to have some fun. I would watch out for Debbie. Her grandma thinks she's an angel, but she's got about forty hands after a couple of drinks. And the woman talks. A lot. If you don't want to have every second of your performance harshly graded, you'll stay away from that one."

He wasn't sure he wanted to go to a funeral reception. He was in jeans and a T-shirt. He still had his beat-up old toolbox in his hand. "I didn't know the deceased. Maybe I should go back to the house."

Shep would be waiting on him. Shep was a big German shepherd he'd brought home with him from Afghanistan after they'd both been discharged from duty. The dog had sat near his truck and looked at him with sad eyes when he realized he was being left behind. Shep wasn't used to being left behind. He was pretty much used to spending every minute of the day with Harry.

"Come on." Cal put a hand on his shoulder. "You've got to meet the fine folks of this town at some point. And no one's real upset about Irene Guidry. That was the single craziest old lady I ever met, and I've met most of Momma's Rotary Club, so that's saying something."

He found himself standing in the doorway of the church reception hall. There were a bunch of people milling about, most with red cups in their hands. "For a crazy old lady, she drew quite a crowd."

"Oh, everyone comes out for funerals in these parts," Cal admitted as he made his way to the big crystal punch bowl and got himself a cup. "There's not a lot else to do so weddings and funerals are big social events." He took a long drink. "And damn, but Zep's got a heavy hand with the rum. There's way more rum than punch. The Guidrys might be trash, but trash around here usually knows how to party."

He wasn't sure he liked his cousin referring to anyone as trash, but he didn't know the family well. He did know he'd heard the name *Guidry* from his aunt's mouth and it was obvious she didn't think much of them. "I think I'll try the lemonade."

"Suit yourself." Cal refilled and looked around the crowd. "I'm going to see what Josette has going on. Now, there's a woman I could spend some time with. Some fun time."

His cousin winked and walked off toward a slender blonde.

He was rapidly discovering his cousin was a bit of a douchebag.

"You're the new guy."

He turned to find his own pretty blonde staring up at him. She was petite, barely coming up to his shoulders, and he would bet half her weight was in that hair. It flowed past her shoulders almost to her waist, and there was so much of it. Thick, honey-colored silk. Sky blue eyes found his own and held him there. Her arms were crossed over her chest, and he noted that she was drinking the lemonade.

"How do you know that? Maybe I've been here all along and no one's noticed me."

Her nose wrinkled sweetly. "Oh, they all notice you. That's how I know you're the new guy. Welcome to Papillon. I came over to give you fair warning. I think single people need to stick together in an effort to stay single despite the societal pressure to give in to the patriarchy. If my mother tries to convince you to let me show you around, she's really trying to find me a husband."

Oh, but he might not mind her showing him the town. She was gorgeous, and he liked the sass she was throwing his way. He was self-aware enough to admit that women had come easy to him. He wasn't hard on the eyes, but finding one who got him was a different story. "That seems to be a theme. The church secretary already tried to have her granddaughter show me around."

A single brow rose over those heavenly eyes of hers. "Debra? Yeah, you have to be careful with her."

"I've heard she's handsy." He nodded. "And she talks a lot."

"Yeah, she also drinks a lot more than Helena will admit, and she's started a couple of spectacular bar fights. She likes to pit her suitors against each other and make them fight for her."

"Good to know." He glanced around, and sure enough, every eye was on him. "Well, I don't suppose you would show me around. Maybe if you showed me around, people would stop offering up their daughters. I noticed no one has asked me if their sons could show me the town. Do the men of Papillon not know their way around?"

"Well, you could say that about a lot of them. But no, it's because there aren't many available men, and when a new one comes to town, it's like a medieval parade of who has the best dowry. You need to remember that whatever my momma tells you, I've got no dowry whatsoever. I come with a lot of baggage. Tons of baggage." She gasped as though she'd just had a thought. "Unless you would rather have a nice man show you around our town. I hadn't considered that and it was awfully backward thinking of me. I know a great guy. His name is Michael Hendricks and he's such a doll. You would get along so well."

Whoa. That had taken a turn. She was smiling, and that smile took her from beautiful to gorgeous. That smile kind of lit up his world, but she was working under a big misconception. "I'm comfortable with women showing me the sights. Did you get excited about setting me up with your friend?"

A hand cupped her hip, and the sass factor went sky high. "Is there a reason you wouldn't like my friend?"

He had to chuckle. This one was obviously a fierce warrior. "I'm sure I would like him but I would only like him, not *like* like him because I like women. *Like* like them."

The cutest frown came over her face. "You're a confusing man."

"So I've been told." Oh, he liked her. A lot. She would be a ton of fun, and not in the way Cal meant it. He would very much enjoy getting to know this woman. "How about tomorrow? It's Sunday. I can take the afternoon off."

Her eyes widened. "Are you hitting on me at my great-aunt's funeral?"

He had probably gone a nice shade of red. He hadn't thought this through, and he definitely hadn't realized she was related to the deceased. He thought she was one of those people who'd come for the gumbo. "Well, that would be rude of me so no, I am not."

She looked him up and down. "It would be rude, and I was only coming over to warn you that my mom will likely try to trick you into dating me. Don't fall for it."

She turned on her heel and started to walk away.

"Hey, you didn't even tell me your name. How will I know who to avoid if you don't tell me your name?"

She glanced back, that blond hair swaying. "Seraphina Guidry. Remember it so we don't have to go through all of this again. Welcome to Papillon, Mr. Jefferys. I hope you enjoy your stay."

He stared at her as she joined a group of women around her age. They all started talking, and that conversation was absolutely about him. No question about it. But her eyes came back up and found his before turning away again.

Seraphina Guidry. The one woman his aunt had told him expressly to stay away from.

She's already ruined one member of my family. I won't let that gold digger take another one from me.

The good news was he didn't have any gold for her to dig. If she went out with him, she would have to take him as he was.

He should stay away. He walked over and got himself a glass of that lemonade and promised he would make good choices.

As he watched Seraphina with her friends, he knew it might be a promise he couldn't keep.

chapter two

The ceiling fan turned overhead, the hum the only sound cutting through Quaid Havery's words. Seraphina had barely heard the man because Luc was squirming in her arms. Her baby boy was in a climbing phase. He climbed out of his crib most nights, terrifying her and keeping her awake. He scaled the bookcases and china cabinet of her childhood home with ease. He climbed up anyone who happened to be holding him as though the child had been born with an innate need to always be at the highest place of any room.

"I'm sorry," she managed to say to Papillon's one and only lawyer. "I should have found a babysitter but pretty much everyone who normally babysits for me is in this room. Noelle LaVigne is at a science camp at LSU. I had to bring him."

It was also hard to find babysitting on Sunday mornings since for the most part everyone would be at church. The irony being if she was actually at church, she could have dropped Luc off at the childcare center and they wouldn't have this problem. But no, they'd been told that Aunt Irene wanted her will read the morning after her funeral and there would be no delay. Her great-aunt was having one last moment of pure stubbornness.

Her oldest brother stood up and held his hands out. "Come here, Luc. I don't like sitting any more than you do. Quaid, how long is this? We all know she was going to give what little she had to that cat shelter."

They were all here, her family. Her mother and brothers, Remy and Zep, and her sweet sister-in-law, Lisa. They were down to the six of them with Luc. She remembered a time when her grandparents and dad had been alive and holidays were big, chaotic events. She'd grown up surrounded by aunts and uncles and cousins, but one by one they'd all left Papillon for greater opportunities, and as the older generation had passed on, the younger ones had lost touch.

The idea of not giving her son what she'd had made her sad inside, but then she had to wonder what her grandparents would have thought of her having a baby out of wedlock.

Remy took Luc and lifted him up. Luc giggled and generally looked at his uncle with worshipful adoration.

At least he knew he was loved.

"Remy's right." Her mother was dressed in her favorite jungle-printed caftan, her hair up in a light blue turban she claimed made her look mystical and wise, but Sera was fairly certain she wore so she didn't have to do her hair every day. "I don't understand the purpose of this meeting. Irene didn't have much beyond that ramshackle house of hers, and it probably should be condemned. The only reason they didn't do it before was everyone knew she had a shotgun and wasn't afraid to use it."

Her great-aunt had been what they liked to call in these parts a "character."

"Did she maybe have a million dollars in cash stuffed in that old mattress of hers?" Zep asked.

Her younger brother was a character, too. "I assure you she did not. I spent the most time with her and she didn't have two cents to rub together."

"Well, maybe a couple of cents," Quaid said in that I-know-something-you-don't-know way of his. Quaid was in his thirties and made most of his money working for the two wealthiest families in the parish. He made enough off the Daroises and Beaumonts that he did a lot of pro bono work. Though Sera was surprised her great-aunt had bothered with a will.

After all, she'd told Sera she wanted her to float her body out in the bayou and let the gators take her because that was the circle of life. Sera had argued that the circle of life didn't normally involve stringing together enough pool noodles to carry a body out to sea . . . or into Otis's belly. She rather thought her aunt simply wanted to frighten the kiddos one last time or to become a legend. The legend of Floating Irene.

They had enough ghost stories.

"So she wrote us all a letter? We should listen to it. It's the last thing she's ever going to request of us."

"Yeah, I wouldn't say that, Sera." Quaid grimaced as he held up a piece of paper. "I have to read this exactly as it's written. You understand that, right? I'm legally obligated to read every word, though her opinions might not be my own."

"What does that mean?" Lisa asked.

Zep groaned. "It means she's got to get her digs in. Go on. It's not going to be anything I haven't heard before. Let's see. I'm going to guess. I'm a moron. I need to stop . . . what did she call it? Spreading my seed everywhere and hoping it grows. See, I never hope it grows. I kind of pray it doesn't grow."

"How about I just get through it?" Quaid looked down

at the piece of paper he held. Sera recognized it. She'd bought her aunt a couple of spiral notebooks so she could write down grocery lists because she refused to use a cell phone and text her order. Apparently the government cared about what kind of denture cream she used.

"Please do." She had a lot going on this afternoon. She was working six days next week and that meant running errands today. Normally she would have gone out to Irene's to make sure she had everything she needed.

She was going to miss her. Even with all her eccentricities, she'd been kind in her own ways. When she was younger, it had been Irene who'd taught Sera to fish, who'd let her and her brothers run wild on her property. When they'd gone out to Aunt Irene's, the only rules had been checking in at supper time and not disturbing the numerous traps she had around the grounds. She'd even told them where the traps were, and her mom had claimed that was how a person knew Irene cared.

"Yeah, let's hear what she had to say." Remy bounced Luc and slid a smile Sera's way as though he was remembering those times, too.

"All right." Quaid sat up in his chair and took a long breath. *"Dear beloved family, If Quaid Havery is reading this, then I am dead and I wasted money on an uppity lawyer because the world is a terrible place. I wanted to leave you with a few words of wisdom while dispensing with my worldly goods."*

"I thought we already dispensed with her worldly goods," her mother said with a shake of her turban. "Seraphina had to rehome all those cats."

She'd worked hard to find a place for her aunt's kitties. She'd run those cats all over Southern Louisiana, but she couldn't put them in shelters. Those cats had been her aunt's babies. She wouldn't have been able to even look at Aunt Irene's coffin unless she'd done her absolute best.

"She left each of you something," Quaid said, looking back to the letter. *"Delphine, you're a ridiculous woman who believes in everything from mystical crystals to swamp men."*

Her mother held up a hand. "Well, I have actually seen a swamp man. Or it might have been Buddy Evers after a bad day of trapping. Sometimes I can't tell, but Irene would have done well to have had a few healing crystals around."

"I'm going to continue," Quaid said. *"You might be some silly thing my brother married despite me telling him it was a bad idea, but oddly you managed to have a couple of decent children, so here's my advice. My brother died a long time ago. Get out and live, Delphine. I didn't because I didn't care to. I liked how I lived. You are not me. You did a good job. You were dumb but faithful. Go have fun, and I don't mean by pulling short cons on tourists. I leave you the ring my brother should have given you. I was selfish and kept it for myself because I was jealous, but now it's yours and not because you married my brother. Because you honored this family by staying when it would have been easier to go. But you're old, girl. You don't have much time left. You should have fun as fast as you can because those wrinkles are catching up no matter how tight you tie that turban."*

Sera bit back a laugh. That was her aunt.

"She left me the ring?" Her mother sniffled and then touched her turban. "And this is much cheaper than Botox and far healthier. Not that I have many wrinkles. But I appreciate the ring. It was her mother's ring. It was supposed to go to your father to propose with but Irene got upset. I didn't argue, but I always loved that ring."

"To my nephew Remy I leave twenty dollars so he can get a haircut. And don't go to Seraphina because she can't cut hair to save her life." Quaid sighed. "Like I said, not my words, man."

Remy chuckled. "That old woman was always on me to get my hair cut, but my wife thinks it's sexy like it is so I'll be donating that twenty bucks."

"It's specifically for a haircut. I'm supposed to verify that you do it," Quaid replied.

"I think we'll survive without the twenty," Lisa said with a shake of her head.

"I could use twenty bucks." Zep sat up. "I'll cut my hair. I look good with or without hair. I have one of those jawlines that can handle any style."

Quaid simply ignored him. Which proved Quaid had been around Zep a lot. *"As to Zéphirin Guidry, I give you a box of condoms and the prayer that you will have the sense to use them. A young man should not spread his seed."*

Zep pointed Quaid's way. "See, I told you. I'll take those condoms, though. Every time I go to buy them at the Fast Mart, Evelyn Gillwater prays for me. Right there in the middle of the store. It's embarrassing since she won't actually give me the box until she's done praying."

Dread crept across Sera's system because she was certain her aunt had something terrible planned for her, too. Irene had always been on her about finding a career and how often she changed jobs, and then there was the unplanned pregnancy when she refused to divulge the name of the father, so Irene had decided he was a married man and Seraphina had brought shame on the family name.

"To my niece Seraphina I leave this advice. You've screwed up your whole life. You didn't try in school. You were lazy about studying. You partied too hard and then you got yourself in trouble."

Tears pierced her eyes and she wanted to push back the chair and walk out. It wasn't anything she hadn't heard before. If she'd been in a big city, no one would have taken any notice of a twenty-one-year-old giving birth out of wedlock. Hallie had been twenty-three when she'd had her baby. But Hallie was married and the town treated it like a big party, congratulating her best friend, whereas they'd all looked at Sera like she was a walking tragedy.

She sucked it up because she wasn't going to run away. She'd done right by her aunt. She couldn't control what her aunt did now.

Quaid looked at her with sympathetic eyes. "It gets better, Sera. Let me finish. *You got yourself in trouble. You can get yourself out. I know all your life people have told you how pretty you are, but you can be more if you choose to. You have to be more because you're a momma now and that boy deserves everything you have. It's time to stop playing around and pretending to be something you're not. You are a caretaker, Seraphina Guidry. You are a person who makes life easy on others, even old women who don't like the world much anymore. To my niece Seraphina I leave my home, my land, and fifty thousand dollars to be used to improve it. It would have been fifty-two thousand but Quaid Havery is extremely proud of that expensive education he got. This is your chance, girl. Sell it. Keep it. Turn it into something beautiful. Thank you for your kindness. Good-bye to you all.*"

Now the tears started in earnest. The words reached into her soul. Could she be more? This was a massive gift and she couldn't take it. Could she? She shook her head, trying to let it all sink in.

"Damn," Zep breathed.

She turned to her youngest brother. How could she take fifty thousand dollars and not share it with her family?

Wouldn't they be upset they'd gotten nothing and she'd gotten a small fortune? It wasn't fair. "Zep, we should talk about this."

Her brother nodded. "Damn straight we should. Quaid here got two thousand dollars for reading a letter. Momma, I need to go to law school."

"There was a little more involved," Quaid protested.

"Aunt Irene had fifty grand?" Remy looked shocked. "She once tried to serve me salad dressing that had expired five years before, and when I pointed out that ranch wasn't supposed to be green, she told me I was acting uppity."

"Guys, I can't take it all myself. We need to split it up." They would sell the land. It made her sick to think about it because she'd always adored that land. It had been her childhood playground. Despite the fact that the place was kind of falling apart, she'd always loved that house. It had a big wraparound porch that looked out over the water and gorgeous columns that dominated the front of the house. Well, they would be gorgeous if they were sanded and repainted. There was a lot of restoration work to be done. It wasn't like she could do it herself.

But if she had fifty thousand dollars, she might be able to make the place shine.

She couldn't spend fifty grand on a home improvement project.

"There can be no splitting up the cash," Quaid said. "I'm executor of this will and the only thing you're allowed to spend this money on is repairing Guidry Place. I hold the purse strings and I wouldn't be doing my job if I didn't honor the will."

"Sera, Zep and I aren't taking any money," Remy said. "This is yours."

"Now wait," Zep began.

Her mother reached out and gently slapped Zep on the chest. "You hush."

"Well, you got a ring and Sera got a house and money and all I got was a box of condoms." Zep seemed to take notice of the look on their momma's face. "For which I will be eternally grateful. Hey, can I cut Remy's hair and get that twenty?"

"You aren't touching his hair." Lisa grinned like she genuinely loved the shenanigans. Sometimes she was sure Lisa viewed the entire town as one big soap opera.

Sera stood up and faced her older brother. Remy had always watched out for her when they'd been growing up. He'd left for a long time, but when he'd finally come home to take over the family restaurant, he'd slid right back into the role of looking out for her. Remy and Lisa were the only people in the world besides her mother and Angela Beaumont who knew the truth of Luc's birth. She took her baby boy into her arms. "I can't take this, Remy. It's not fair."

"Oh, I think it's entirely fair." Her brother stared down at her with soft eyes. "You were the one who went to Aunt Irene's place three times a week to check in on her despite the fact that you had a job, were going to school, and were also taking care of a baby. You were the one who ran Irene's errands and picked her up for holidays to make sure she actually got out of that place every once in a while. She wants you to have her home. You always loved it. I'm not saying you should go out there and make it your home, but it's special and shouldn't be torn down and made into a fast-food place or some rich Texan's second-best fishing getaway."

"But how would I even find the time to work on it? I don't have the skills."

"That's why she left you money," her mother said. "You do have the skills and the smarts to hire someone. And you can do some of it yourself. You helped Lisa and Remy pull up the carpet at their place and put in hardwoods. You know how to do small things. Sure, you can't fix that shower of hers that looks like it's raining blood down on a person, but that's what you pay for."

She was overwhelmed and Luc seemed to get that. He put his hands on either side of her face. It was something he'd done since he'd been able to hold his head up. He would put his hands on her cheeks, prompting her to look into his eyes, and he would stare with such love that she would know they could handle whatever came their way.

She hugged her baby tight. She'd done one good thing. She could do another.

"Okay then, baby boy, looks like we've got a big project ahead."

And maybe, just maybe, she could give him the life he deserved.

Harry sat down at the overly large dining room table he was sure impressed guests with its sheer length. He was impressed with the craftsmanship that had gone into the Colonial-period antique, even though it was a bit overwhelming as a breakfast table. But then he wasn't used to having servants set up a buffet every Sunday morning.

He grabbed a muffin and some coffee and slid into the chair opposite his cousin Angela, who was already up and ready to face the day. He wasn't sure how they managed it, but in the days he'd been at Beaumont House, he hadn't caught either Angela or his aunt Celeste looking anything less than perfect. It was like they didn't ever leave the confines of their bedrooms without the full Chanel treatment.

He would bet that pretty blonde he'd met the day before

would look awfully cute all tousled from sleep, with hair flying everywhere.

He'd thought about her all night long. It had been a while since a woman had occupied his thoughts.

"I can't believe Mother let you bring Shep in the house." Angela reached a hand out as his big German shepherd lumbered over to greet her. "Growing up, we never had dogs."

"That wasn't my fault." Celeste strode in the room dressed in a chic sheath and sky-high heels he had no idea how anyone walked in. She was dressed for church, a thing that seemed to happen a lot around here. She settled into her chair and the maid brought over an elegant carafe and filled her cup. "Your grandmother believed animals belonged outdoors." A smile curled up his aunt's normally placid face. "I've missed having dogs. We had several growing up in Texas."

Shep always seemed to know when someone was willing to give him a pet. He walked over to his aunt and offered up the top of his head. Celeste stroked him. "You're a pretty boy." She glanced Harry's way. "Your mom and I had a big old mutt we called Sparkles. He was the ugliest, meanest-looking thing in the world, but he was so sweet. Scared off anyone who didn't know him, but that dog was the kindest soul."

"Mom talked about him a lot. She kept a dog most of the time," Harry explained. "Sometimes more than one. She would go volunteer at the shelter and come home with some sad-sack mutt she knew no one would want."

"That sounds like my sister," Celeste said, nodding to the maid, who slipped out of the room. Celeste straightened up. "Angie and I are going to church and then to a meeting with the florist. It won't be too long now before she's walking down the aisle."

Angie smiled, a soft pink flushing her skin. "Sometimes it seems like it's coming so fast. I want to remember it all."

His cousin seemed sweet, and he'd liked her fiancé. Austin was a lawyer in New Orleans. They'd met through a mutual friend and dated for a few years before he'd popped the question. "The church secretary is looking forward to it. I believe she called it the social event of the year."

"Precisely why we need our Harry to make the gazebo beautiful again," Celeste said. She frowned briefly Angie's way. "Darling, don't forget you have a fitting on Tuesday. You don't want too many carbs."

Angie's face fell so briefly if Harry hadn't been looking at her, he would have missed that expression of shame that took over before she was right back to placid. As her mother continued to talk about how Harry would save the day, Angie's napkin made an appearance and she pushed her barely touched plate out of the way.

"So what are you doing today, Harry?" his aunt asked. "I understand you can't get the raw materials for the project until next week. You should get out and see a bit of the town. Angie, don't you have a friend who can show him around? Not that little fat one. And not the boring one. Maybe we could ask one of your sorority sisters to come down for the afternoon."

It seemed like everyone was going to try to set him up. Shep had given up on the human conversation and had settled himself at Harry's feet. "I think I can take a look around on my own."

"I'll take him out this evening, Mother." Calvin yawned as he walked in and made a heaping plate for himself.

"Maybe you should think about staying in once in a while, son." Celeste's tone had gone frosty.

His cousin was wearing the same clothes he'd worn the

night before, but Cal didn't seem to care that he was doing the walk of shame. Cal merely gestured for the maid to fill his coffee cup as he took a place at the other end of the table from his mother. "Why would I do that? You're the one who told me a young man should have a social life. Thank you, Annemarie."

The maid nodded and disappeared again.

Harry wondered if she hovered right outside the door, waiting to be called on. It was weird and made him feel awkward since he was perfectly capable of getting his own coffee. It was good to connect with his family, but he was never going to fit in here.

"We have different definitions of that term, son." A thick layer of frost had come over his aunt's voice. "When I discussed you having a social life, I meant attending parties and meeting the right people. I did not mean barhopping with lowlifes. You know how I feel about those Guidrys and yet you hang out at that bar all the time."

"It's a restaurant." If Cal was bothered by the ice his momma was sending his way, he didn't show it. "And Zep is a friend of mine. I know you don't understand the concept of friends and raised us to view people as chess pieces to use or discard based on their social status, but we can't all be as perfect as you."

Celeste leaned forward as though she was about to give her son a full-on lecture, but she seemed to remember they weren't alone. She gave Harry a tight smile before sitting back in her chair. "Well, you know how best to spend your time. You seem to know everything at the tender age of twenty-seven. Of course, at your age I was already married and had you, but certainly the younger generation knows better."

A smirk hit his cousin's face. "Yes, I certainly do since

I managed to not get tied down with a whining, stinky kid so far. I can say that because I'm talking about me. Angie was a sweet baby, and we all know Wes was perfect."

The very name seemed to make the whole room freeze in place. Even Shep seemed to understand something had gone wrong. He lifted his head and Harry reached down to put a hand on the dog.

Cal set his mug on the table. "I'm sorry, Mom. I promise I'll take Harry out tonight and we won't go near Guidry's. And I'll have him back at a decent hour. I don't think Harry wants to be set up yet. Let's give him a chance to settle in before you start parading proper young women in front of him."

Celeste seemed to take Cal's words as a peace offering. "As long as you don't parade improper ones in front of him." Celeste turned Harry's way. "I heard from some of my friends that the Guidry girl was sniffing around you yesterday at her own aunt's funeral. The gall of that girl. It's no wonder she got herself in trouble. You should stay away from that bit of trash."

"She wasn't hitting on me. She warned me that her mom might try to set us up." What exactly was his aunt's problem with the Guidrys? After his encounter with the sassy Seraphina, he'd spent some time talking to her brother Remy, who had served in the Navy. He found he naturally migrated to the ex-military crowd. He felt more comfortable with them than discussing small-town politics or gossip. He'd liked Remy and his pretty wife, Lisa. He'd definitely liked the gumbo.

Celeste pushed back her chair. "Well, of course Delphine is trying to catch a man for her daughter. That girl is trouble, Harry. And she's not smart enough to protect herself. Or she got pregnant intentionally to trap whoever she was sleeping with at the time. What I'm trying to say is

Seraphina Guidry is a single mom. She's not the type you should be around, and you should guard yourself around that whole family. Angie, I'm going to check my makeup. I'll be ready to go in half an hour. Don't be late, and you should change your shoes. Open-toed shoes in church is rude."

His aunt strode out having never touched a bite of food.

Angie sent her brother a glare. "You had to bring up Wes, didn't you?"

Cal sighed. "I'm sorry. She was pushing me. I had a long night."

"I'm sure you did," Angie shot back. "But you're not the one who has to spend all day with her. She'll be on edge and short with everyone."

"Y'all don't ever talk about Wes?" He'd found it odd. There were pictures of Wes everywhere. His youngest cousin had died roughly three months after he'd shipped out to Afghanistan. He'd been killed in an accident.

"Oh, she talks about him but it's usually to let me know it would have been better if I'd died instead of Wes," Cal replied.

"That's not true." Angie stood and crossed to the buffet, grabbing a muffin.

"Really?" Cal looked at his sister, a skeptical expression on his face. "And when she said, *You know I wish Wes was here instead of you*—what do you think that was a meta-phor for?"

"Damn," Harry breathed.

"She was tipsy and she didn't mean it." Angie sat back down and turned to Harry. "Mom got drunk on the anniversary of Wes's death last year. She was harsh on all of us, but she apologized the next day. She certainly doesn't want Cal dead, just a bit more serious about life."

Cal smiled, but there was no humor behind it. "When

Wes died, Angie became the angel. My mother only seems to be able to truly love one of us at a time. It might have been different if Wes hadn't gotten sick."

He knew a little bit of the history. "He had cancer as a kid, right?"

Angie nodded. "He was diagnosed when he was four. My mother pretty much devoted herself to him from that point on. He went through a lot at a young age. It was awful, but he got the best care, and by the time he was seven or eight, you would never have been able to tell he'd been sick at all. He was healthy. Wes recovered from his cancer. Mom never did."

Cal sighed. "Wes was her perfect child, her miracle baby. Well, with the singular exception of his choice in friends. If you want to know why Mom wants you to stay away from Sera, it's because Wes was crazy in love with her."

Angie shook her head. "They were friends. That's all they ever were."

"Yeah, well, Wes wanted more." Cal looked tired as he sipped his coffee. "My younger brother was a good guy, but he was used to getting what he wanted. He chased after Sera for years. My parents sent us to public school at first. Some of the older kids at the school used to bully Wes. Sera stood up for him. She was his only friend in the beginning. I often think he imprinted on her, but she never liked him that way."

"Like I said, they were friends," Angie agreed. "She's not bad. Sera's actually pretty nice. She's a little on the unlucky side. She does have a kid."

"Lots of people her age have kids. It's not like she's a teen mom." He was confused about a lot of things. "Why does everyone treat it like she did something scandalous? We're not back in the 1800s. Women have kids without getting married."

"Not in polite society in a small town." Cal picked up his fork. "Don't get me wrong. There are parts of this town where no one cares, but the Guidrys are odd. They're not poor and they're not rich. They're mainstays of the town, but you won't see them at Mother's parties. She considers them beneath her."

"Do you?" He wanted to know if the snobbery went all the way through this family he found himself in.

"I hang out with Zep all the time because he's a good guy and he's fun as hell. You'll find that walking on that side of town is way more amusing than this one," Cal admitted. "Sera's problem is she wouldn't tell anyone who the father of the kid was, and that means one thing. He's married. Every married woman in town is watching that kid to see if it was her husband who cheated. So far he looks more like his uncle than anyone else. If Sera's serious about taking that secret to her grave, it'll be best for everyone if Luc continues to look like a Guidry."

"How old is he?" So that was what she'd meant by baggage.

"I don't know," Cal replied with a shrug. "Two or three. I only know that I don't play around with single moms, so she's off the table and that's a shame because she's fine. Even after she gained that baby weight. I'm pretty sure it went to all the right places, if you know what I mean."

Something about the words made him sit up taller. "I do not. She seemed like a nice young lady, and honestly, even if she hadn't been, you shouldn't say things like that."

Cal rolled his eyes. "Yep, Captain America is in the house. You're going to be fun to hang out with, cos. We'll get some beer in you and see if we can get that stick out of your ass."

If being polite meant he had a stick up his butt, he was all right with that.

"I don't know. I like how Harry acts," Angie said with a smile. "I actually think he and Sera would get along. She needs someone nice in her life. She was dating that Jackson fellow from two towns over. I heard he dumped her when she wanted to introduce him to Luc. Said he was only having fun and didn't want to raise some other man's kid."

Jackson sounded like a moron. Not that he was interested in anything serious. But Seraphina Guidry was intriguing. If there was a spark, he wouldn't mind seeing if it grew into something that could be good for both of them. He certainly wouldn't rule out a relationship because she came with a kid. "Well, she made it clear she wasn't interested in me."

Except there had been a definite chemistry between them. He'd been around long enough to know there was attraction and then there was heat. He and Sera had heat. Whether or not that was enough to build a fire, he couldn't know if he didn't spend more time with her.

It would be a mistake because he wasn't staying here in Papillon. He only had a couple of weeks here. Six at the most. Maybe two months. Then he would be on the road again, seeing the country, doing odd jobs. What did he have to offer a single mom who should be looking for someone to take care of her?

Of course, *care* didn't mean cash. It didn't necessarily mean a life of ease. No one really got it easy. Life was about how a person handled the tough times. For his family, taking care meant being around when times were tough. His father hadn't had money most of the time, but he'd had a hand his mother could hold.

"That's a good thing because my mom would throw a fit if she even thought you were interested in her," Cal said, seeming to get his appetite back. "Besides, she's going to have her hands full. They read the will earlier today and it turns out Old Irene didn't leave that decaying mansion of hers to the cat sanctuary like she said she would."

"Mom's been trying to get that place condemned for years," Angie explained. "I think it's beautiful, but Mom thinks it's an eyesore. Personally, I think Mom just wants the land. It backs up to our property and has way better water access. The rumor is back during Prohibition, the Guidrys were bootleggers and there's secret rooms all over the place. No one's been in it for years except Irene and her family, and from what Sera's told me, a whole lot of the place is boarded up. Who did she give it to? Tell me she left it to the historical society. Mom's the head and she'll find a way to snap it up. She might be able to get it for cheap."

"That doesn't seem fair," Cal replied. "That house has been in their family for a hundred and fifty years. They weren't always middle class. Mom forgets that from time to time."

"Aunt Celeste wasn't always rich. She forgets that, too." His aunt could be kind to him, but he didn't like how she talked about Seraphina's family. It wasn't his place to correct her, though, since he barely knew the woman.

"Yes, she likes to forget that entirely." Cal nodded his way. "She doesn't ever mention that when she met our dad, she was a stewardess."

"Flight attendant," Angie corrected. "They're called flight attendants these days."

"Well, in those days she was a stewardess and she had an affair with a businessman who married her when she got pregnant with me, so she was merely luckier than Sera," Cal pointed out. "Don't tell her I know that, by the way. She always tries to tell me I was a preemie. Grandmother Beaumont slipped that story in whenever she wanted to let me know I was half poor. Like that came in my DNA or something. You know, now that I think about it, Sera's the lucky one since she's the new owner of Guidry Place, all the land, and according to whoever Josette was talking to this morning, a crate of Confederate gold."

Angie rolled her eyes. "You listened to the rumor mill? You know by the time it gets to anyone willing to talk to that mean girl that it's likely all crap."

He shrugged slightly. "Yeah, there was also something about a bunch of dead bodies and having to hide Irene's serial killer past in order to take possession of the house, but I just figured it had already gone through Gene."

Papillon was an odd place. "So Sera's inheriting a mansion?"

"It's a mansion in name only," Angie explained. "It was a mansion back at the turn of the twentieth century. Sometime in the fifties, most of the family moved into town and bought the house Delphine and Sera still live in. They founded the restaurant, but Irene wasn't interested in it so she took care of the ancestral home. When the grandparents passed, they left Sera's side of the family the restaurant and Irene got the old property. Everyone assumed she would sell it off at some point or leave it to charity. I'm surprised she bequeathed it all to Seraphina."

"Sera's the only one who ever gave that old woman a moment of her time," Cal replied. "I'm not all that surprised."

"I wonder if that's why she did it." Angie pushed her chair back. "I've got to go change shoes. I'm not going to be the one to tell Mother that Seraphina is now our neighbor. She can find that out on her own. I hope it's merely a rumor because if it's not, Sera's inherited more than a house that will likely fall apart around her. She put herself in between my mom and something she wants, and that never goes well. See y'all after church, and it's not fair that I have to go and you don't."

"I'm not the one getting married." Cal yawned and sat back. "I don't have to impress the priest. Harry here isn't even Catholic. He's the luckiest one of all. He can watch all the football he wants every Sunday."

"Hopefully there will be football in Hell," Angie said with a wink. "Bye, boys."

Harry still had some questions. "Why does Aunt Celeste hate Seraphina? You said she was friends with Wes. I get she didn't want them to date, but according to you, they didn't."

"Nah, Sera wasn't interested in him that way. My sainted brother wasn't her type," Cal said. "She was more into bad boys, if you know what I mean. Sera got around in high school. Never could convince Wes that it wasn't going to happen."

"And your mom hates her because she didn't want Wes?"

"Nah. She hates Seraphina because she blames her for Wes losing his damn mind and going into the Army."

Harry stared at him. He got that Wes hadn't needed the Army the way he had, but he still didn't think joining up achieved a level of crazy.

Cal sighed. "I didn't mean it that way. It would have been great if serving his country was truly what Wes was doing, but it wasn't. He was running away."

"From what?" As far as Harry could tell, Wes's life should have been very good.

A grim expression crossed his cousin's face, a serious look he rarely saw there. "Wes was in his last year of college. Sera was working but for some reason she went up to Baton Rouge and they had a big fight. I don't know exactly what happened. I think Wes probably gave her some dumbass ultimatum. I told him he should be patient and eventually she would give in and sleep with him. I mean, he couldn't actually marry her, but he could have a good time. Like I said, I don't know what happened, but he came home and told Mom and Dad he'd dropped out and was going into the Army. He said he would prove to Seraphina that he could be man enough for her."

Harry sighed. "Damn. That explains it. He gives up his degree, and all over a woman. Why would she do that? Why tell him to go into the Army?"

"Who knows?" Cal shrugged like it no longer mattered, the sad look in his eyes turning back to the devil-may-care expression he wore like a mask. "Maybe she wanted to get rid of him. Wes could be annoying. Sera was one of the cool kids in high school. By that time Wes was in a private school. He would have been back in Papillon after he graduated. Maybe she didn't want the nerd to ruin her social life. None of it made sense to me, but Mom blames Sera for Wes's death, and she will not like Sera setting up house in our backyard no matter how big that yard is. She'll put the pressure on if what I heard is true. Though if Sera really has all that gold, she might make it a fight. Either way, it'll be interesting."

He didn't like to think about the woman with the high-voltage smile convincing his cousin to drop out of college, but he'd known women who lived to manipulate. Men, too. They weren't happy unless they were in control, and sometimes they drew satisfaction from ruining lives.

It didn't make sense, but it didn't have to because he was going to stay away from Seraphina. He wasn't going to cause a rift in his family over a woman he'd barely met. "Well, I'm going to work on a couple of things. I'll be out in the shop."

"I'll be in the media room. The Saints are playing. Come on up if you want to hang," Cal offered. "And I was serious about tonight. We're going to this bar outside of town. You'll like it."

He probably wouldn't, but at least he would know his cousin would get home all right. He pushed his chair back and started to pick up his plate. The maid was at his side before he could take a step. She took the plate out of his hand and swept away the mug.

"Thank you," he said.

She didn't look back.

It was a strange, strange world. He was happy when he and Shep got out to the shop and back to work.

Celeste stepped out of the dining room and forced herself to take a deep breath. She wasn't going to get emotional. When had it gotten hard to shove her feelings down? She'd had years to perfect the fine art of swallowing down every bit of rage, sucking up all her sorrow, and curbing her joy.

It might be Harry causing it all. Seeing him again, having him in her life, reminded her of who she'd been before she'd got it in her head that she could be someone else, someone more.

"Oh, she talks about him but it's usually to let me know it would have been better if I'd died instead of Wes."

The words floated out of the dining room, causing Celeste to stop in her tracks. Cal. Cal was talking.

"That's not true." Her daughter's voice was quieter.

"Really?" Celeste could practically see the expression on Cal's face. He would be staring at his sister with that arrogant look he'd inherited from his father. "And when she said, *You know I wish Wes was here instead of you*—what do you think that was a metaphor for?"

She forced back the need to walk into the dining room and apologize. One foot in front of the other. The maid walked by and Celeste nodded as though she hadn't just heard her son talk about how terrible she was.

She'd stopped drinking the day after that terrible night. Oh, she would have a sip or two of wine, but she wouldn't indulge. Indulgence had led to her mask slipping and her rage spilling out and striking her children. Cal had every right to be angry with her.

She hadn't mentioned it since that stiff apology, but her words were obviously still there and she had no idea how to address them except to give him some space. She wouldn't say a thing about him taking Harry out tonight. Honestly, she felt better with Harry there, his steady hand keeping Cal in check.

She glanced in the mirror. The face staring back was practically perfect, but that thought gave her no comfort. It was a mask.

Shouldn't a person's face change over time? Not that she'd allowed it. The first time her husband had mentioned the lines around her eyes, she'd gone to the plastic surgeon and had them taken care of. Every line or wrinkle was dealt with ruthlessly because perfection was the only proper outcome.

No one should be able to see her age, her grief, her happiness.

Her lipstick had faded. It wasn't the vibrant red she always wore. Her signature.

It didn't look so bad. Her lips were on the thin side, but they were rather nice. It would be a long walk to fix it and her feet hurt.

Her mother-in-law wasn't around to enforce the codes anymore. That was what she called her mother-in-law's rigid rules of behavior. The codes. Always look perfect. Never smile too brightly. Clothing should be understated but expensive. A lady never raised her voice or complained.

Why was she still following those rules? And why the hell couldn't Angie wear her cute shoes to church? Everyone else did. Did God truly care that her daughter was showing some toe cleavage?

But she'd followed them for so long, she wasn't sure what she would do without them. Those rules had become a road map of sorts, a way to live without risking too much.

Those rules hadn't saved Wes.

She took a deep breath. The well of her grief seemed never ending, a dark pool that she couldn't seem to climb out of.

"Mom?" Angie stood in the hallway.

She shook her head. How long had she been standing here staring at herself in the mirror? "Yes?"

"Are you all right? I'm going to change my shoes and then we can go. Unless you've changed your mind. No one will care that we miss a single Sunday."

Oh, but it was only weeks before Angie's wedding and their absence would absolutely be noted. There would be gossip, and avoiding gossip was the foremost of the codes. She smoothed out her dress and reached for her handbag. It was a sedate Louis Vuitton that went with practically anything. A show of her wealth. "Of course we should go. We need to talk to the priest about changing the candles in the sanctuary before the big day. He's being unreasonable."

"I think he's trying to follow church rules," Angie replied.

Celeste waved that off. Some rules were made to be broken, especially when an incredibly large check was involved. Money might not be able to purchase happiness, but it could buy candles in the proper color scheme. "It will all work out. I assure you. But, Angie, those shoes are fine for church."

Her daughter's eyes went wide. "What?"

It was time to find some compromise with her children. Maybe if she'd . . . No. She wasn't going there. She was focusing on the future and that meant her living children. She strode to where her daughter stood, looking at her like she'd grown two heads. "I said the shoes are fine. Let's go."

Angie stared for a moment more before a slow smile crossed her face. "All right, then."

It was good to know she could shock her children in good ways from time to time.

And it was good to bend the rules a bit. She took a deep breath as they walked into the morning air. This afternoon she would pay a call on Quaid Havery and inquire about whatever crazy feline organization old Irene had left her house to. Then she would see about finally getting the Guidrys out of her life.

It would be a good day.

chapter three

❧

"Okay. I haven't been out here in a long time. Wow." Sylvie Martine stood in front of her car, her heels sinking slightly into the ground since Irene had never bothered to have the drive paved. It was still the same dirt and gravel drive that had been there since Sera's great-grandpa's days. Hallie's car was parked beside Sylvie's flashy sedan.

Sera had called Sylvie for a lift because her car needed a new battery and she couldn't afford one. Again.

Hallie had come straight from mass to support her, though she had texted that she'd already done that by praying the house was still standing when she got there.

"Are you sure this is okay?" Hallie stared up at the house, a look of abject horror in her eyes. "I mean should we go in there? Or should we have hard hats? Maybe I should send Johnny in first. Or we could call Zep. He doesn't have a child to raise."

Though he was a pretty good uncle since he was hanging out with Luc this afternoon so she could come and survey the house she'd so recently inherited.

It wasn't that bad. Sera stood beside her two best friends as the afternoon light illuminated the task in front of her and told herself everything was going to be all right. After all, her aunt had lived here for years and nothing had fallen down around her. Mostly. "I'm pretty sure it's solid. My great-great-grandfather built it to survive hurricanes. It's still standing so I think it's fine. Most of the problems are cosmetic."

At least she hoped they were. Fifty thousand dollars sounded like a lot of money, but repairs and upgrades were expensive. She might need to take out a loan to get this place into real shape. Could she even get a loan?

Sylvie shook her head. "It's gone downhill since I was out here last." She sighed. "It's been years and years. I feel bad. I should have come out here and seen Irene. I got busy."

Sylvie was particularly busy because for the last several years she'd served as the mayor of Papillon. Like many of Sera's friends, Sylvie left the small town they'd grown up in for college. She'd gotten a degree in public administration. She'd been planning on going to DC, but when the mayor of thirty years had died suddenly, she'd come home to take care of her town. Her chock-full of crazy town. How Sylvie managed to get through a single town hall, Sera had no idea.

"She would have met you with a shotgun." Sera didn't want her friend to feel guilty. Her aunt had been isolated in her last years. "She knew you took over the mayor's office. She pretty much threatened anyone from the government. You know how she liked to think everyone was out to take her land and force her into medical experiments."

Sylvie chuckled. "That sounds like her. Still, I played out here, too, back when she didn't mind having ragamuffin kids running all over the place."

"Does it have electricity?" Hallie hadn't moved more than a couple of feet from her shiny new SUV. Unlike Sylvie, Hallie hadn't played here. Hallie's mother had been in a longtime feud with Irene over a banana bread recipe and wouldn't allow Hallie anywhere near the woman who'd accused her of culinary thievery. Not that Hallie would have played in the mud and caught crawfish. Even from a young age, she'd been worried about the state of her hair and nails. Hallie was definitely the girly girl among them.

"Of course it does." The electricity was unreliable at times and a whole lot of the lights blinked off and on, but they worked. When they wanted to. "And it's got AC and plumbing and everything. You don't have to come in. You two can go if you want to. I've got some things I want to check out. I'll call Remy and have him pick me up when he's done with his shift at the restaurant."

"That's hours from now," Sylvie pointed out. "Besides, I'm curious about what it looks like inside. How much crazier could it have gotten? I remember she used to have a collection of ceramic owls. They always creeped me out. I kind of want to face it again as an adult and maybe I'll stop having nightmares about owls."

The owls were still there. And they were still creepy and weird.

Hallie moved in beside her. "You love this place, don't you?"

She'd kind of expected that Hallie wouldn't want to stay long, and Sylvie always had something come up. Sera had come fully equipped with a notepad, her cell phone, and a pen so she could start making lists. Probably long lists. Long, expensive lists. "I do. I love it a lot. I know it looks run-down, but it's an amazing house and it's got a gorgeous view of the bayou."

It had a lot of land around it. Sera had always thought her aunt could have done amazing things with all that land. In her mind's eyes she saw a big patio with an outdoor kitchen and a firepit. She could throw parties where tourists could enjoy the beauty of the bayou with all the amenities of a great bed-and-breakfast. She could have lovely weddings out here.

She could raise a family here, like her grandmother had.

"Have you given any thought to living here?" Sylvie asked. "Not that you've had much time to think at all. It's a lot to take in, but I remember you talking about what you would do with this place when we were kids."

The whole estate had seemed magical when she was a kid. Back then she hadn't seen the disrepair. All she'd seen was the beauty. The whole world had kind of been that way. She wanted Luc to have that, to see the world the way it should be before he had to face the way it truly was.

"Really? Live here?" Hallie wrinkled her nose like she couldn't imagine the thought. "I mean I know you can't live with your mom forever. But this is so far out of town. I always thought you would get one of those duplexes out near me."

Hallie lived in a small neighborhood mostly filled with families of oil rig workers. Her particular neighborhood was one of the nicest in town because it was where the engineers and drillers lived. There was another neighborhood, though close to Hallie's, that was made up of manufactured homes and duplexes and fourplexes that served as housing for the roughnecks and their families.

Sera couldn't afford either. She couldn't afford renting a room somewhere, not that she would because she wanted Luc to have something more than a bathroom down the hall. "It works to stay with Mom and Zep. It cuts way down on the need for day care. I tend to work days and Zep works nights. He's surprisingly good with Luc, though I worry he's already trying to teach him how to charm the ladies. He might be actively using Luc to help him pick up women. Wow, I'm basically a walking stereotype. Twenty-five years old, living at home. Single mom in a small town. Barely finished high school. Can't seem to keep a job."

"Hey, you've been at Miss Marcelle's for six months," Hallie pointed out. "You've settled in real nice there."

"And you get your hair done in Houma." That fact had not been lost on Sera.

Hallie blushed. "Well, I've been going to Darlene for years. It would be rude to ditch her now."

Sylvie held a hand up. "And my momma would be real upset if I didn't go to her. Black girl hair right here."

Sera wasn't all that great with white girl hair, either. She hadn't expected Sylvie would be a client. After all, her mom—Miss Marcelle—did run the salon.

Hallie had complained about Darlene and her overuse of the scissors for years, but Sera simply sighed because she didn't blame her friend. The truth was she wasn't good at her job. She could do a serviceable haircut, but she wasn't all that creative. She pretty much offered everyone highlights, and that was all she had. "Yeah, well, I do more cleanup than I do styling these days. I'm not very good. I don't have a passion for it. I tried but the only people who still come in and ask for me are Lisa and her sister Lila. My clientele has become mostly men, and they stare at my boobs. Marcelle ran one out last week."

"I heard she chased him out with a broom because that was how she took out the trash," Hallie said.

Sylvie frowned, an expression Sera had seen her friend use on the most annoying of constituents. "Momma was so upset," Sylvie added. "She tried to get the sheriff to track that jackass down. Then she tried to get me to make a city ordinance, since I *am* the mayor. I had to explain to her that grabbing a woman's ass is already illegal and we don't need an extra law."

It hadn't been a great day. Sera had been left in tears

after that jerk had hit on her. "He grabbed my butt and asked if I did private haircuts. When did I become this girl?"

Hallie turned to look at her. "What girl?"

"The bad girl. The one men think they can play around with until the one they marry comes along." It hadn't been like she'd had a bad reputation in school. She'd dated Ben Reed for three years until he'd gone off to college and hadn't come back. She'd never cheated on him, though he hadn't liked Wes hanging around all the time. She'd made one mistake and it looked like she would pay for it forever.

Sylvie's eyes had gone soft and sympathetic. "You aren't that girl. No one really is. Men are jerks. At least a lot of them are. Most of them can't see what's standing right in front of them because they're always looking off at something in the distance."

"Oh, I think it's more than that." Hallie leaned against her car. "You want to talk about this? Because I avoid this subject like the plague, but I have thoughts."

Sylvie stared Hallie's way. "Hey, she's had a day."

Hallie shook her head. "Nope. If she's ready to talk, then we should talk. You know it."

Was Sera ready? If she wasn't by now, she wouldn't ever be.

"You think I should have told everyone who Luc's father is." She knew it bugged the hell out of her best friend that she wouldn't tell her the secret.

"I think whoever Luc's daddy is needs to step up, and it would go a long way to quiet down the rumors," Hallie said.

Sera knew what the rumors were. "I've never slept with a married man. I told you. It didn't even happen here. It happened when I was in Baton Rouge."

"It shouldn't matter," Sylvie insisted. "It's Sera's business and no one else's."

"Don't be naive. You grew up here, too. This is a small town and an oil town," Hallie pointed out. "You know how the wives can be. They're very territorial. When you find a man who can take care of you, you protect your marriage. At least that's the way these women work. You remember when the company sent out a single female engineer? They went crazy. The woman literally made twice what their pot-bellied, middle-aged husbands made and they thought she was going to steal one of them. Like she spent four years at Texas A&M getting a degree in petroleum engineering so she could steal a rigger from the arms of his wife."

That poor young woman had had a time of it, and she'd hauled herself right back to a nice cushy job in Houston the minute she'd been able to. Sera didn't have anywhere to go. "I've never dated a married man. I've barely dated at all. I turn down almost everyone who asks me. I liked Jackson."

Hallie sighed. "Yeah, I did, too, until he turned out to be an ass. I wish I'd never introduced you to him. He seemed like such a nice man."

She'd learned some guys were good at hiding their intentions. "I'm sure he's great with Johnny. He was great with me until I wanted to get serious."

Sera, you can't think this is going anywhere. I want to get into management. I know it sounds stupid, but wives can make or break a career here. You would break mine. But we can have some fun.

"I didn't like that man," Sylvie said. "He was pretty and all, but he had my jerk alarm going off. Sera, you can't let a man like that take you out of the game."

"It's not just him." She blinked back tears, pushing the humiliation down. "You would think in this day and age that no one would care. I'm not the only single mom around here. It's like I'm wearing a scarlet letter."

"But it wouldn't be if you would fess up about who Luc's dad is," Hallie insisted.

No, if she told who Luc's daddy was, the town might explode. And according to Angie, she might lose custody of her son. "I don't remember his name. It was a crazy night and I can't even regret it because I love Luc."

Would things be different if she moved? She looked up at the house she'd loved since she was a child and realized this might be what her aunt had wanted. For her to leave Papillon behind and start all over again. If she moved to Houston or New Orleans, no one would care that they didn't know who her baby's father was. She would be one more anonymous woman trying to make her way in the world.

Though it made her heart ache, she might have to sell this place. Not might. She knew what she had to do. There would be no gorgeous B and B where she served muffins and planned weddings, where Luc ran wild all over the bayou. She would have to take everything they could get out of this place, move to the city, find an apartment and a job she would likely hate, and survive.

"There's nothing wrong with you." Sylvie was always a positive voice in her life. Despite everything she'd been through, somehow Sylvie always saw that silver lining. "It's their problem."

"It will get easier." Hallie sighed as though she knew she'd gotten everything she was going to get.

"Will it?" There were things Sera hadn't considered. "Or will it get worse as Luc grows up? Will everyone be watching to see if they can see their husband in my kid's face? How will they treat him?"

Hallie's eyes went wide. "They won't be nasty to Luc. I

can't believe they will. You've got friends. No one is freezing you out. It's just the stuff with Jackson that's bringing it all back. And who cares what those crazy women think. Once you meet someone great and settle in, they won't see you as a threat. Right now you're a gorgeous blonde who does yoga every Wednesday. It's intimidating when you've got three kids and a husband who's gone most of the time. You'll see. Now, I know I made a mistake with Jackson, but I was thinking . . ."

Sera put her hands up. "Absolutely not. I'm done dating. I'm going to work on this house and try to figure out where to go from there. No more men."

She gasped as something moved behind Hallie. The overgrown bushes shook and she could hear the sound of leaves rustling. Sylvie backed up.

Hallie turned and grabbed her arm. "What is that? Is it a gator? I heard rumors that Irene had them trained to attack. She found them as babies and raised an army."

Sylvie snorted. "I could see that happening."

Her aunt hadn't been the mother of gators, but they were close to the water. It certainly wasn't unheard of for something scaly with big teeth to lumber through the area.

"Okay, we'll get in my car." Sylvie touched the button on her keys and there was a chirping sound as it unlocked.

They were closer to the car than the house. If it was a gator, he would mostly just hiss and look scary, but it was never a good idea to hang out with one. Unless it was Otis, but he stayed closer to the wharf.

The bush rustled again and a big creature rushed out, but Sera relaxed. Normally the sight of a German shepherd running her way would scare her, too, but this one had the goofiest, happiest look on his face. His tongue was hanging out and his tail wagging like he'd been playing a game and he'd won.

"Hey, boy." Sera got down on one knee.

Sylvie breathed a sigh of obvious relief. "I'll take dog over gator any day. I know I've lived here most of my life, but I will never get used to massive reptiles running toward me."

Hallie took a step back. "That's a big dog you don't know."

Hallie obviously didn't speak dog the way Sera did. The big guy scampered up and treated her like an old friend. "Nah, this is a sweet boy. And he's got a collar."

Sylvie reached out to give the dog a pet. "He's a pretty boy. Or girl."

She was betting this was a boy. "What are you doing out here, buddy? Did you get lost?"

"No, but I might have," a deep voice said. "And he's a boy. You can tell from the way he finds every woman he can and tries to get her to pet him."

She looked up and into the eyes of Harry Jefferys. Gorgeous, stunning Harry. He was more casual than he'd been yesterday, wearing a tank that molded to his muscular frame and showed off beautifully sculpted arms. He'd traded the jeans for basketball shorts and boots for sneakers. She stopped at the sight of metal where his right leg should have been. The shorts were long, covering his knees, but there was a metal rod in the place of his calf, ending in a sneaker. He had pulled the ear buds out of his ears and they dangled around his neck.

He glanced down to his leg. "Sorry. I wasn't expecting to meet anyone out here. We were going for a run. Shep, you should leave the nice ladies alone. Again, sorry, he's never met a stranger. I also don't have a leash. I didn't think I needed one out here. I thought I was still on my aunt's land."

It was so good he'd reminded her who he was. He was

far more than a hot bod and a face to die for. He was a Beaumont. Oh, maybe not in name, but he was Celeste Beaumont's kin and that meant they were on opposite sides. She straightened up. "No, you're on my land now."

Sylvie grinned. "Ooo, you said that like a lady boss, Seraphina. My land. I like that."

Harry put his hands on his hips as he surveyed the house. "Yeah, Cal mentioned you'd recently come into some property. You should get it fixed up before they appraise it. It looks like you've got a couple of areas to work on."

For some reason his comments stung. She wasn't sure why since she didn't care what he thought. "Thank you for pointing it out to me, Mr. Jefferys. I will be sure to do that. And you're more than welcome to run through here if you need to. We don't have fences up for a reason."

She bet Celeste would be putting one up the minute she found out who her new neighbor was, though.

"But you should look out for traps," Hallie said.

Harry looked back at her. "Excuse me?"

"There are no traps." The last thing Sera needed was parish inspectors coming out to make sure her aunt hadn't left a bunch of traps in the woods for tourists to run into. Sera had gotten all of them. She hoped. If Harry mentioned that to Celeste, she might get to thinking about creative ways to make her life hell.

"That's only a rumor," Sylvie explained. "Irene Guidry was what we like to call a character. She was kind of isolated, but she was a lovely soul."

Yes, there was Sylvie's positivity. And Irene would have been far more likely to take a shot at someone she considered an intruder. She'd kept her trusty shotgun with her all the time. She'd even refused to go into a nursing home at the end because her shotgun hadn't been welcome. Or at least that had been her excuse. Sera rather thought she'd simply wanted to die in her own home. Irene hadn't liked to go into town much. She'd been happiest here where she'd grown up and lived all her life.

Had she been afraid to get out and see the world? It was funny because Sera was afraid she wouldn't get to stay. She didn't want to leave. She loved this place, but it was starting more and more to look like staying wasn't a good idea.

"Seriously, I don't joke about things like traps or mines." Harry frowned her way. "How do you think I lost this leg?"

"I'm so sorry. I didn't realize," Sylvie offered, the politician in her trying to smooth things over.

Hallie turned a shade of pink no human being ever should. "I'm so sorry. It was a joke."

Harry's lips curled up in the most spectacular smile. That smile could light up a room. Maybe a whole house. "I was, too. I heard a bunch of stories about this place. You're all crazy, but that doesn't scare me. I like a little crazy."

Sera took a breath. At least they hadn't completely offended the man. "I was worried you had lost your leg to a mine."

"I did," he replied. "Blew it right off, but the good news is I can't lose much more of it, and I would bet any mines your great-aunt could get here aren't as bad as the ones I came up against in Afghanistan. I'll try to make sure if I step on one, I only lose the prosthesis. It's surprisingly replaceable and they're always innovating. I wouldn't mind checking out the new ones. I have my eye on a sweet new C-Leg. Besides, Shep here used to sniff out mines and munitions. He's pretty good. I know I wish he'd been with me that day."

"I'm so sorry." Sera needed to be nicer to the man. Just because he was Celeste Beaumont's nephew didn't make him a bad person. "We shouldn't joke about things like that."

"Hey, if I can't laugh about it now, why did it happen?" He'd moved in closer to her, and though there was still at least a foot of space between them, she swore she could practically feel the heat from his body. He'd been running and a fine sheen covered his skin. It did nothing to make him less attractive. "I have a whole repertoire of one-legged jokes. Well, it's really more like one and a half. I still have my knee and the thigh. I have some spectacular scars. Does the leg bug you? I normally wear full-length pants."

She found everything about the man fascinating, but then she thought he probably got that a lot. "The leg doesn't bother me. I'm sorry I stared. I haven't seen one like that before. My brother has a couple of friends with prostheses. He was in the Navy."

Harry smiled again. "He was a SEAL. He *was* the Navy. Yeah, I talked to him yesterday. He seems like a great guy."

"Remy's the best," Hallie said, staring at him like he was a rock star and she was a twelve-year-old girl with a crush. "And thank you for your service."

Harry nodded her way, but Sylvie was muttering something under her breath about marriage, to which Hallie again reminded everyone her eyes still worked.

If Harry was bothered by the shenanigans, he didn't show it. "Are you going inside? You should take an inventory first. Did the lawyer do that for you?"

"No, and knowing what Quaid charges per hour, I'm glad he didn't," she explained. "It was a real simple will. She had items for my mom and my brothers, but everything else came to me. I feel like I'm being selfish."

"You took care of her," Sylvie said softly. "You were the one who visited her and made sure she had food."

"And dealt with those cats." Hallie wrinkled her nose. "Did anyone clean up all that kitty litter or did you inherit that, too?"

Oh, she'd dealt with it. "The cats are in happy homes. And luckily my brothers feel the way y'all do." It was time to make her retreat. She turned to Harry. "Like I said, you are more than welcome to run through here. Now I need to go inside and make a few lists. It was nice to see you again."

"If you would like, I could come in with you," Harry offered. "Old houses like this are a hobby of mine. I might be helpful. Why don't you let me see inside, Seraphina?"

When his voice went low like that, her mind went a little blank. If he'd only been gorgeous, she could have dismissed him, but he was charming, too. And Remy had talked about him after the funeral, telling her stories of how he'd earned his medals while he served his country.

But he was connected to the Beaumont family and that meant he was off limits. Totally and completely, full stop.

She held her notepad up like it was a shield. "I wouldn't want to take up your time. Thank you. Good afternoon, Mr. Jefferys. Hallie, Sylvie, I'll be inside if you want to come in. If not, thanks so much for coming out here with me."

She didn't look back as she started toward the porch. The sooner she got this place ready to sell, the better.

Harry stared as Sera walked away from him. It seemed to be the way they ended every interaction.

The pretty woman with the halo of curly dark hair and perfect skin held out her hand. "She forgot to introduce us. I'm Sylvie Martine. I'm the mayor. Well, it's honestly more like being a warden sometimes."

He shook her hand, his mind still on the woman slowly making her way up the steps as though she expected them to give way underfoot at any moment. "Harry Jefferys. Nice to meet you."

He was a fool because only this morning he'd made the decision to stay away from Seraphina Guidry, but here he was knowing he wasn't about to continue with his run. He was going to follow her into that house and see how bad the situation was.

He should put his earbuds right back in, crank the volume up, and try not to break his good leg as he ran across uneven ground.

If he fell, would she help him up? Maybe offer him a water and sit with him while they waited for the ambulance. Could they get an ambulance out here?

"Uhm, I don't know that she should go through that place on her own." The blonde with short hair started reluctantly walking toward the house. "I guess I should go in with her. After all, she did go with me that time when I snuck away to New Orleans to see the Jonas Brothers. I don't know that it's the same. We only got grounded, but she didn't even like them and she went. We'll be even then, right? Walking into a haunted house pays off the debt for getting grounded for a month because I was in love with Joe. I'm Hallie, by the way. Hallie Rayburn. I've been friends with Sera since we were kids. If I don't come back out, tell my husband and daughter I loved them very much."

"Absolutely." Well, now he couldn't walk away. He never left a woman in danger. And he wouldn't mind getting a look inside. The house itself was stunning. Or it could be. The porch did need some refortification, and the roof definitely needed work, but that house had been built with love. It was there in the details, in the vintage corbels and porch swing. He'd been wrong about the stairs. They were surprisingly solid, but it looked like someone had used a different wood in some spots. The whole thing needed to be sanded and repainted. He would bet the steps that were different had been "fixed" by nonprofessionals, likely Irene Guidry's nephews, or maybe Irene herself.

"I'm not worried about ghosts," Sylvie said as she put her hand on the railing. It looked like it needed a coat of paint, too. "Critters are another story. I'm worried the rodent population got the message there is no longer an army of cats waiting to take them out and they've moved in. She didn't merely keep those cats as pets, you know."

"Would you feel better if I took a look around with you? I'm pretty good with home repairs and Shep will scare off most critters." The German shepherd was big enough he wasn't even worried about gators. Shep had a decent sense of self-preservation. He knew when to run and he was fast. "I really could help her figure out what the place needs."

He'd made his living for the last few years working on houses. He'd always been good at building things, and he'd spent time with some experts learning plumbing and electrical. He'd discovered there was always a job in construction wherever he went.

What would it be like to have a shop of his own? To build the furniture he saw in his head? He loved to work with reclaimed materials, to make something lasting out of what others considered trash.

"Yes, that would make me feel so much better," Hallie agreed. "Especially if there are serial killers hiding inside. Or clowns. Doesn't this place look like a murder house?"

No. It looked like a beautifully built Creole-style plantation home that needed a whole lot of TLC. It honestly wasn't that different from Beaumont House. A bit smaller, but he would bet it still had a lot of the original amenities. Beaumont House had been modernized on the inside. "I think it's got potential. It needs some attention, but this place was probably a jewel in its prime."

Shep bounded up the stairs.

Hallie followed behind him. "I will be honest, I always thought it would be an excellent place for a bed-and-breakfast."

"Oh, that would be perfect," Sylvie agreed. "We need more hotels, and I would love something nicer than that No Tell Motel outside town. That's really its name. Someone wasn't very creative. On the other hand, we have the Royal Garden Motel, which thinks way too much of itself. The health inspector finds violations all the time. A local B and B would be great. Especially around festival time."

Opening a B and B had been his mother's dream. She'd always wanted to run one, but she'd never had the money to invest.

"I worry Sera is looking to flip it, but she would be great at running a B and B," Hallie said. "I think it would be the perfect job for her. She's one of those jack-of-all-trades and master of none, if you know what I mean."

He knew. That old phrase pretty much summed him up. He wasn't a plumber, but he could deal with a lot of plumbing issues. The same with electrical. More important, he could tell when someone else knew what they were doing. Sera was going to have to hire contractors, and there were contractors out there who would take one look at the sweet-faced blonde and see dollar signs. If she picked the wrong one, she could get taken for everything she had.

He put a foot on the first of the steps, satisfied it held his weight without sagging. "How much does she know about rehabbing a house?"

"I watch a whole lot of HGTV," a prim voice said.

He glanced up and Sera was standing in the doorway, that clipboard in her hand and Shep sitting at her side, tail thumping.

"You're serious about fixing this place up?"

"Yes," she replied. "I have to fix it up or I don't get to keep it. It's in the will. My aunt wanted me to take the money she left and turn it into a home again. I know it would make a great B and B, but I don't have enough to take it to that level. I've got to make a profit off this place."

"You don't want to live in it?" He'd seen the way she'd looked at the house. She'd definitely looked at it with love in her eyes. He wouldn't be surprised to find out she'd spent time here when she was growing up. Childhood memories were powerful things.

She stepped back on the porch and let Sylvie join her. "I don't think I can afford to keep it. I have to put everything my aunt left me into the house. Maybe that gets it habitable, but I would have to pay taxes and insurance, and the up-keep on a place like this is pretty steep. I don't think the pittance I bring in cutting hair would be enough. Besides, it's a big old house for me and my son."

Yes, her son. She had a kid. That didn't scare him off at all, but he found it interesting that she obviously wasn't thinking past the next few months or years. She was a young woman. She was beautiful. She would get married and have more kids at some point. Unless she absolutely didn't want to.

He finally hit a stair that buckled. Yeah, it looked like they'd been replacing them as needed rather than redoing the whole staircase like he would have. Uniformity was very important in some cases. He bounced the step a bit. It held but it likely wouldn't when they started bringing heavy equipment in. "This one needs to be replaced. And you're going to have to paint the whole thing."

She frowned. "It seemed fine when I was on it."

"You don't weigh what I do," he pointed out. "And if you're going to fix this place up, you'll have a lot of big guys coming in and out. You want to make sure they can actually get inside the house to work."

She wrote something down in her book. "All right, then. Porch stairs."

"Those won't be too hard." Sylvie was walking around the big porch, taking it in. She glanced at the wood furniture and obviously decided not to try to sit. "We might need to update some of the décor."

Sera shook her head. "I don't think I can afford that. Maybe I could go to a garage sale."

"Nah, I can fix these." He reached the top step and moved to the rocker. It was beautifully done, just a bit worn. "I can refinish and repaint. You can get some new cushions for cheap and it'll look good as new."

"Really?" Sera asked, her eyes wide. "You can . . . I mean, that seems like a good idea. I will consider that. If I can sell the place furnished, that would be good. Well, except for the owls. I'll probably lose the owls."

He liked when she got distracted. She forgot to put up her walls, and she let him see a hint of the woman under her protective gear. She didn't like owls. It was good to know. Luckily he wasn't partial to owls. He glanced up and saw that the ceiling was painted a soft bluish green. Or it had been at one point in time. It was a pretty color, but odd for exterior paint. "Huh. I've seen a couple of porch ceilings painted like that around here. Is it a tradition?"

Sera looked up. "It's called haint blue. It didn't start here in Louisiana."

"It's a tradition among the Gullah," Sylvie explained. "When they were brought over as slaves, they brought their traditions, too. They believed this color would hold off the haints, or haunts as you would call them. Painting your porch a color like this would protect the whole house. It started in South Carolina and Georgia, and now it's kind of a Southern tradition. You'll see it all over town. My momma tells the story to anyone who moves in. Don't believe her. She gets a kickback from Gil at the hardware store."

"Momma told me they stopped doing that," Sera said with a frown.

"They never stop," Sylvie replied with a shake of her head. "Those two are going to be the terror of the nursing home one day. Sorry, Harry, Sera's mom and mine are kind of the bane of the town. My mother runs a successful salon and Delphine's family has the best restaurant in Papillon, but they're not happy unless one of them is convincing a tourist she's a voodoo priestess who put a whammy on him and the other is charging fifty bucks to take it off."

Sera had gone a nice shade of pink. "They like to think of themselves as entrepreneurs. Anyway, that's why many started painting their porch ceilings blue. My aunt did it for the other reasons Southerners use this color. She swore it kept the wasps away. She said they would think it was more sky and not bother to stop here. They would keep flying."

"Wouldn't they notice the overhang?" Hallie asked, looking up. "I would think they'd try to fly up into the ceiling and get confused as to why the sky stopped there. I would be."

He liked these women. They were fun. "Well, now they would think the sky is broken or maybe that the cracks in the paint are a wormhole or something," he said. "But only if the wasp is good at astrophysics."

Sera laughed, the sound magical to his ears. "I wouldn't want to confuse the wasps."

He stood beside her and looked up at the ceiling again. The color was quite beautiful, and he liked that there was tradition behind it. "I think I prefer the story about it keeping out ghosts. Maybe the ghost sees the color and thinks that's the way to heaven. You know sometimes the sky isn't as pretty as that color. It's nice to have something beautiful to look at. Maybe it helps the ghosts find their way home."

She was quiet for a moment and then she looked to him, a sheen of tears in her eyes. "I like that, too." She sobered and he missed the emotion on her face. "I should get inside and get to work."

He had to make a choice. His aunt wanted him to stay away from her, but she needed help. He wasn't the type of man who refused to aid a person in need and he had the prosthesis to prove it. Just because he lent her some advice on a subject he was well versed in didn't mean he would fall at her feet and beg her to date him. Even though his dog was already madly in love. "I'll help you."

She had her hand on the door. "Oh, I can make a list. It's easy. It's pretty much everything that needs fixing."

Hallie clapped her hands as she made it to the top of the stairs. "Excellent. Oh, I feel so much better with Harry here."

Sera looked at her friend. "I'm glad you do."

"I don't know, Sera, he might be useful," Sylvie said. "And he said the dog would chase critters away. We have no idea what's hiding in there."

Shep's tail thumped as though he was ready to jump into action.

Hallie's hands went to her hips. "He's an expert. I assure you Celeste Beaumont didn't bring him in to touch that precious gazebo merely because he's her nephew. He's good and you need someone good."

She shook her head. "No, I need someone cheap."

He could help with that. "I'll do it for free. I'm only consulting, after all."

And refinishing those rockers. And maybe fixing the porch steps.

"I don't need a consultant. I was going to call Herve down at the shop. He has a cousin who does home repairs," Sera replied. "He can handle all the stuff I can't. I'm making a list and then I'm going to fix all the stuff I can fix before I call him in."

"You're going to need to prioritize," he explained. "Unless you have an unlimited budget."

"That's what I was saying. I'm going to figure out what I can fix myself and do all of that and then bring in the big guns."

"The big guns being Herve from the auto shop's cousin." He wasn't sure she'd thought this through, but then she'd only found out she owned this place earlier today. Still, she should understand that a project this big needed an experienced manager. "Have you ever met him? Is he a licensed contractor?"

She snorted, a sound that shouldn't have been so cute. "It's Southern Louisiana. We're a town of six hundred people. No one is licensed."

"You are," Hallie pointed out. "You had to go through all sorts of hoops to be able to cut hair. Shouldn't Herve's cousin do the same to be able to fix your roof and make sure the house doesn't fall down?"

"And no, he's not a licensed contractor," Sylvie added. "He's not even really a contractor at all. Not like what you need. He's a handyman. He does odd jobs when he needs beer money. You have a real contractor right in front of you."

Sera pointed Harry's way. "Well, he's not even from Louisiana. I bet he doesn't have a license, either."

"I am a licensed contractor in Texas and Louisiana." He didn't mention he'd only gotten the one in Louisiana because his aunt had insisted and paved the way a little. He rather thought it was because she wanted to give him a reason to stay.

That seemed to stump her. She was quiet for a moment and then nodded as though coming to a decision. "That is a kind offer, Mr. Jefferys."

"It's Harry, please." He knew it was a mistake, but something inside him flared to life when he realized he was going to spend time with her. Something about Seraphina Guidry made him feel. He hadn't realized how numb he'd been. This was a big job. It could take months to get this house rehabbed. He would be around her constantly. He could figure out what it was about this woman that got to him.

"Harry, it's kind of you to offer, but I have to turn you down." Her jaw had gone tight. "I have to do this myself. I hope you have a nice day." She turned and started for the inside but stopped and put a hand on Shep's head. "You, too."

She disappeared behind the door.

That hurt more than it should.

Sylvie had an apologetic frown on her face as she opened the door Sera had closed. "I should follow her."

Someone should. It apparently wouldn't be him.

"Shep, come on, boy." He knew when to retreat.

The dog looked back at where Sera had disappeared before he whined and moved down the stairs.

He knew the feeling. She'd wanted to say yes to him. It had been there in her eyes. She'd wanted to invite him in and get his advice, but she'd turned him down even when it was to her own detriment.

Something was going on and he didn't entirely understand it. He understood why his aunt was upset. Why was Seraphina? Was she afraid of his aunt?

Hallie was staring down at him. "I'm going to get her to change her mind. She needs help. She's not thinking. She's had a long week, and a funeral is always exhausting. I hope the offer will still be open because she's going to realize how much she needs you. She's being stubborn is all. She's got it in her head she needs to be independent."

He rather thought *he* was the problem. He would bet if someone else had offered to help her for free, she would have been all over that deal. As he'd never done anything she could have found offensive, this had to be about his family. It had to be about his aunt or maybe even Wes. Was she carrying a torch for the boy she'd rejected? Or guilt because she'd rejected him in the first place?

He wanted to tell himself it was a mystery he didn't need to solve, but he knew he wouldn't be able to leave it alone.

"I'm around if she changes her mind." He reached and got his earbuds. "Even if she only wants to talk. I'll send her some resources. Come on, Shep. This run isn't going to finish itself."

He took off, jogging slowly, but his mind was back on that house and the woman inside it.

Not even the air-conditioning and breeze of the fan in Quaid Havery's elegantly appointed office could cool down the fire Celeste felt licking along her every nerve ending. "What do you mean Irene left the house to her niece? Which niece are we talking about, because it better be someone from out of town. Some long-lost niece no one in the Guidry family talked about? One who never chased after my son and clawed his heart out? It better be that niece."

Angela was seated beside her, and her daughter shook

her head. "Quaid didn't have anything to do with who Irene Guidry left the house to. You don't have to breathe fire his way."

The man who'd been the family lawyer since he'd taken over for his father four years before actually looked intimidated, and that wasn't an expression she normally saw on the thirty-two-year-old's face. "I absolutely didn't tell Ms. Guidry who to leave her house to. I merely served my function and wrote the will."

And that was where he'd made his mistake. "You wrote the will and knew Seraphina Guidry would inherit that house."

"Yes, I did." Quaid straightened up and seemed to shake off his surprise. "When one writes a will, one tends to need the names of the people inheriting, Mrs. Beaumont. Like when my father wrote your husband's will and put your name there on the list."

She felt her eyes narrow because she knew what he was poking at. "Yes, it's lucky for me that you put off that appointment with my husband before he could change the will and leave everything to Calvin. Is that what you're trying to say? Don't you try to intimidate me, Quaid Havery. Angela and Calvin both know what happened."

Angie leaned over, looking the lawyer in the eye. "We're happy Dad didn't rewrite his will. Cal didn't want that responsibility, and he certainly didn't like the way my father treated us like we were back in the eighteenth century and everything should be held by the eldest son. My mother can handle the Beaumont holdings and has done so brilliantly. Don't think you can split us up over that. There are many other ways to go about sowing dissension among the Beaumonts."

Sometimes her daughter could be obnoxious. "Angela."

She shrugged. "Well, you make me go to church, and we're all supposed to be honest. It would be way easier to sway me to his side if he offered me some carbs."

Quaid sighed and sat back. "I wasn't trying to sway anyone. I was merely pointing out that writing wills is my job. Irene Guidry paid for my services and I wrote her will. It was not my place to tell her who to leave her property to."

"It is your place to watch out for this family's best interests." She was well aware of the ice in her words. She used the voice she spoke to badly behaving board members with. "The Beaumont family makes up a large part of your business."

"Yes, and I'm the only lawyer in town," Quaid countered.

He was underestimating her will in this. "Business can be conducted over the telephone these days. I assure you there are plenty of lawyers in New Orleans who would be thrilled to represent my interests. My daughter's fiancé is a lawyer."

Angela raised a hand in a vain attempt to call her off. "Momma, Austin is a prosecutor. He doesn't do business law."

"Well, Quaid here does everything. I'm sure Austin can, too." She would send him right back to law school if she needed to. "I don't want that tramp in my backyard. I've made it plain that I want to buy Guidry Place for years."

"And I took your offers to Irene," Quaid replied. "At great personal risk. I was lucky that old woman's eyesight was going."

She waved it off. He was being a baby. "I told you I would pay for the Kevlar vest." She sighed and sat back. It was obvious the man was going to be useless for anything but basic information. "So Seraphina is planning on living in that rattrap?"

"That rattrap is worth a lot of money." Quaid settled in as though he realized the real danger had passed. He really was the only option in town. "As for Seraphina's intentions, I don't know exactly what she's planning on doing with it."

Celeste knew. The young woman would use it as a weapon to torment her. She would parade that family of hers around like they had the right to be there. Delphine hadn't lost her boy. Delphine, for all the mistakes she'd made, still had a loving family around her. Seraphina had done her best to ruin Celeste's family, but she'd still gotten a sweet baby boy out of whatever man she'd chosen over Wes.

If only Wes had lived, he would have seen Sera for who she was. He would have seen that Seraphina was a woman who slept with married men. It was the only reason Celeste could come up with for her not telling the world who the father of her child was. She was ashamed, and she should be.

She ignored that prickle of unease that nagged at her. What would her sister have said? There but for the grace of god . . .

It had only been her mother-in-law's desperation for a grandchild that had caused her to allow Ralph to sully the Beaumont name by marrying a flight attendant.

"If I had any other options, I would take them, Celeste," Opal Beaumont had said the day of Celeste's wedding. *"You won't ever be a real Beaumont, but after I'm done with you, no one else will question it. But you and I will always know that you're a gold-digging imposter."*

"I can't imagine Sera is going to live there, Momma." Angela was using her soothing tone.

It set her on the edge because she didn't want to be soothed. She wanted never to have to see Seraphina Guidry again. She wanted that woman to stop haunting her every day of her life.

Quaid leaned in like he was telling her a secret. "If it helps, I don't think she's going to live there, either. I think she's going to fix it up and sell it. Give her some time and you might be able to get that property."

Sera would never sell to her. Or perhaps she would, but only if she paid far more than that ramshackle place was worth. There was no reason to fix it up when she was going to raze it to the ground and build something new. She forced a smile on her face. "Of course, you're right. Angela, we should go or we'll miss the appointment with the florist. Quaid, if you hear anything about Guidry Place going on the market, please let me know."

He nodded, but there was suspicion in his eyes. "I will do that."

That suspicion proved he wasn't a dumb man. She had zero intentions of letting the situation lie until Seraphina had the upper hand. She needed a plan. She would have to find a way to win this war she found herself in.

Then it could be over. Then Sera would leave and she wouldn't have to think about her again.

But as she walked out, she wondered about that girl who haunted her dreams. Sometimes that face of Sera's became someone else's. Her own.

She shook the thought off and began to plan.

chapter four

❧

Sera hadn't stopped thinking about Harry all day. Sending him away had been harder than it should have been, and it wasn't merely because he would have been incredibly helpful.

She wanted to spend time with him. She liked how he smiled and how he flirted with her in a way that didn't make her feel like he was only thinking of one thing. She flat out liked him. And his dog.

She rocked for a moment, Luc's little body draped over her torso and shoulder. He was getting so big. One day—way too soon—he wouldn't be able to lie on her like this. He wouldn't need her to rock him to sleep.

One day she might not be able to rock her baby while she listened to the sounds of the evening, to the cicadas singing, her mom listening to country music while she did the dishes, the wind coming through the big cypress trees outside their house. One day soon she and Luc would be alone in the city and the only sound that would matter would be the alarm clock telling her it was another day to get through.

She did not want to leave Papillon.

She wanted Luc to be surrounded by family the way she had. Remy had only been home for a year. She wasn't ready to leave her big brother again. They just felt complete, but she had to consider the fact that Luc was getting older and he would hear the rumors about his birth.

Would it help if she made up a man? Maybe she could find one on Craigslist. He could show up and claim to be Luc's father, and then they could have a huge fight and break up and he could leave, never to be seen again.

What was she going to tell Luc? Did she have the right to keep the secret of his conception from him?

I love you, Seraphina. I always have.

She could still hear Wes that morning after she'd gotten drunk and landed in the bed of her best friend. When she'd explained it had been a huge mistake, he'd gotten so angry with her. There had been an undeniable potential of violence in him that morning. She'd known Wes Beaumont most of her life, but in that moment, she'd been afraid of him.

The chime of the doorbell brought her out of her dark thoughts. She glanced at the clock on the dresser. Almost eight o'clock. It wasn't very late, but late enough for her to wonder who would come to their door. Zep had already left for the night.

She stood up and gently placed Luc in his bed, hoping he would stay there for once. Her boy liked to climb and he wasn't afraid of falling. Nope. That was her fear. She left her sleeping baby and walked into the hall as she heard her mother opening the door.

"Well, hello, Angela," her mother was saying. "Come on in. Is everything all right?"

Sera sighed. She should have expected a visit. Naturally Angie Beaumont would show up after dark, and she'd likely walked so no one would see her car parked outside.

It wouldn't do for the sweetheart of Papillon to be seen talking to the bad girl.

She stepped out into the foyer, where Angie was standing.

"Not at all, Ms. Delphine." Angie was dressed in slacks and a blouse. Beaumonts didn't do casual.

Although one of them did. One of them wore shorts that showed off his legs, and yes, she'd thought the prosthesis was sexy, too. He'd had a scar on his right arm and a couple of whispery ones that ran from his jawline to his shoulder blade. The scars made him real. Without them he would be almost too perfect. With them, she could remember he was more than a pretty face and a masculine body. He was a man who'd been through a lot.

Sometimes she wished the world could see her scars so maybe they would remember she'd been through a lot, too.

"I wanted to pop in and talk to Sera," Angie continued, glancing to Sera. "I heard you all had a busy day."

And she was here to make sure that day wouldn't ruin the secret they kept. "Why don't you come on into the kitchen and I'll tell you about it. You want a glass of wine?"

Angie gave her a wide smile. "I've been wedding planning with my mother. I could use a whole bottle."

Sera led Angie back to the kitchen and picked up a bottle of Pinot Noir that Remy had left for them to try. There were perks to having a restaurant in the family. She could always take a shift if she needed cash, and someone always wanted them to try wine. "How are the plans going? Is Austin happy with them?"

Sera had met Angie's fiancé but only because they'd both been at a church function and it would have been rude not to introduce him. She was sure if they'd been somewhere else, Angie would have ignored her the way Celeste would want.

"Austin wants it all over with." Angie took a seat at the round breakfast table, crossing one leg over the other and showing off the red sole of her shoes. "Sometimes I think we should have eloped."

"And deprive the town of the wedding of the year?" Sera expertly uncorked the wine and poured two glasses. "That would be cruel."

Angie gave her a long sigh and took the wine. "I suppose so. I know my mother would be disappointed." She glanced around as though looking to make sure they were alone.

"Momma's gone to her bathroom. She'll be at least an hour or two." Her mother took long baths during which she read old romance novels and soaked in lavender-scented bath salts. She had a gorgeous claw-foot tub. There was one at Guidry Place, though like everything there, it needed to be refinished.

Like Harry had offered to refinish the rockers she'd loved as a child. She'd stood there as he'd run a hand over the arm of the chair. Like he could feel the thing, see himself bringing it back to its old glory. Harry had the most beautiful hands.

She took her own glass and sat down opposite Angie. "How did your mom take the news?"

There was zero question in her head why Angie had shown up this evening. The news that Sera now owned Guidry Place, a property close to Beaumont House, would have made the rounds. Celeste likely had heard it at her Sunday luncheon.

Angie's expression went tight. "Not well. She's upset. She thinks you're going to move in."

"I might have to for a little while." She'd been overwhelmed by the amount of work she was going to have to do. It would take months to get the place ready to show. "It's a lot of work. I have to do some of it myself because I don't think Irene understood how much repairs and refurbishing cost these days."

"Or you could sell it to my mother." Angie leaned forward. "You know she's wanted that place for a long time."

"I know she's talked about tearing it down." It was stubborn of her because she knew Celeste would buy it, but she wasn't about to sell her childhood paradise to a woman who hated her. A woman who would only see it as a piece of trash to be removed.

"She would like to build a new guesthouse and a pool," Angie said, as though that was completely reasonable. Everyone needed two guesthouses. "She would give you a good price."

"No, she wouldn't. She would try to screw me over and you know it."

"I won't let her. You have to see you're in over your head. You're not ready for something like this."

She wasn't but she had to find a way to make it work that didn't include selling out to Celeste. "Tell her I'm going to fix it up and I will likely sell it, but only to a family that plans to live here, or Sylvie talked about selling it as a bed-and-breakfast. We need more hotel rooms around town."

"I don't know that Mother will like that idea."

"I don't care." She was tired of being afraid of Celeste.

Angie's eyes widened. "You need to. You know why you should." Her voice went low despite the fact that they were alone. "Sera, I like you. I've always liked you and that's why I've tried to protect you all these years. Mom only knows you rejected Wes. She doesn't know you slept with him, and she definitely doesn't know Luc is her grandchild."

"I don't honestly think she would care. I've thought

about this for years." She was tired of keeping secrets. "The woman hates me. She wouldn't want Luc to come anywhere close to her precious name because he's half mine."

She'd stewed over it all afternoon as she'd walked through the house. Maybe Hallie was right and she should come clean. It would cause a scandal for a while, but then it would die down and maybe she wouldn't have to leave. She would have to explain to Luc why half his family wouldn't spend time with him, but it would be okay. Her family would give him all the love he needed.

Angie put her glass down. "If you think that's true, then you don't know my mother. I want you to think about this. In the three years since Luc was conceived, she's lost Wes and my father. She's actively trying to tempt Harry into coming here to live, and that second guesthouse she wants to build is so Austin and I will stay here. She honestly thinks Austin won't mind commuting hours to New Orleans. She's terrified of having an empty nest, and Luc is a sweet little bird who won't fly away for a long time. She won't care that he's half Guidry. She'll take him and make him all Beaumont."

Make him hate his own mother. Or worse, teach him she wasn't even worth thinking about. "The courts wouldn't have a reason to take Luc from me. I'm a good mom."

Angie's gaze turned sympathetic. "I know you are. You're a genuinely good person, and I honestly think if my brother had lived, you two would have found your way back to each other."

She hoped they could have been friends again, but she'd never felt a spark with Wes. She'd loved him. She genuinely had, but she hadn't been in love with him. What would have happened if he'd lived? There was no question in her mind that he would have asked her to marry him. She might have done it since she'd been terrified at the thought of having a child on her own. She'd made the decision to tell him when he came back on leave, but he'd never come home. Would she have married him and fallen in love with her husband? Had she been foolish to want passion and romantic love in her life?

"I don't know about that. It doesn't matter now anyway."

Angie took a long drink before sitting back. "No, I suppose it doesn't, but I think about it. I think about what would have happened if Wes hadn't died. I wonder if my mother would have even bothered with my wedding. She didn't pay much attention to me while Wes was around. Well, except to tell me how I should dress and how I was embarrassing her. It's like she remembered she had other children when Wes was gone. I hate that I think those things, but you need to remember that my mom was obsessed with Wes. And just because you're a good mom doesn't mean my mother won't try to get custody of Luc. She'll think she can give him a better life."

"The courts won't take him away from me without cause."

"Maybe, but will you have the money to fight her?" Angie asked. "You'll need a lawyer, and one from out of town because Quaid has represented our family for a long time. You'll have to find a lawyer and he'll want a retainer. My mother is patient. She can keep the legal battle going for years."

It was her worst nightmare. The thought made her stomach turn. This was the conversation she'd had with Angie when she was six months along and she'd decided to let the Beaumont family know she was carrying Wes's baby. She'd thought it would bring them some peace, to let them know Wes wasn't entirely gone.

Thank god Angie had stopped her. Angie had opened the door that night and had hustled her out. They'd talked over tea in the back booth at Dixie's Café, and Sera had realized how close she'd come to making a huge mistake.

Was she still trying to make that same mistake? Still trying to believe that somehow she could find her place here again, be enough for anyone outside of her family?

Angie stared at her with sympathetic eyes. "Let me help you. I can talk to Mom. If I let her know you're not going to stay, she won't have a problem with it. Let her make you an offer."

"I can't sell it until I restore it. It's not allowed by the terms of the will. Technically it's not mine until I've spent the money Aunt Irene left on restorations. Quaid has to sign off on everything. Tell her I'm going to honor the will and then I'll sell it." She still wouldn't sell to Celeste, but she would sell. "And then I'm probably leaving town."

"Oh, I hate that, but I know it's probably for the best." She reached out and put a hand over Sera's. "I love you like a sister. I wish my mom could see how good a person you are. She's not capable of seeing past her own grief."

"I didn't make Wes join the Army. I didn't even suggest it."

"I know that, but she won't believe you," Angie argued. "She can't believe that her perfect boy could be so reckless. Besides, he did tell all of us he was joining up to prove to you that he was a real man."

She shook her head. "I never suggested he wasn't. All I ever told him was I didn't want to be his girlfriend. I made a mistake that night and I hated the fact that I hurt him, but I couldn't pretend to feel something I didn't."

Angie sighed, a weary sound. "And he couldn't stand the fact that he didn't get what he wanted. I blame my mother for that, too. There was a lot to Wes you didn't see because he was in love with you since you were children. He could be petulant."

She'd seen that side of him the morning they'd last spoken. Maybe she needed out of here if only to get away from the ghosts that haunted her.

Maybe the ghost sees the color and thinks that's the way to heaven. You know sometimes the sky isn't as pretty as that color. It's nice to have something beautiful to look at. Maybe it helps the ghosts find their way home.

Harry's words floated through her brain. Was she still carrying Wes around? Was he still here with her? Would she leave him behind if she finally left Papillon? Or would she simply relocate them all and be stuck with the same problems as before?

She wanted to spend time with Harry like she hadn't with anyone in years. But Wes was still here, still between her and happiness. Or something like it. "Tell your mom I'll be gone in a year if she can leave me be. I know I can't stay here. Luc already has Wes's eyes."

Angie gasped. "I hadn't noticed."

"He's got Remy and Zep's coloring, but if you look close, those are Wes's eyes staring back," she admitted. Sometimes, when she wasn't angry with Wes, she missed him. He'd been a good friend for years. Had he only been that way because he'd wanted her? Did it matter why he'd been there for her?

If he'd lived, would they still be friends? Or would he have taken Luc from her if she hadn't fallen in line?

It didn't matter. The past was the past and she needed to focus on the future.

"I'll make her understand," Angie promised and looked down at her glass. "Now, this is delicious. Tell me Remy's going to stock it. I have to go to Guidry's to get any kind of decent wine that doesn't come from my mother's cellar. She dispenses that wine with the same graciousness as she gives out compliments."

Sera chuckled and forced herself to talk about anything but the sorrow that had opened up inside her heart.

The Back Porch was a ridiculously tacky bar in a prefab building right outside the parish line. It was full on a Sunday night, and it was obvious these were not churchgoing people. He'd already seen the bouncers stop two fights, and he was fairly certain whatever was going on in that bathroom might end in an STI.

"You want a beer, soldier?" There was a big guy behind the bar. He had to be at least six-seven, with dark hair that brushed his shoulders.

"Ex-soldier, and how can you tell? And three of whatever's on tap."

"I'm excellent at profiling customers," the bartender replied. "Mostly because I need to know who's going to give me trouble and who won't. We're on our own out here. It's precisely why my boss opened this bar. He didn't want to have to deal with Sheriff LaVigne. Of course, the owner is a lazy bastard and doesn't deal with much of anything, so I'm on my own."

"And what kind of trouble will I give you?" Harry held out his hand. "Harry Jefferys, by the way. I suspect you're ex-military, too. I think that's a Navy tat I see on your arm."

The big guy shook his hand. "The name's Cain. Cain Cunningham, and I did my time. Now, you're not going to give me trouble unless someone offends you, and it might take a lot to do that. You're not the type who cares what other people think. You're confident. If someone hurt a person in your circle, you could set a man on his ass. The problem is you're with Cal Beaumont and he's always looking for trouble. Zep Guidry doesn't have to look for trouble.

It finds him. Is there a reason he's not at his brother's bar instead of mine?"

Zep Guidry had explained that beer tasted better when his brother wasn't keeping track of how much he drank. "I think he wanted a change of pace. And my cousin wanted out of the house. He wouldn't care where we are as long as he's not at home listening to his mother remind him he's got to go to work in the morning."

Cain looked a bit skeptical. "Does he actually work or is this one of those things where he's got a title and an office and no real power?"

"He's learning the business." Slowly, from what Harry could tell. Cal didn't talk much about work, and in the time he'd been here, Cal seemed to take Fridays off. "No one expected his father to pass as early as he did. Cal was barely out of college."

And from what he could tell, Cal wasn't handling the stress of suddenly inheriting a company well.

"Yeah, and I remember when he lost his brother. That couldn't have been easy. I grew up in these parts. I left for a couple of years, went into the military, and when I came out, I worked in Atlanta," Cain explained as he poured the three beers Harry had ordered.

"What made you come home?" From what he could tell, most young folks who left didn't come back.

"What always makes us come home? I had a family member who needed me," he replied in a gravelly tone. "Is that why you're in town? I hear you're Cal's cousin but you've never been here before. I thought the Beaumonts were all tight."

He wouldn't call the family tight in an emotional way. There was a careful distance between them all, and he worried it was more about grief than anything else. They seemed to be stuck in a cycle. "Celeste Beaumont was my mother's sister. I'm not from the wealthy side of the family. I grew up in Texas. We didn't get down here a lot. Did you know them as kids? My cousins, that is."

A single shoulder shrugged as he placed the final beer in front of Harry. "I'm a bit older than Cal, but sure, I knew them. It's a small town. Everyone knows everyone else. And Cal has always been a little wild. Wes was quieter. It was obvious he was the favorite. He was smarter. Everyone thought he would take over the company one day. It was a shock when he up and joined the Army. And Angie was just kind of there. She was a shy girl. She kind of blended in wherever she went. But they seemed like solid kids. Cal wouldn't let anyone bully his brother or sister. He was a pretty good guy. And then he started drinking."

He stared pointedly at the beers.

"Yeah, I don't think he's going to stop anytime soon." His cousin partied pretty hard, and it was obvious it was starting to be a problem. Harry picked up two beers in one hand and one in the other. It was not his first rodeo. "I'll see if I can keep him under control tonight."

"Try, because I do not need the sheriff up my ass if Cal causes trouble. He might not come out here often, but if a Beaumont gets hurt in a bar fight, I assure you I'll get a visit," Cain said with a frown.

"I'll make sure he's cool." It was the only reason he'd agreed to come out this evening. He hadn't wanted Cal driving. He turned to the table his cousin was sitting at and caught sight of the third person in their party this evening. Zep Guidry. Yeah, maybe making sure Cal got home all right wasn't the only reason he'd done it.

How many times did that sweet-faced blonde have to turn him down before he got the message? He started for the table. He wasn't going to pursue her. Not romantically.

He'd received that message, but he got the feeling there was something more to the feud between his aunt and Seraphina. He also worried it was a battle Sera wasn't going to win.

He set the beer in front of Cal and Zep and slid into his chair.

"So you met Cain," Cal said, taking a sip. "Watch yourself around him. He's on the dangerous side, if you know what I mean."

"I do not." He'd seemed pretty cool.

Zep leaned in. "There's a rumor he works for a drug dealer. Now, I stay away from all that stuff because beer works fine, and no one ever lost their teeth from drinking beer."

Cal shook his head. "I don't know about that. Herve lost his front two teeth in that fight and it was all because he'd been drinking beer."

Zep rolled his eyes. "You know what I'm saying. I don't do anything to hurt this face of mine. It's my moneymaker. It's how I bring in the tips."

"You have to play the handsome card because you're the world's worst waiter," Cal pointed out. "If your brother didn't own the restaurant, you would have been fired long ago."

Zep simply shrugged. "That's fair. But like I was saying, I'm not into the drug scene, but the word is Cain is part of that world. His sister was. Suzy Cunningham was a nice girl until she got involved with drugs. Died of an overdose. I would have thought that would teach Cain, but he's a stubborn fool. And hopefully he didn't hear that because he can also be a violent fool from what I've heard."

Harry hadn't gotten those vibes off the man, but hiding his true nature would make him an excellent criminal. "I have to ask why we're here, then, if it's so dangerous."

"We're walking on the wild side, cos," Cal said with a grin. "Guidry's is full of families. Hell, they have a playpen in the middle of the dining room. We're men. We need our space."

Couldn't their space include a regular cleaning? He wasn't a fussy man, but he liked things to have a certain level of hygiene. He didn't need to walk on the wild side. He'd already seen the darkness the world could offer. He tried to always look for the light, but Cal seemed determined to push boundaries. A rock song started to pulse through the place and Cal stood up.

"I'm going to go and see if any of those lovely ladies over there needs a dance partner," Cal said with a smirk, looking over at a table of six women who had been doing rounds of shots. "Come on, Harry. Let's live a little."

He patted his right leg. "I'm not such a great dancer. You go on."

There it was. That silver lining he liked to find. Yes, he'd lost a leg, but on the bright side, he had the perfect excuse not to dance.

If Seraphina wanted to dance, he would try it. Especially if it was a slow song he could sway to.

"Suit yourself." Cal strode up to the table and immediately had two dance partners.

"You can join him. I'm fine here," Harry said to Zep.

Zep sat back. "Nah. I'm not much of a dancer. And I'm not looking for a date tonight. Though you should know I could find one if I wanted to. I guess this isn't really my crowd. The truth is I like Guidry's bar. Maybe I'm getting old, but fighting and waking up next to someone whose name I can't remember has lost a lot of its appeal. But Cal is my friend and I can't let him come out here alone."

It was good to know someone was looking out for Cal. "How long has he been doing this?"

"Since Wes died and he realized he was trapped," Zep replied.

"Trapped?" He had to lean in to hear Zep over the music.

"Yeah, Wes was supposed to take over the business," Zep explained. "I know Cal has a business degree, but he never wanted to manage his dad's company. He liked marketing. He wanted to move to New York and try his hand with one of the big corporations. He wanted to get out of that house and out from under his mother's thumb. Wes was the one who was groomed to be the CEO one day. Cal acts like an ass some of the time, but he's trying to hold it all together. First Wes loses his damn mind and blows up all his parents' plans, and then he dies. Then not a year later, Cal loses his father. It's been rough on a lot of people, but Cal hides behind beer and women."

"It seems to me like Wes's death was rough on everyone." He wanted to understand what was going on. No one seemed willing to say more than Sera had been mean to Wes and Wes had run away. It didn't make sense.

"Yeah." Zep's expression had lost its normal lighthearted look. "Town like this, losing a kid is hard. He wasn't someone anonymous. He was more than a name in a paper, even to the people he wasn't close to around here. And given that he was a Beaumont, everyone had expectations."

Even the rich had their troubles. No amount of money guaranteed a perfect life. "That he would take over the company?"

Zep nodded. "And that he would marry young and start a family like his father had. Honestly, I thought he would marry my sister."

"From what I've heard, he would have." He'd only met Wes a couple of times, but now he remembered that even as a kid he'd talked about his best friend and that she was a girl and so very pretty. He must have been talking about Sera.

"Sera and Wes were always close, but I think she viewed him more like a puppy who imprinted on her at a young age. I was all Team Wes because my sister does not have the best taste in men. Her high school boyfriend never intended anything serious with her. He dumped her the day before he left for college. Wes always treated her right. I knew she didn't love him, but couldn't she have given him a chance? That was a lot of money she walked away from." He waved it off. "I'm joking. Mostly. I doubt the Beaumonts would have allowed Wes to marry Sera even if she'd wanted him. They've got their ways."

"What does that mean?"

"Everyone knows Celeste will move heaven and earth to make sure her children marry the right people, associate with the right people. I know she bought off two of the guys Angie dated before she settled down with Austin. His family owns a bunch of apartment buildings around the South. He went to a good school and got into a profession Celeste approves of. His older brother is growing their real estate empire. That's the right people in Celeste's eyes."

"She's not as bad as you make her sound," Harry argued. "She's been very welcoming of me. After all, I assure you I don't own some company. I've basically got nothing but my truck, my tools, and my dog."

"But you're blood and you're a war hero." Zep studied him for a moment. "I saw you talking to my sister the other day and then she mentioned she saw you earlier this afternoon. Were you looking for her?"

Ah, he was about to get the brotherly lecture. He should have expected it. "I was out for a run. I didn't realize her new property was so close to ours. It was a coincidence, but I was happy to see her. Your sister is a lovely woman."

Zep's eyes narrowed slightly. "My sister is also a vulnerable woman. She's got a kid, you know."

"She's also got a life. I don't see how her having a kid means she shouldn't date. I've got a dog."

"I'm saying there are a lot of men out there who don't want to raise someone else's kid," Zep drawled.

He'd heard that from more than one of his friends who wouldn't date single mothers. He'd never understood the excuse. "He wouldn't be someone else's kid."

Zep raised a brow.

He was moving too fast and not explaining himself well enough. "I'm not saying I'm looking to get married. I'm only saying that a woman having a child shouldn't be a big deal. If I wanted to date a woman, had a connection with her, her having a kid wouldn't matter. If I married someone with a kid, the kid would be my kid, too. That's how family is supposed to work. I know you put the word 'step' in front of 'father,' but 'father' is the important part."

Zep was quiet for a moment as though taking the words in. "Well, her last boyfriend didn't see it that way. She hadn't dated since Luc was born, and then Hallie set her up with this walking bicep who basically wanted to play around. I've heard he's been talking about her around town. I would very much like for him to do that to my face. I apparently have to actually witness the behavior in order to give him the ass kicking he deserves."

"What's he been saying?" Maybe there was a good reason Seraphina wasn't interested in dating.

"The normal guy stuff. I don't know," Zep admitted. "People tend to shut up when I walk in, but I know they're talking about her. I hope this house helps. Sera's smart, but her plans for the future kind of fell apart when she had Luc."

"The dad's not in the picture?" According to Cal, no one knew who the dad was, but her brother would likely know more.

Zep shook his head. "No, and let me tell you that's a guy I'd also like to have a discussion with. Sera says she doesn't know. I mean she knows, but it was a one-night stand thing. But I find it odd. Sera is more of a monogamist, if you know what I mean. She's also not a big drinker. I worry that she got drunk at a party and someone took advantage of her. But again, I'm not allowed to kick anyone's ass. Luc is great, though. I love that little guy. Wouldn't have said I liked kids, but that nephew of mine is sweet as pie. He's always into something."

"How old is he?" He shouldn't keep asking questions. Every single answer led him back to the truth. Sera should be off limits for more than one reason. It would upset his aunt if he dated her, and he wasn't planning on hanging around long term. He would leave and be one more man who'd failed her.

"Luc is three."

Somehow he'd thought the kid was younger. "So Sera was pregnant when Wes went into the Army?"

"Yeah, I know what you're thinking," Zep began. "Sera got pregnant, Wes asked her to marry him because honestly, he would have taken her any way he could. Sera said no and that's what set him off. It was a crazy thing to do. But then Wes, for all his money and the power of his family name, had a chip on his shoulder."

"Why?"

Zep huffed like he knew what he was about to say wouldn't explain a thing. "He wasn't good at sports. That's a big thing around here. Even when a kid is small, he usually plays baseball or soccer. Cal was big enough no one messed with him. Wes was a scrawny thing. He was more brainy than anything else. It's the kind of thing that turns on a man, if you know what I mean. Karma. In high school it's all about jocks, but then high school is over and the jock ends up working on an oil rig and Wes takes over a multimillion-dollar company. He hadn't quite gotten over high school."

And now he never would.

Zep continued as the song changed and Cal kept dancing. "Like I said, I know his death was hard on Sera. They'd been friends for years, and your aunt wouldn't even allow her to go to the funeral. I know that's haunted her."

It was the one thing he couldn't understand about his aunt. The snobbery had been taught to her, the leftovers of a mother-in-law who hadn't thought she was good enough. "My aunt hates her. I don't get it. I don't understand how she can blame Sera for something Wes did. Even if Sera did say something to him, it was Wes's choice to leave school."

"I agree with you, but your aunt has a lot of sway in this town," Zep explained. "It's not like she can turn Sera into an outcast, but she can make her damn uncomfortable. How did she take finding out Sera inherited that house?"

"Not well." His aunt had been angry at dinner this evening, though in a restrained way that made Harry far more nervous than if she'd let it out. "But there's not a lot she can do about it."

Zep took a sip of his beer. "She can do more than you think. Celeste can be creative. I know she's convinced a lot of her friends to abandon Miss Marcelle's salon since Sera started working there."

"She wouldn't." Celeste might call her lawyer and yell, but surely she wouldn't actively try to hurt Sera and take her job. That would be overkill.

"Sera's had five jobs in the last three years," Zep pointed out. "She thinks she gets fired or laid off because she's bad at them. I think Celeste had a hand in her losing them all. I was hoping with Angie getting married that Celeste would forget about her vendetta against my sister."

"I'll look into it." He wasn't sure what he could do about it, but he couldn't simply let it lie. He'd never been the type of guy who could see a wrong being done and shrug and walk away.

"Good," Zep said with a nod. "Now, are you going to ask my sister out or what?"

"Whoa. I think that would put her in a worse position than ever. My aunt's already upset about the house."

Zep leaned in, his voice going low. "Yeah, but Sera was smiling this evening when she talked about you. I haven't seen my sister smile like that in years. She likes you."

He'd felt it. He'd felt her watching him, felt her curiosity, but he'd also known it was tempered with wariness. "She's been clear that she doesn't want to have anything to do with me."

"And yet tonight at dinner she went into detail about how graceful you are." Zep smirked and rolled his eyes. "It was over the top and nearly made me lose my appetite. *Harry's so graceful*. Yes, she used that word. Graceful. She said you ran like you never lost a leg. How would she know that except she watched you for a while. She also said you offered to help but she had to turn you down since she was sure you already had enough work because you're doing a bunch of stuff for the wedding."

"I'm only working on the gazebo, and I can't even start for a few days," he explained. "I'm waiting for some wood I ordered to come in. I've got to drive to New Orleans to pick it up along with a bunch of other materials. I have some time to help her out."

"Good. She's taking a couple of weeks off so she can get things started on the house. Though if you ask me, Marcelle sounded a little relieved. Another job bites the dust," Zep said under his breath. "Maybe you should run through those woods again and, oops, you happen to be carrying your tool kit. You could do that for strength training. And somewhere in all that helping, you convince her to go out with you."

Harry held his hands up because Zep was moving pretty fast. "I don't know that my dating Sera would be good for her. I'm not staying. I'm only here until after Angie's wedding."

"And then you'll go home?"

He didn't really have a home. "I'll hit the road again."

"That's going to get old after a while," Zep pointed out with a shake of his head. "You know, Papillon is a nice place to settle down. Lots of room. Good food. Who knows? Maybe you'll like it here. You won't know unless you try. And hey, we're growing. Lots of work for a person who knows how to build things. It's something to think about. We even have a clinic with a nurse practitioner who knows what's she doing now."

It was his turn to get suspicious. "You really want me to ask Sera out. Won't that cause more problems for her?"

It could definitely cause problems for him.

Zep set his beer down. "Sure, but sometimes problems have a way of solving themselves. Sometimes when you put two problems together, they get tied up so tight they make something. But hey, what do I know? I'm only saying Sera can be stubborn but she deserves some happiness. Patience is the key with her. I hope she doesn't kill herself fixing up that house. I went by this afternoon to pick her up and one of the porch steps gave way. Now you have to hop over it. And she told me I broke it so I have to fix it. That's not fair.

She got all the money and the house. I got a bunch of condoms and my aunt is mean. She bought regular size. I can't
even use them. Because I need the extra-large kind."

Those stairs needed help. They should be the first thing
on her list. Or his. "I'll fix the steps. I'll go out there early
tomorrow. I've got some wood that will fit for now. She
should rebuild the whole thing at the end of the project, but
the first thing we need to do is fortify them or no one is
getting in that house."

Zep sighed in obvious relief. "Thank god. I was worried
I would have to work on my day off." He hoisted the mug
and drank. "Whew, I was taking it easy because I didn't
want to have to pound nails when I had a hangover. Now I
can drink. I think I'll go dance, too. Cal, don't take all
those ladies. Leave a couple for me."

Zep pushed his chair back and winked Harry's way.

It looked like the party had started. Harry sat back. He
wasn't taking everything Zep said to heart. Sera really
didn't seem like she was into him, but that didn't mean he
couldn't help her out. He would simply do it quietly, and
that included making sure his aunt didn't do something she
shouldn't. And if Zep was right and all Sera needed was
time to get to know him and figure out he wasn't a jerk like
her last boyfriend, then he would be in place when she was
ready.

After all, it wasn't like he had to leave Papillon right after
Angie's wedding. He could hang around, do some jobs, save
some money. Zep was right about it being nice here.

He sat back and mentally made a list. Maybe patience
and some manual labor would pay off.

chapter five

◠

Sera took a deep breath and tried to understand the words Sylvie was saying over the sounds of Luc giggling at something his uncle was doing. She glanced back in to where Zep was drinking his coffee and Luc was having lunch because it was eleven in the a.m. and he'd been up since dawn. Zep had dragged himself in at some insane hour and was only now thinking about getting ready for the day.

It must be nice to be able to sleep in. She honestly didn't miss going out to bars and partying, but she did miss sleeping until ten in the morning.

"Sera? Are you listening to me?"

She forced herself back to the conversation at hand. "I am. What's going on? You said something about codes."

"Yes." A long sigh came over the line, a sure sign that Sylvie was getting frustrated. Or anxious. "I was down on the second floor and they were talking about sending out code enforcement."

"Sending them out to where?" She was running late as it was. She didn't need city hall gossip. She needed to get out to Guidry Place and start working. She'd gotten online the night before and she was fairly sure she could change a couple of boards on the porch stairs. It wouldn't be pretty, but hopefully it would be enough so workers could safely get in and out of the house.

Not that she had workers yet.

"Sending them to your place."

She groaned at the thought. Sometimes her mom had some kooky schemes that led to her using their front yard in ways the neighbors didn't approve of. Like the time she'd decided to drag out all the Christmas lights for a Christmas in July extravaganza, as she called it. She'd tried to charge for it, though Sera rather believed all those lights coming on at ten p.m., because that was when it was dark enough to see them, was really what had set the neighbors off. And using dried mashed potatoes to simulate snow had brought out a not-surprising amount of critters. "I'll find Momma. I have no idea what she's planning, but I'll shut it down."

Like she didn't have enough to do, but this was her life now. Adulting sucked.

Would she see Harry today? Would he run by the porch and give her a wave? What would she do if he stopped and offered to help again?

Turn him down. That's what she would do. It was the only thing she could do. No matter how much she could use the help to get those steps ready.

"Why would you find your mother? This is about you."

Sylvie's words effectively stopped the whole Harrison thread going through her brain. "What? Why? What did I do?"

She quickly went down the line of possible violations. The yard was mowed because she'd nagged Zep enough until he'd done it. Oh, she'd had to start doing it herself, but Zep had just enough shame that he'd taken over. They hadn't violated the burn ban since her momma held that women's healing seminar where she'd had everyone burn away the pain of their past by setting gifts from their ex-lovers on fire.

"It's nothing you've done," Sylvie said. "I think it's all Celeste's doing. You had to know she would come after you once she realized you're the new owner of Guidry Place. I kind of thought she'd offer to buy it, but it looks like she's going to get nasty."

Celeste? This wasn't about her mom? It was about her. "I can't sell until I fix it up. And how could I have code violations? I only inherited the place yesterday."

Sylvie's voice went soothing. "Honey, you didn't violate the codes, but the house isn't up to standards, and we all know it. I'm afraid you're going to get a visit, and that will put you on a timetable. I have to do some research because I'm not sure how long you'll have."

"Before what?"

There was a long pause that ratcheted up her anxiety before Sylvie continued. "Before they try to condemn the property."

Nausea rose, but it battled with complete confusion. "Can they do that?"

"I don't know. I mean, yes, they can if there's cause. If they decide the structure itself is dangerous to live in, they could absolutely condemn the property. That's why I wanted to give you a heads-up," Sylvie was saying. "I think it might be best if you're out there when the code inspector shows up. They've got a backlog they're working, but they fast-tracked your house. I'm going to look into it, but I happen to know that the head of Code Compliance is in Celeste Beaumont's women's Bible group."

Nausea was definitely winning. She should have known

Wes's mom would never allow her to have a house so close to her own. Celeste would never want her to have anything good at all. "Is there anything I can do?"

"Sera, there are rules to this that not even the Beaumont name can change. I let Margret know that I would be looking into corruption in her office if I got even a whiff that she was doing this to make Celeste Beaumont happy. Unfortunately, she's got cover on this one because Guidry Place has been in disrepair for years. But I did manage to convince her to send Darnell Ward out. He's completely honest and fair."

But she might need someone bribable because her house probably should be condemned right now. In a couple of weeks, maybe it could pass, but not today. "What should I do?"

"I think you should get out there and be working when he shows up. If you prove to Darnell you're working on getting the place up to code, he'll give you a lot of leeway."

Would he once he figured out she was completely in over her head? Would he take one look at her and know that most of her experience came from watching HGTV? She only knew it wouldn't help at all if the man thought she was lounging around while her house was crumbling. She so hoped it wasn't actually crumbling. "I'll get over there now."

"Let me know what happens."

She hung up and shoved her cell in the front pocket of her jeans. At least she was dressed. She'd been planning to wait until her mom had returned from her morning meeting, but her plans had changed. "Zep, I need you to watch Luc until Mom gets back."

Zep sighed as though relieved that he would get out of doing any manual labor. "Now, that I can do. Hey, buddy.

Maybe we should go to the park. I hear there are tons of pretty ladies out there."

"Don't use my son as a pickup tool. And you better come and help me this afternoon. You owe me porch steps," she said, tossing her purse strap over her shoulder and leaning down to kiss her baby.

Luc grinned up at her with the gaze of a boy who was constantly amused by the world around him. "Momma, park. Park."

Zep sent her a knowing look. "It's not just me. He checks out the toddler set. That boy is going to be a player. And I don't think you'll have to worry about those porch steps."

He was so obnoxious sometimes. But then he winked at Luc and made her remember that when she'd needed him, he'd been there. Zep had been a single male in his twenties having the time of his life and he'd stayed home those first few months and learned how to change diapers and burp his nephew. He could be annoying, but when she really needed him, Zep was there. "Take him to the park, but you better pay attention to him. I'll call you later, and seriously, I need your help on those porch steps. They're probably not up to code and that's a real problem now."

"I bet it's not."

She raced out the door because her brother wasn't right about this.

Ten minutes later her heart was racing because she could see a car in the drive. It was a new-model SUV and probably belonged to the man who could shut down all her plans. She wasn't sure how much time she would have if Darnell Ward decided she wasn't serious about fixing the place up. Anxiety arced through her because it wasn't like many people took her seriously in the first place. They tended to see blond hair and decent-sized boobs and treat her like she didn't have a brain in her head. No one thought she could do anything but wear a T-shirt well.

What the hell was she going to say to him? She only vaguely knew Darnell. He was smart and a deacon at the Presbyterian church. He liked fried shrimp and ordered his gumbo local-hot. He had the occasional Sazerac. Could she use the Guidry brand to help her out? Yes, Celeste could offer him a bribe in the form of cash, but she had an in when it came to the best gumbo in town.

Why hadn't she made it here before he did? She might have been able to figure out a way to distract him from in-specting a couple of the rooms that were more problematic. Did she really need to check out the back study, where she was pretty sure a couple of raccoons were nesting? If he was standing on the front porch waiting for her, he would likely want to see everything.

She had to get it together. She had to look like she knew what she was doing. Like she was competent.

She *was* competent. She could do this. All she needed was a little time.

If he'd tried the porch steps, though, she was probably already done. Darnell Ward was a solid guy, and he'd likely put one foot on the step and gone straight through it. He could have even been hurt.

Her mind was awash in pure anxiety when she heard the front door open.

He'd gotten into her house?

She watched as Darnell stepped out wearing khaki slacks and a collared shirt, a clipboard in his hand.

"You've got quite a job ahead of you," Darnell was say-ing. He was an attractive man in his mid-forties, and if she remembered correctly, he had three kids and a wife who worked at the elementary/middle school.

She was about to answer when she realized he wasn't talking to her. His head was turned and another big body moved from inside the house to the porch. Harry. He was a reassuring presence, and the deep rumble of his voice could be heard even with the distance between them.

"Yes, but once she's gotten it all done, it's going to be a jewel of a house," Harry proclaimed.

Darnell looked up at the ceiling. "Yeah, there aren't many of these old Creole places left. You said she's not living here, right?"

"I'm not," she said, moving gingerly on the first step.

Shep banged out of the house, pushing his way through the rickety screen door. He bounded down the stairs and right to her.

"Hey, Seraphina," Harry said, sending her a pointed look. "Darnell here is from the city. I was going over all the ways we're working to bring this old place up to code, starting with getting those porch steps fixed this morning. Everything all right at home? I explained that you went back to your place to have some lunch with your son."

Darnell was all smiles. "How is that boy of yours doing? He must be growing like a weed."

She glanced down at the steps. They were completely redone, each one looking solid. Though they needed to be painted and sealed, they were safe to walk on.

Harry. Harry had done that and now he was covering for her, and the parish official who should have been worried seemed perfectly comfortable. Harry had done that, too.

She gave Shep a pat and started up the stairs. "Oh, he is. How are your kiddos?"

Darnell held out a hand as she reached the top step.

"They're doing well. My oldest started high school this year. Time flies. I think it's nice that you make sure to go home and have lunch with your son. You know, one day this could be a great place to raise a family. But you're also smart to not move in."

"Oh, no. I love this place, but it needs so much work," she said, shaking his hand. "And I don't know that I'll ever live in it. It's way too big for me and Luc, but I love this house so much. I grew up here."

Darnell's lips curled up as he watched her move to Harry's side. "Well, you never know. What seems too big now can feel just right down the line. Yes, this will make a fine home for someone. I'm going to send you a copy of this paperwork, but Harry here went over all the plans. You seem to know exactly what you're doing. There are definite violations, but I'll give you some time. I'll be back out in ninety days, but I have no doubt you'll get everything done. You have a nice afternoon."

Ninety days? She had ninety days. Her hands were shaking, and she realized they had been from the moment she'd understood Celeste Beaumont was coming after her. She'd thought she would have to fight, have to beg, have to explain why she hadn't even fixed the steps needed to get inside the house.

She watched as Darnell got into his truck and drove away.

"Sera, I'm sorry I didn't call you, but I had some time earlier today and . . ."

He didn't get much past those words when she burst into tears and threw herself into his arms.

Harry felt the breath leave his body the minute she was against him. The move had shocked him because she'd seemed perfectly composed the moment before. If she'd been surprised he was there, she hadn't shown it at all. She'd taken his every cue, and there was no question in his mind that the compliance officer had been happy with both the inspection and the fact that Seraphina Guidry knew what she was doing.

She didn't, but she was smart and she could figure it out if she was given the time she deserved.

"Hey, it's okay." He gently put his arms around her because she seemed to need some affection. Yeah, it didn't have anything to do with how soft and warm she was. With how good it felt to hold her.

Right. It felt right to hold her, like he was supposed to comfort her when she was sad.

"Sylvie told me they were going to try to condemn the place," she managed.

So she'd known what was going on. He let his hand find her hair. "He's not trying to do anything but make sure the place is safe. I found him to be reasonable. It's all going to be okay."

She cried, holding on to him like he was the only real thing in the world. It broke his heart, those sobs of hers.

Shep sat down, looking up at him and whining because he couldn't stand to hear her cry, either.

He also couldn't stand the thought that someone else could drive up and see her pain. She was a private woman. Even though he hadn't known her long, he'd figured that out about the lady. Though it seemed like the house was isolated, it wasn't. While he'd been working on the steps, he'd been interrupted by three different people, two who'd been on the water and his cousin, who was on her morning run. Angie had stopped long enough to give him a lecture on how her mom wouldn't like the fact that he was helping out, but she herself thought it was a great idea.

If anyone found them like this, there would be gossip, and while he couldn't care less, Sera would.

He leaned over and pressed his arm under her knees, lifting her up. She gasped but her arms went around his neck before she started to cry again.

"I'm sorry," she managed through her tears.

He got the door open and carried her inside. "There's nothing to be sorry about."

If she'd known about Darnell, then she'd likely been worried about the visit. He didn't know why she'd stayed away this morning, but he would bet she'd gotten here as fast as she could after she heard the news. She likely hadn't thought she would walk in on him talking to the man who could shut her whole operation down.

She had to have been overwhelmed. Just the size of the job would be overwhelming, but knowing someone was trying to stop her seemed to have sent her over the edge.

He carried her to what he'd come to think of as the formal living room. There was a mid-century modern sofa complete with plastic covering over all the pillows that would make it very uncomfortable to actually sit on, and a china hutch that displayed an astonishing array of ceramic owls.

He lowered himself carefully down, forced to think about every move because the last thing they needed was for him to fall. He eased onto the sofa as she was starting to relax in his arms. "It's going to be okay."

How much responsibility had been placed on her slender shoulders? She truly believed this house was her shot at giving her son a bright future, but she was trying to take it all on alone. She had to feel so isolated.

She shuddered and her chin came up. Her face had gone red, every bit of emotion stamped there, but it didn't make her less appealing. In fact, it dialed his attraction up a few notches because she was so real and raw. Because she wasn't holding back. There was something about this woman that called to him, and he didn't even want to think about all the reasons he shouldn't be here.

He wanted to be here for her. Whoever her son's father was, he'd left her alone to deal with raising a kid and having someone's entire future in her hands at an age when she should still be figuring out who she was and building her career. He wanted to be someone she could count on.

She sat on his lap and closed her eyes. "I'm sorry I lost it like that, but I didn't know what I was going to do."

"It's okay." He didn't want this moment to end. She would realize that they were too close and then she'd put that careful distance back between them. This might be the only chance he ever got to hold her, and he wanted it to last. "You've got time."

"You fixed my steps. I was going to do that. I was going to make my brother help me, but I was going to do it first like you said I should," she said, her gorgeous eyes on him.

"I didn't have anything to do this morning and I had some extra wood," he explained. "It's nothing I would use for the latticework on the gazebo. It was to support the base."

"You took it from Beaumont House?" She'd stiffened in his arms.

She was so touchy about anything to do with his family. "I bought that wood myself. It wasn't expensive. I wasn't even going to ask her to pay me back. Don't worry about it. It's okay. It's okay to need to lean on someone. I want to help you."

She relaxed again. "But you shouldn't."

"I shouldn't want to help you?"

"No. You're a good person, but you should stay away. It would make things so much easier."

"It wouldn't make things easier on you," he replied simply.

She seemed stumped by that, and he had to wonder how many people outside of her family she could truly count on. She shook her head, seeming to come to some kind of decision.

"Harry, I know it's dumb, but I want you to kiss me. It won't mean anything except I want to know what it feels like to have you kiss me just once."

His whole body went still, anticipation nearly overwhelming him. She'd asked him to kiss her? He could do that. He'd dreamed of doing that since the moment he'd seen her. Even as he'd gone over all the reasonable arguments why it would be a bad idea, his hands had itched to touch her. He wasn't a player. He liked relationships, but the last few years his vagabond lifestyle hadn't led to long-term bonds. He wanted that with her, wanted more than the mere physical.

She didn't want that. "It will mean something to me."

She shook her head. "Then I should get up."

Nope. He tightened his arms around her. He would take whatever scraps she would give him. "Just one kiss? That's all you want?"

"That's all I can let myself have."

"Then I'm going to make it count."

He stared at her for a moment, catching her gaze and memorizing how blue her eyes were, how gorgeous she was all flushed with emotion. He let his hand stroke her hair and revel in how soft she was. And then he lowered his mouth to hers and closed his eyes, allowing touch to lead him.

If he'd thought her hair was soft, her lips were even softer. Warm and lush, he gave himself a moment to explore. He felt her palm run along his jawline up to the back of his neck, making his skin come to life everywhere she touched him. His whole body tightened with anticipation he knew damn well wasn't going to be assuaged.

He started to pull away because the last thing he was going to do was take more than she wanted to give.

"Not yet," she whispered, pressing her lips to his again, needing more.

He gave in, hauling her closer. He deepened the kiss, letting his tongue run along the seam of her lips until she sighed and opened and let him in. He felt her tongue come out to tentatively touch his own and it was over. He couldn't stop himself from invading. He took over the kiss and felt the moment she softened around him, offering herself to him in the sweetest way possible.

He let his hand move to her hip as she molded her body to his.

"Harry." She whispered his name, her voice hoarse, and he knew he was about to go over an edge they couldn't come back from. Because that whisper of hers wasn't a *stop*. It was a *go further*.

And he knew. He knew she would shut him out if they went much further. She wasn't ready for anything serious.

He pulled back and took a deep breath. "Well, that went about the way I thought it would."

Her eyes widened and she sat up, scrambling off his lap. "I can't believe I did that. Harry, I'm sorry. I was . . ."

There she was. There was the skittish, scared Seraphina who hid under all that sass. "You had a rough morning and you needed some comfort."

Her face was flushed. "Comfort would have been a hug."

He forced himself to stand. That kiss had just about done him in. There was nothing he wanted more than to pull her back in his arms and show her how much comfort he could give her. He shoved his hands into his pockets so she wouldn't see how they were shaking. "You're too hard on yourself. It was a kiss, nothing more. It was a great kiss."

Her eyes flared. "Great?"

He smiled her way. "I can't help it. I'm a really good kisser."

She snorted, a sound he shouldn't find so adorable. "Arrogant much?"

He forced down a sigh of relief. If she was sassing him, she wasn't embarrassed anymore. "I'm only being honest here. I have it on the highest authority that I'm a world-class kisser."

"And whose authority is that?"

"Suzy Perkins. She was my girlfriend through the last couple of years of high school and my Army days. She would write me long letters about how much she missed kissing me."

"Then she should have married you. Yet I don't see a ring on your finger."

"She really wanted a guy with both limbs." It was actually easy to joke about it now. Suzy had been a sweet girl, but she hadn't been able to handle what rehab had been like. She hadn't liked hospitals and doctors and dealing with his grumpy ass. Somehow he kind of thought Sera wouldn't have wilted like Suzy had. Sera would have yelled at him when he hadn't wanted to do the work it took to walk again. She would have been strong enough to handle it.

Sure enough, her eyes flared and her shoulders went straight as an arrow. "She left you because of your leg?"

There was the lioness who would defend those she loved. "I don't think it was really about the leg. I think it was more about the fact that I wasn't the most lovable guy at the time."

"You had just had your leg amputated," she said with righteous indignation. "You were in pain and shock. You needed her. You didn't even have your mom. You were alone. Who took care of you?"

"You don't want to hear it." God, he wanted to touch her again.

"Oh. It was Celeste."

He didn't want to make more of it than there had been. "She came to see me in the hospital, and then she paid for a nurse and a physical therapist."

"You needed someone who loved you to be with you."

"Yeah, well, Suzy didn't love me. But I am an excellent kisser, and I've obviously worked my magic on you because you aren't crying anymore."

She reached out and put a hand on his arm. "She was wrong for you. I'm glad Celeste came to visit you. I might not like her, but I'm glad she was there for you."

"Me, too," he replied. It would have been so easy to lean over and brush his lips against hers again. It felt like the right thing to do, but he forced himself to take a step back. "I've got a week before I'm going to have to split my time between here and the gazebo. The stairs and the porch are solid now. I'm not going to repaint until the end of the project, so what shall we work on next?"

"I don't think that's a good idea."

"I can help you." He wanted to. "I'm waiting on the special wood I need for the gazebo. I'm at loose ends, and I'm not good at sitting around. I like to work."

"Harry, I'm so glad you were here, but you have to know it was your aunt who called in code compliance on me."

He wouldn't put it past his aunt to call around and put a bug in someone's ear. "She wants to buy the place. And honestly, they probably would have come around at some point."

Sera shook her head. "She won't stop, and she'll be angry when she realizes you're helping me."

"I wasn't planning on telling her." He also wasn't planning on hiding it. He wouldn't bring it up, but if she asked, he wasn't going to lie. His aunt's morning routine didn't lead to a lot of conversation. She was in the office by eight a.m., and unless it was a Sunday, she didn't eat breakfast. He'd barely said hello to her before she was running out the door today. Cal had left for New Orleans and wouldn't be back until Friday. Angie was wrapped up in wedding plans. No one even bothered to ask him what he would be up to. He didn't think that would change.

"It won't work," she insisted.

He shrugged. He wasn't sure it could work, either, but he wasn't about to leave her alone to handle this job, especially now that she was on a clock. "I'm going to see if I can fix the wiring in the kitchen. It kind of sparks at odd times."

"Harry." She stared up at him, the saddest look on her face. "It can't work."

He knew what she was talking about, but he wasn't going to argue with her. If she kicked him out, he would stay away. But he would also give her an out if she couldn't ask him to stay. "I think it can. Oh, it will likely require an entire rewire, but that weird lamp will work again. I promise. The only thing I'm better at than kissing is fixing things."

Her eyes rolled. "You're not that good at kissing."

"Oh, I can try again."

She gave him a flustered smile. "Go look at the wiring, weirdo. I'm going to get my tool kit. I got new locks since I can't find my aunt's keys to the old ones. I think she might have buried them somewhere."

Shep followed her out.

And Harry got to work.

* * *

Celeste stared at the phone. She had it on speaker since she was alone in the space she used at Beaumont Oil's small but elegantly appointed office in the town square. There was a larger office in New Orleans that served as the main corporate headquarters, but the family had always kept this building in Papillon for everyday work. Cal spent four days a week at the New Orleans office, staying in the French Quarter house that had been in the family since they'd moved to Louisiana from Texas.

She was glad he was there now because she didn't particularly want anyone to overhear this conversation. "What do you mean she has ninety days?"

There was a pause on the line that let Celeste know her tone had been heard and properly received. Margret Hawkins cleared her throat before she began speaking. "Well, there are rules, you see."

"Then bend them."

"Well, uhm, you see I wasn't able to send out the man I would normally send out. He's more willing to listen to reason," Margret said in a breathy tone. "I had to send out Darnell, and he's a real stickler for the actual rules we have in place. He said it wasn't as bad as he'd expected and felt that Ms. Guidry had a real handle on things. He liked her contractor a lot. Said he was a solid guy."

"I would like to know the name of that contractor." She would find out the name and then hire him right out from under her. There weren't many contractors around, not ones who could stop everything they were doing to put all their eggs in Seraphina's not-well-funded basket.

There was a shuffling sound. "It's not in the paperwork. We don't require that a homeowner have a contractor. Most of the time they can do the work themselves or have family helping them. You know our rules are actually pretty relaxed."

"Then someone should tighten them," Celeste ground out. It was obvious Margret was a moron, but then she should have known that little mouse couldn't get the job done. And now there was paperwork, and she knew how government entities functioned. She hung up before Margret could say another word.

She was about to dial up her attorney when there was a brusque knock on the door, and suddenly Sylvie Martine was striding in past her useless assistant, who might be looking for a new job soon.

"I'm sorry, Mrs. Beaumont," Carla was saying. "She insisted. I tried to tell her you were on an important phone call, but she walked right by me."

Celeste made a note to herself to hire a quicker, wilier receptionist. She would bring in the coach of the local football team to teach her how to tackle unwanted visitors like the one she found herself face-to-face with now. Sylvie Martine was young to be a mayor, but there was no way to mistake the air of authority the twenty-seven-year-old exuded. She was dressed in slacks and a chic blazer, the silk blouse beneath of an acceptable style. Sylvie would be someone Celeste would tell Angela was a suitable friend, even a suitable potential daughter-in-law, despite her working-class roots. If only Sylvie chose her friends well.

"It's all right, Carla," Celeste said, sitting down in the chair she'd bought when she'd taken over after Ralph passed on. "I always have time for our mayor."

Sylvie stood in front of the desk, her arms crossed and obviously ready for a fight. Before the door had even closed, her eyes had narrowed. "I would like to understand why you're attempting to bribe city employees."

She was going to take that route? "I assure you there was nothing exchanged between me and Margret. I was simply asking about a property that happens to be close to my own."

"A property that also happens to have changed owner-ship to a woman you have had problems with in the past," Sylvie pointed out.

In the past? Her son was still dead, so there was no "past" about her problems with Sera Guidry. How could there be when the woman paraded herself around town constantly? It would have been bad enough if she was like many of the other young adults who only came home for holidays and visits, but Sera was always around. She was a cockroach nothing seemed to drive away. "I assure you my only thoughts are about safety. You know Guidry Place has been falling into disrepair for years."

Sylvie wasn't backing down. "Yet you only decided to call code compliance in when Seraphina took over the deed."

She'd sat up thinking about how she would sidestep that particular point. It wasn't like she didn't know Sera had a friend in city hall. Sera, Sylvie, and that pudgy blonde with the baby were always hanging around together. "Well, I certainly wasn't going to turn an old woman out of her home."

And she'd believed Irene Guidry when she said if Celeste tried anything, she knew how to cut brake lines.

"Of course, this is all about you being an upright citizen," Sylvie said with a shake of her head. "I'm here to explain to you that you will not intimidate city employees into doing your dirty work."

"I was unaware that enforcing city codes was dirty work, Madam Mayor. It sounds more like you're bending the rules for your friend." Any argument could work both ways, Celeste knew. Turnabout was fair play. "I'm sure that might come up in your next election."

Sylvie snorted. "Bring it on, Celeste. If you want to im-port a ringer to be mayor to all the crazies of this town, I welcome it. I can go back to my original plans. And you can deal with the fallout when whoever you bring in resigns six months in."

She did have a point, but it was terrible not to have someone she could intimidate at the mayor's office. The younger generation did not pay the proper respect. "Well, you should understand that I do expect to live next to properly maintained homes. I'm certain Angela will be thinking about a family after she gets married. I won't have my grandbabies endangered because the Guidrys can't take care of their own property. And if code compliance can't enforce its own rules, then I'll take that up with the city council."

"I assure you Darnell's reports will be perfect. He's a straight shooter. Per the city's codes, Sera has ninety days to come into compliance. Code compliance is about making sure everyone is safe. Not kicking out people you don't like or condemning houses we all know you want to buy."

Celeste sat back. Sylvie might have youth on her side, but Celeste had found that sometimes patience was a far better tool than anything else. "It's not the house I want. I assure you Sera is wasting her time since I'm going to raze the entire thing and build something new."

"She's working hard on that house," Sylvie argued.

"You know she won't be able to afford the taxes and insurance on that place." Maybe there was another way to win this particular war. If Sylvie could convince her friend to sell, she would make leaving Papillon a condition of the contract. "Not to mention the upkeep on a place like that. She certainly can't afford it when she can't seem to keep a job."

"You know exactly why she can't keep a job. Don't think you can use city hall to force my friend out of town." Sylvie turned and strode to the door before turning back. "I know you think that the Beaumont family is as respected as the Daroises, but you're wrong. This town adores Pamela Darois, and they love her son just as much. They fear you. That's the only reason they defer to you."

"Well, you know what Machiavelli said." And yet she'd always hated that quote. *It is better to be feared than loved if you cannot be both.* She wasn't sure anyone could be both. Hadn't she always hated the fear her mother-in-law brought every time she walked into a gathering, how every single woman there knew she was about to be judged and found wanting?

Sylvie glanced around. "I'm surprised you didn't take over your husband's office. It has a much better view."

"I'm only here until Cal settles in."

"Really? Because you've been running this place since Ralph died. I heard you implemented a few changes and last year the stock was up. Cal never struck me as the type to take over such a large operation. He was always happier being creative."

Celeste felt her shoulders go rigid. "Cal will be a wonderful CEO. Ralph always meant to leave the company to one of his sons. That's been the Beaumont way for a hundred years."

Sylvie seemed to think about that for a moment. "Well, you're the last Beaumont standing, Celeste. It's your family now. How are you going to run it? Maybe you should stop worrying about Sera and start being who you could be. Start setting an example for the women of Papillon, and not the one your mother-in-law set. You're good at running Beaumont Oil. The town could use a female CEO."

Celeste stared at the door as it closed.

Sylvie was wrong. The job was Cal's and she wasn't going to take it from him.

And when he took over? What would she do then? She

was sick of the endless rounds of socializing, tired of always trying to look perfect, be perfect.

A CEO didn't have to be perfect. He only had to be good at his job. That's what Ralph always said. He left perfection to the women of the family.

But none of that mattered because her son would do what Beaumonts did. He would take over the company and then she would fade into the background.

She would concentrate on her home. That's what Beaumont women did. They made perfect homes.

Perfection, in this case, started with getting rid of Seraphina Guidry.

chapter six

❦

"What do you mean you rented the truck to someone else?"
A fine edge of panic went through Seraphina as she looked
at Jerry Nichols, who owned the local gardening center/
feed store that also hired out a fleet of service vehicles. At
least that was what he called it. Sera wasn't sure a tractor,
two backhoes, and an old moving van that still had *U-Haul*
on the side of it counted as a fleet.

In Papillon, stores often served more than one purpose.
Also in Papillon things went sideways on a daily basis, but
she couldn't have this go wrong.

"I didn't do anything, hon," Jerry said with an apologetic
smile. "It's my daughter. She set up this whole Interweb site
thing. It's newfangled nonsense if you ask me. I can take a
reservation just fine on the phone, but she insisted it would
work better this way."

"It does work but only if you actually turn the computer
on." LaTonya walked in from the office, giving her father a
tired shake of her head. "If you had looked, you would have
seen the moving truck was reserved for today and won't be
back until tomorrow morning. Also, payment's already
been made in full. Dad can refund your down payment or

we can shift your reservation to tomorrow when we will actually have the truck back."

"The truck is still here. It's out in the parking lot." Tomorrow morning would be far too late. She held up the rental agreement. "But I have paperwork. And I have cash."

"Yeah, Dad's good with paperwork," LaTonya agreed. She pointed to the computer monitor. "However, this rental agreement was signed and agreed to twenty-four hours before yours."

"But the other person only talked to a computer," Sera argued, desperation starting to sink in. "I talked to a person. People trump computers, right? I mean, I had the courtesy of actually coming in here yesterday and talking to you, Mr. Nichols. You remember how we talked about the Saints and how they're going all the way this year?"

Mr. Nichols nodded. "I do and it was nice of you. People should communicate more. It's why the world is going to hell in a handbasket. Computers. They're the real problem. You can't look a man in the eyes over a computer."

She might still have a chance at this. "I agree. You don't even know who rented the truck. It's just a name on a computer screen. You don't know that this person won't drive away with the truck and never come back."

"I promise to come back," a deep voice said. "I was not going to flee with the truck."

Sera groaned inwardly because she knew that voice. It was deep and musical and haunted her dreams lately. Harry Jefferys, of the gorgeous face and the handy ways. It had been a week since she'd told him it couldn't work. One week since he'd kissed her like she was the most important woman in the world. She'd called him arrogant, but he was right about his skills. The man could kiss, and she hadn't wanted him to stop. There had been a big piece of herself that had wanted him to keep kissing her and stroking her, and if they found themselves horizontal, then she could have blamed it on her emotional state.

He'd been a gentleman, and now she dreamed about his hands on her. After he'd managed to rewire the kitchen lights, she'd told him he didn't need to come back in the morning, that she could handle it. And every single day he showed up during his morning run. Every single day she told herself she would smile and send him on his way. And every single day he ended up fixing something, and damn but that man was even sexier when he was holding a hammer.

He'd fixed the porch steps, making it possible for her to safely enter her new property and buying her ninety days with the city. On Tuesday she'd been smart and hadn't been outside when she knew he would come through. He'd knocked on the door and explained that Shep really needed some water and could she help a puppy out? He'd then stayed four hours to work on the kitchen sink, which now gave her access to clean water and not brownish sludge. On Wednesday he'd caught her in town buying the wrong screws for the repairs to the light fixture in the living room. It threatened to fall on her head every time she walked under it. He'd helped her get the right ones and followed her back because he assured her it would be a two-man job. It hadn't been. He'd handled it all by himself while she'd made a couple of extra sandwiches because the man could eat. By Thursday, she waited on the porch for him because that furniture wasn't going to move itself. On Friday she'd let him help her fill the back of his truck with donations to the local women's shelter, and when he'd claimed he needed lunch, she'd gone to Guidry's with him and they'd eaten gumbo in the kitchen and drunk sweet tea.

And the weekend. This weekend he'd helped her pull the carpet out of the living room and hallways, and it had been a bit warm so he'd taken off his shirt. Then it had been even warmer.

She liked him. Really liked him. She couldn't stop thinking about the man, and it was getting annoying.

She turned and there he stood in jeans instead of his usual athletic wear. He had on a T-shirt that hid all those muscles of his, but the sight was imprinted on her brain forever. Shep sat at his side, tail thumping against the floor.

"Is there a problem?" When Harry moved, the dog shifted with him. The leash wasn't really needed, but Harry tended to attach it when they were in town.

She already knew way too much about his habits. She knew how he liked his coffee. A splash of cream. A lot of sugar. Knew he hummed when he got lost in work, and he was usually humming some country song. Knew he was a baby when it came to cayenne pepper.

She definitely knew she was developing a soft spot for a man who should be totally off limits. "You already have a truck. I need this one, Harry. The flooring store in New Orleans is having a sale today on the hardwoods I need, but they won't hold it until tomorrow. If I don't pick it up by four, they'll release it for sale. It's sixty percent off."

"That's an excellent discount." Harry handed his driver's license to LaTonya, who already had the keys in her hand. "You should definitely move on that. I browsed through the catalog you have and that hand-scraped oak will look beautiful and it doesn't look too hard to install. I'm picking up the wood I need for the gazebo. The individual pieces are too long for my truck and it's supposed to rain this afternoon. I don't want it wet before I stain and finish it. So I rented the moving truck."

"But I rented the truck." She held up her paperwork.

Harry was always super fair. "See. I even paid a down payment."

He picked up the pen on the desk as LaTonya pushed some papers in front of him. He glanced down at the contract. "I paid the whole fee up front."

Tears pulsed behind her eyes. What was she going to do if she couldn't get the flooring? She would have to pay more or go cheaper. The oak was perfect. It would catch the light from the big bay windows and it would look golden. "You can have it tomorrow. Or I could drive real fast and try to get back here by afternoon. Would that work?"

He glanced her way. "It's two and a half hours to New Orleans, so that means it's also two and a half back. It'll take a while to pack up the truck and get all the business stuff done. You couldn't possibly return in time for me to get to the store before it closes."

"Couldn't you get it tomorrow?" He wasn't even paying for it. His aunt would be paying, and she didn't need a discount. Celeste Beaumont didn't clip coupons and only eat the specials at the café.

He turned her way, his lips quirking up in a smirk. "I'm on a deadline. Gotta get my cousin married off and all." That smirk turned down as he looked at her. "It's going to be okay. I'll drive. You can navigate. And that means they need to refund your deposit."

She blinked back tears. "What?"

He sighed. "It's a big truck. You're picking up what? Fifty boxes of flooring?"

"Seventy."

"It will all fit with room to spare," he said. "But we'll have to drop Shep off. I don't know anyone's home right now, but I can probably talk the maid into watching him. The cab will be too crowded with two of us and a big dog. Besides, he's a little gassy. Too many treats."

He was willing to share it with her? And she got her deposit back? "I can pay for half."

"Or you can navigate because I don't know the roads around here and half the time there's a gator lounging in the center of whatever road I need to be on. Also, the sheriff is quick with a ticket."

"That's Armie. I heard the fridge at the station house has been acting up so he'll ticket everyone until they can get another," she explained, her heart rate back to something normal. Well, normal when she was around Harry, which was still elevated. "He's married to my brother's sister-in-law so I can usually get away with a warning."

"See, you're already helpful." He signed the final contract with a flourish. "If I have to stop back by Beaumont House, we need to get going. Shep, you're getting shut out for a girl, buddy. Sorry about that."

Shep simply wagged that tail of his.

Sera had a better idea, an idea that did not involve her being seen with Harry anywhere close to his aunt's house. She had no illusions that the staff wouldn't report to Celeste that Sera had been in the truck when Harry dropped Shep off. "My place is closer. It's on the way out of town. My mom wouldn't mind having a friend for the day, and I know Luc would love it. He's good around dogs. He won't try to climb him or anything. He's been around Lila's dog."

The softest expression came over his face. "You want me to meet your kid?"

"Well, I don't know that we'll have a lot of time to meet anyone." She was right back to shy again. Maybe it wasn't such a great idea. Her mom would take it all wrong. Her mom would tell Remy, who would likely be all big brother about it when there wasn't anything to really protect her from since they were only friends.

Of course, she had a baby with her last male friend, so there was that.

"Maybe we should think about this."

He shook his head. "You think way too much. It's my place or your place. We need to hit the road or it'll be late before we get back."

"There's a storm coming in," Jerry warned.

"It's only rain, Daddy," LaTonya argued. "The weatherman said there was only a fifty-fifty chance."

"It's coming." Jerry rubbed his right elbow. "I feel it in my bones and they're far more reliable than some degree from a university. Like I said, you kids these days depend far too much on technology."

He walked away grumbling about how computers were taking over the world.

LaTonya shook her head. "Don't listen to him. Although he might be right about the weather. That elbow of his should be granted a degree in meteorology. Keep an eye on the forecast. The bridge into town floods this time of year. You two be safe."

Sera had to make a decision. What was more important? Getting the flooring or having to explain to her family that she wasn't dating Harry Jefferys?

The lunches they'd had while they were working were not dates. Talking to him on the phone late at night because she had a question about the best tile to order wasn't a date, even though it ended up with her talking to him until two in the morning about everything from his favorite movies to why she was genuinely afraid of birds. They were rats with wings, and they attacked from above.

Not dates. Not at all.

"We'll stop by my place." They were friends. Nothing more. Her mother would understand that.

"Good." Harry was back to smiling. "And we can grab dinner in town. I haven't been in the French Quarter in years. I'll call and make us reservations someplace nice."

She hurried after him and swore she was going to keep the whole day platonic.

Harry knocked on the door to their motel room as the rain poured down, beating against the roof. He huddled under the awning and hoped Sera would let him in. After all, he was the reason they were stuck outside Papillon. If he hadn't insisted on dinner in the Quarter, they wouldn't have gotten stuck in traffic. If they hadn't gotten stuck in traffic, they would have been safely home before the road into town flooded.

They wouldn't be here in a cheap motel where there was only one room left and he was going to end up spending the night sleeping on the floor.

If she let him in at all.

He knocked again. He'd run over to the convenience store across the street and procured toothbrushes, some snacks, and a bottle of wine as an apology.

The door came open and she stood there, her eyes rimmed red.

"I can't get a cell phone signal." There was a panicked look in her eyes.

"Okay. I'll see if I can get one." He walked inside and made a beeline for the bathroom. He was soaked through.

"There's two bars, but the call won't go through," she insisted. "It's got plenty of charge. I always make sure it's charged. I wouldn't leave my mom without a way to get hold of me if something were to happen to Luc."

He put his hands on her shoulders. He knew the start of a panic attack, had had a few himself. "Sera, it's all right.

Everything is going to be okay. Take a deep breath with me." He stroked his hands down her arms. She'd relaxed a bit the minute he'd touched her.

She took a long breath. "I'm sorry. I'm acting crazy."

He shook his head and smoothed her hair back, not missing the way her eyes closed at the contact. Zep had told him she hadn't dated in a long time. She'd been deprived of much-needed affection. "You're not. You're acting like a mom. There's a landline here. Your mom has a landline at her place, right?"

He was pretty sure he'd seen one on the wall of the kitchen. He'd liked Sera's home. It was comfortable. It wasn't a museum like his aunt's house, and yet it had been beautifully decorated. There had been pictures all over the place, and plants and books. He'd stared for a long time at the picture of Seraphina in her majorette uniform. She'd practically shone in that picture, a light in her eyes that couldn't be denied.

Life had dimmed her light, but he often saw it sputtering back to existence as though her spirit could only be dark for so long.

Her shoulders were right back up to her ears. "I can't remember the number. How stupid is that? I push a button on my phone. Mom. The landline doesn't have a button for my mother."

She'd been on edge ever since she'd realized they wouldn't make it back to Papillon and she was separated from her son. It was more than that. She'd gotten to the flooring place and they'd tried to jack the price up on her. They'd seen a pretty blonde and figured they could take advantage of her. Harry had set them straight, but he would bet that hadn't been the first time Sera had to deal with men who thought pretty meant dumb, and dumb meant they could do whatever they liked.

He pulled his shirt over his head and set it on the sink before grabbing a towel and drying off as best he could.

She took a deep breath. "Or I could calm down and look it up in my contacts. I'm sorry. I do know how a phone works. I didn't think about the landline. I never use it. I'm panicking. It's my first real time away from Luc and this storm looks nasty."

She picked up the phone and dialed the number.

"Hey, Mom," she said. "I'm afraid Harry and I got caught on the wrong side of the bridge. I'm so sorry. I should have been home hours ago. Is Luc okay?"

He stepped back in the bathroom to give her some privacy. He could hear her talking quietly but he shut the bathroom door and leaned against it.

He was falling madly in love with this woman and he was blowing it. He should have thought about her and what she needed, but no, he'd made the selfish choice to have her all to himself. He'd known exactly when she was renting that truck. She'd made a note of it on that endless list of hers and he'd used it to his advantage. He'd gone in and rented the truck right out from under her, though the wood had come in days ago. He'd done it because he'd wanted to spend the day with her. He'd spent most afternoons with her lately, but being on a road trip together was different. She couldn't ignore him in the truck. He'd been able to turn on the radio and talk to her about the kind of music she liked. He'd had hours with her without the fear of getting caught. That hadn't gotten past him. He knew why she'd taken him into the kitchen at Guidry's when there had been plenty of open tables in the dining room. She was nervous about his aunt finding out they were spending time together. He could have told her that he didn't intend to lie about what he was doing. His aunt hadn't asked where he spent his afternoons. She was far too busy working on the wedding or the business. She'd been going into the office the whole time Harry had been here.

But when she eventually asked, he was going to tell her because he wasn't ashamed of Sera.

He was kind of ashamed of himself, though.

"Harry? Are you okay in there?"

He opened the door. "Everything all right at home?"

She nodded. "Yeah. Luc and Shep are getting along great. Lila's going to bring over some food for him. Zep is there in case anything happens, so they'll all be fine. I'm sorry I freaked out. I don't spend much time apart from Luc. I haven't ever spent the night away from him. He's in a climbing phase and I worry a lot."

"I'm the one who's sorry. I should have brought you home sooner. I shouldn't have made you have dinner with me."

"You didn't make me do anything," she said. "Is that wine? Because I could use it."

"Yeah. I figured I got you into this situation, the least I could do was try to make you comfortable. I'm sorry there wasn't much of a selection. I did get toothbrushes, and I found a T-shirt for you to sleep in. I'm going to warn you, though. It has a big beer can on it."

She picked up the bag and took it out to the king-size bed that dominated the room. "Big beer can it is, then. Beggars can't be choosers."

He stepped out as she opened the bottle. Naturally the selection had been weak, to say the least. He'd gotten her a screw-top bottle. "Sorry about the cheap wine. I assume you grew up around the good stuff. My choices were red or white or pink. The red needed a corkscrew."

She sniffled and held up the bottle. "My brother is the

wine snob. The older one, that is. Zep is more of a beer guy. Don't feel bad about it. Feel bad that this place doesn't even have glasses. Cheers."

She held the bottle up and took a healthy swig.

"Sera, I'm sorry. I didn't listen to you. I was selfish and I sincerely apologize."

She seemed to think about that for a minute. "You knew I had rented that truck, didn't you? You walked in knowing full well I would have a problem and you could solve it."

Well, he'd never thought she wasn't smart. "Yes."

"You set this whole thing up so you could get me alone in a place where I wouldn't put you to work."

"Well, in my defense, I did not arrange the storm." If he had, he would have been smart enough to put an extra set of clothes in the truck. He was going to be stuck in cold, wet boxers all night. He could wait until Sera turned off the lights and strip down. He wasn't going to have her think he would take advantage of her.

"But you got out of your shirt fast enough." She looked him up and down. "You do that a lot, you know."

He felt himself flush. "It's hot around here. I can certainly stop doing that."

"And interrupt the daily entertainment? My friends would be upset at the thought. Did you notice that Hallie and Sylvie show up every day to check and see if I need anything? Neither one of those women has ever picked up a hammer in her life but suddenly they're all about home repairs."

"They're your friends. I'm sure they're only trying to help you out."

"Yeah, no, they come over to catch a glimpse of all that." She moved her hand around, indicating his chest. "You know every woman in this town is either crazy about you or thinking about setting you up with their daughter or sister or unattached friend. I heard you caused a fuss at Dixie's the other day. Momma said you had two women fighting over who got to bring you coffee."

He winced. It had been embarrassing, but two of the younger waitresses at the café had taken a shine to him, and they were quite aggressive in their attentions. "I've found that being single in a small town has its disadvantages. Of course, I also get invited to dinner a lot. A lot."

And he'd turned them all down because he only wanted to be with one woman.

"Has Josette asked you out yet?" Sera asked, her tone deceptively bland.

He knew a minefield when he walked on one. He had the half leg to prove it. Josette Trahan had been at several of the events he'd attended. She was lovely, but there was something cold about the woman. "She asked if I wanted to go out to her place for drinks. I declined."

"She used to be my sister-in-law, you know. She was married to Remy until she found a better prospect." Sera took another drink. "She's probably the most beautiful woman in town."

"She is not."

"Really?" Her brows rose. "Is this the moment when you say I'm the most beautiful woman in town?"

"I don't have to say it for it to be true." He'd screwed everything up. Maybe it was time for outright honesty. "I'm not interested in anyone but you. I sat in that café getting my coffee mug refilled every three minutes and thought about the fact that if you had been there with me, I'd be safe."

She set the bottle down on the nightstand. "You wouldn't be safe at all. Your aunt would throw a fit."

"I'm a grown man. I don't let my aunt tell me what to do."

Her blond hair shook. "And if she kicks you out of the house? Have you thought about that at all?"

He shrugged, the thought not bothering him much. He felt far more comfortable in that ramshackle place of Sera's, and something was always falling apart there. "I've lived in my truck before. I can do it again. I'll put the camper on top, park on your land, and stay until you don't need me anymore. With all the bedrooms in that place, I can fix one up and stay there. I sometimes can't sleep and find work soothing."

She stood up and grabbed the T-shirt he'd bought for her. "It can't work, Harry. I'm not going to lie. I'm incredibly attracted to you but I don't think it's a good idea. You're an amazing guy. The funny thing is if you were willing to have an affair, I might do it. I want you that much. But you would want to get involved."

Honesty could sometimes hurt. "I'm only here for another couple of weeks, but yeah, I would want to get to know you."

She stared at him for a moment. "If you get to know me, you might not leave, and then I'll be the one to cost you the only family you have. Hell, I don't know if I can do it to Celeste after everything she's been through. I know I'm supposed to hate her, but I also kind of understand her. She put everything she had into Wes and she needs a reason he's gone. She needs a villain she can pin it on. It's too much to understand that some things are random and we can't control them. The world gets infinitely more scary when you have a child. I can't imagine losing Luc."

"You are being so much kinder to her than she is to you." He wanted to kiss her. He wanted it so badly he ached with the longing.

"Yeah, well, I've thought about it a lot. I know she

wouldn't believe it, but I miss Wes, too. He was my friend for so long it was hard to move on without him."

"Did you love him?" He'd wanted to ask the question for days, but it was a touchy subject all around.

Her eyes came up, a depth of misery there. "I did, but not the way he needed me to. I think that I might have ruined two lives when we fought that day."

"It didn't ruin your life at all. It might have made it harder, but you're going to be okay." He was starting to understand her. "You feel guilty, but you didn't force him to leave school."

"No, but I didn't ask him to stay, either. I was angry with him, too. I never expected him to do what he did. I can't imagine him in the Army. Wes was gentle." She seemed a bit shaken. "Not that you're rough, Harry. I didn't mean anything by it."

"I went into the Army because I didn't have anywhere else to go," he explained. "I'm glad I did. It helped me a lot. I think it might have helped Wes, too, but the truth is the world can be random and unsafe. Even if he hadn't gone into the Army, he could have gotten killed. He could have gotten into a car and taken a wrong turn one night and ended up in the same place. We can't know these things. I understand Celeste needs someone to blame but that shouldn't be you, and it shouldn't come between the two of us. I can't promise you where this is going. I'm not supposed to stay past the wedding, but you're right. If I want to, I will stay. I don't know what the future is going to bring. I only know that being with you feels right to me. If my aunt doesn't like it, that's her problem. We make decisions in life and we live with them. I can live with this decision. I want to try with you but I don't want to hide it. Nothing flourishes in the shadows. Especially not you. You should be in the light."

There were tears in her eyes as she looked up at him. "You might not think that if you knew the truth."

"Then tell me."

She took a deep breath and shook her head. "I'm going to take a shower. You should try the wine."

She slipped into the bathroom and closed the door between them.

Harry stared at that closed door. What had she meant about the truth? He didn't understand any of it. Cal was spiraling. His aunt had the worst priorities he'd ever seen. Only Angie seemed to have moved past Wes's death.

Sera definitely hadn't, and despite the fact that she said she hadn't been in love with him, the man was still standing firmly between them.

And now his leg ached. Well, his stump ached. He'd slipped on the wet floor and banged into the front desk of the motel. He was screwing up a lot today.

He grabbed the bottle of muscadine wine and took a drink. It looked like sharing a bottle was going to be about as close as he would get to Seraphina.

chapter seven

Seraphina stepped out of the shower and knew she would regret not spending the night with Harry for the rest of her life, but did she honestly want to wreck another of Celeste Beaumont's relatives?

She moved in front of the mirror, looking at the girl reflected back. Girl? She wasn't a girl at all anymore and hadn't been from the moment she'd realized Luc was growing in her belly.

Or maybe it had been that moment that she'd realized she would have to let Wes go, that minute she knew she'd gone too far and they couldn't go back. She'd finally understood it wasn't fair to him to even try.

Did she have to pay for that one mistake the rest of her life? She stared at herself in the mirror and wondered who she'd become. Was she the woman who peaked in high school and never quite found her footing after? She'd watched most of her friends start their lives, find careers, get married, leave for brighter prospects, but she felt stuck. It wasn't that she wanted to leave. She didn't, but she wanted something that made her feel like she was moving forward. Purpose.

She'd found it in restoring that old house. The last week had been the best she'd had in a long time. She wanted to get up and get to work. There was a bounce in her step and the place was starting to look good. It was starting to look like a place that could really work as a B and B.

Harry was a part of it. He didn't pat her head and tell her to call a man in to do all the work. He taught her. He was patient with her. She'd started to think about what she would do with the money from the house. What if she took that money and bought another place, a place that needed work? She was damn good at making a place look pretty. Harry was good at the practical stuff. She could study real estate. Maybe get her license. They could build a business out of their skills, and she would do something she genuinely loved.

She groaned. She had only kissed the man once and she was practically married and running a business with him.

Her phone rang, startling her since it hadn't been working before. She glanced down, her heart seizing a bit. Her mom. She slid her finger across the screen to accept the call. "What happened?"

"Nothing," her mom said. "Sweetie, I was calling to tell you everyone is fine here. The rain's let up and you should be able to get back in the morning. Luc is sleeping and that dog won't leave his room. I've been watching the baby monitor and every time Luc gets up and tries to climb out of bed, the dog gently nudges him back. We should steal that dog, Seraphina."

She liked the dog almost as much as she liked his owner. "We're not stealing Shep."

"Maybe not steal, but you could do that thing where you bat your eyes and all the boys do what you want."

Yeah, that hadn't worked since high school. "Momma, I'm not stealing that man's dog, but I will think about getting Luc one. Is everything really okay? I'm sorry for not getting home."

"I'm not. You could use a night away. Now let's talk about how you're going to take that man down. Zep told me he is very interested in you. It's been a long time since you seduced a man, and quite frankly, you are out of practice."

"Mom." Sometimes her mother could still shock her. "I'm not seducing him."

"Well, you never will with that attitude of yours. I swear if I was twenty years younger, I would be all over that man like jelly on peanut butter, and it would be the crunchy kind. There would be nothing plain about it."

She coughed. "Mom . . ."

"Don't you pretend like he's not the most gorgeous thing to walk into Papillon in years." Her mom was quiet for a moment. "Is it because he's related to Celeste Beaumont?"

"You know how she feels about me."

"I know that you've let her bully you for years because you feel guilty about what happened to Wes. You have to stop that. I've let you wallow, but it's time to be my sassy, take-no-prisoners daughter again. You were a girl who knew what she wanted and went after it."

That was where her mother was wrong. "But I didn't. I didn't go after anything. I got lost after high school, and I haven't figured out what I want to do with my life. Everyone else seemed to know."

"Not everyone. It only seems like you're alone. Life threw you a curveball. You needed a couple of years to adjust, but it's time to get back into the game. If you don't, you're going to find yourself like me." Her mother's voice softened over the line. "Don't get me wrong. I love my life and that it's surrounded with friends and with my family, but I wish I'd taken the time to explore more. I wish I'd dated. I told myself I needed to concentrate on you kids, but now I know the truth. I was scared. It was easier to hide away after your father died. It was easier to lock my heart up, but I regret it now. I know that Jackson fellow hurt you, but that's his loss. If you're interested in this man, you should go for it. Don't use Luc as an excuse to not take care of yourself. You're a good mom, Seraphina. You're a good person. You deserve to have a life as much as that Celeste Beaumont does."

Tears pulsed behind Sera's eyes. Her mother was pointing out all the worries that simmered under her surface, everything that kept her up at night, kept her mouth closed when she would have spoken up. She had changed since Wes died, since Luc was born. She'd pushed aside all of her own hopes and dreams in favor of making herself less of a target.

She'd made herself small and now she was allowing her guilt to keep her from something that could be wonderful. Harry.

"He stole the truck out from under me," she said with a sniffle. "He manipulated everything so he could spend time with me. He's a sneaky bastard, and I think I could really like him."

She might be able to love him if she let herself try.

Her mom chuckled. "He's a man who obviously knows what he wants."

"He's says he's going to leave, but I'll be honest, I think I'm more afraid that he'll stay."

"No one gets through life without facing their fears. Unless you want to end up like your Aunt Irene. You know there's always a story under the surface. Irene wasn't born hating the world. She wasn't born a hermit. Something happened to her when she was a young woman. I don't know what it was. I only know that your great-grandmother said she changed after she went away for college. I think someone hurt her and she came home and never left again, never dated. I don't want that for you. Take a chance. Even if this isn't something that lasts forever, it's something you need. Unless you don't think he's worth it."

That wasn't the problem at all. "I could cost him a relationship with his aunt. He won't let us hide if we're dating."

"I knew I liked him." She could practically see her momma smiling. "He's a man, Sera. Let him make his own choices. If you've talked about this and he's made the decision, then you're the only one holding you back. And you're the only one who can free yourself. I love you, baby. I'll be by your side no matter what you do, but I think there's a reason you got caught with him tonight. Although I know that motel. Couldn't you have gotten caught at a five-star in New Orleans?"

Sera laughed at the thought and wiped her tears away. Her mother had a point. Maybe it was time to start taking back some of her life. "What if I'm making another mistake and it ends up hurting people?"

"Are you going into this with any thought to hurt someone else?"

She was trying desperately not to. "No."

"Then do your best and know that we love you. Know that your family stands by you."

"Hey, Momma, are you trying to get Sera to jump Harry's bones?" She could hear her brother in the background. "Because that would help me out enormously. I need to get that brother off the market or I won't ever get a date again. You go for it, sis. Help baby brother out. Hey, I even have some condoms for you."

Zep was the most obnoxious member of her family. "I'll see you in the morning, Momma."

She hung up.

What did she want? She wanted to stay here and live at Guidry Place, at least for a while. She wanted to build some kind of a future for herself and her son. She wanted something sweet in her life.

She wanted Harry.

She smoothed back her hair, happy that at least the place had a working hair dryer. Yes, she was wearing a T-shirt that had a massive beer bottle on it and she'd washed away all her makeup. Yes, she was in a motel where someone had likely been murdered recently. And yes, she didn't have a lot to offer the man sitting outside, but she was going to walk out there and offer it to him anyway.

She stepped out of the bathroom and stopped because Harry was sitting at the small desk, his prosthetic leg propped against the bed. He'd taken off his jeans and sat there in a pair of boxers. His face was tight as he looked down at the place where they'd amputated.

All thoughts of being seductive and bold fled and her heart softened. She rushed to him. "What's wrong?"

He grimaced. "Sorry. I didn't want you to see me like this."

"You've got a cut." She touched his leg right above his knee, a few inches from the scrape he'd taken. "We need to take care of it. Is it rubbing against the prosthesis?"

"No. It's a little above where it sits. I slipped in the rain and scraped against something."

"We need to get you in the bathroom and clean it up." It wasn't bad, but he definitely would need some soap and water. "You're chilled all the way through. I'm sorry I took so long."

He looked at her and there was a weariness to him that made her ache. "I heard you talking to someone. Is everything all right?"

She nodded. "Yeah, I've got three bars now, so that

makes me feel better. Though you should know my momma wants to steal your dog. According to her, Shep is a baby whisperer." She stood up. "Come on. I'll turn on the shower and help you get in."

He glanced down. "I need a minute to get my leg back on."

He would only have to take it off again. "Or you can lean on me. It's not far."

"Sera, I . . ."

She stared down at him because they needed to get a few things straight. Whatever happened between them wouldn't be some fast and furious affair where they spent more time in bed than out of it. If they were going to be friends, be more than friends, then she had some firm beliefs in how that would work. "You said you wanted to get to know me. This is part of me. I want to help you. I want to be something more to you than a pretty face and a body in bed. If there's one thing I've learned, it's that life is rough, and you better be strong enough to help the people around you. You also better be strong enough to accept help from the people around you. You told me I'm the most beautiful woman in town. Well, I wonder if you'll think that when you see my scars. I've got a nice one at my bikini line because Luc was a ten-pound baby, and I wasn't built for that."

The sweetest smile came over his face, lighting him up. There was something special about Harry, some inner goodness that shone through. "I'll think that scar is beautiful because it's a part of you."

"Then don't expect me to think less of you because you're about to awkwardly hop to that barely functional bathroom and clean yourself up. I'll think you're brave because you went through all of it and there's no bitterness in you."

His hand came out, reaching for her own. "Oh, don't think I woke up this way. It took a lot to get past my bitterness. After I came home to Dallas, I worked for a little while in a restaurant that gave jobs to injured vets. It's where I learned how to make the best grilled cheese sandwich in the world. It's also where I met a great therapist who guided me through those first rough months when I thought the world was over. I was angry and bitter and I hated everyone for a while. But I got through it with some help. I'm glad to take yours, sweetheart."

She balanced him as he managed to stand. She glanced down at his foot. Even that foot was oddly sexy. It was big and solid, like the rest of the man. She eased her arm around his waist and his arm came out to close on her shoulders. She was the perfect height to balance him. It was funny because she'd always bemoaned how short she was, but now she was happy to be his crutch.

She'd been right. It was horrifically awkward, but Harry laughed as they wobbled and hopped and weaved their way to the bathroom.

"We are not going to be winning any three-leg races," he said as they made it past the door.

"I bet we could if we practiced. They have one every year at the Founder's Day picnic, and Herve and his brother always win. I think it's because they've had so much practice helping each other out of bars when they're drunk." She turned on the hot water as he balanced against the sink.

"We'll have to practice, then." He was staring at her, his eyes steady as though he didn't even want to think about looking away. "Sera . . ."

This was the moment when she had to make her choice. But then, she'd pretty much already made it. "You're sure?"

"More sure than I've been of anything in my life."

She went up on her toes and let her lips brush his. "Okay, then. Let's get you cleaned up and we'll deal with everything else."

He grinned down at her. "And I can take you on a proper date?"

She nodded, a warmth flaring in her heart. She was going on a date with Harry Jefferys. "Yes."

"And not to your family restaurant. Somewhere else."

She nodded. "There are a couple of places we could go. I can show you around. I've heard you've turned down the other tour guides."

"Yeah, I was waiting for the right one."

He was so heartbreakingly gorgeous. And that was what would happen. He would break her heart and she was still going to try with him. She gently brushed her lips against his once more. "I promise to be diligent about showing you around town. Maybe you'll like it there. Well, when we can actually get back into town. Now sit down and let me clean this up for you. I've got some bandages in my purse, and a tiny first aid kit. Luc gets scrapes all the time. I'll be right back."

Harry proved to be an excellent patient. He was still while she cleaned the wound, not even wincing when she rubbed the antiseptic over it. "What made you change your mind? I thought you would be done with me when you figured out my evil plot."

"To take me to a nice dinner? To help me deal with those jerks who wanted to jack the price up? Strangely, I didn't find that so evil."

"Do you get that a lot?" he asked.

"Men who think because I'm blond and have breasts that I obviously don't have a brain in my head? All the time," she replied. "It's not bad at home. They all know me, but we get a lot of tourists. I was a waitress for a while. I lost that job when I poured a whole pitcher of iced tea on a man."

"And what did he do to deserve that?" His voice had gone deep.

He was going to be overly protective. That was easy to see. "He seemed like he needed cooling down. That was all. He actually wasn't doing anything to me, but Hallie was working there, too. It was when we were just out of high school. He got handsy and she froze. So I took care of it. It wasn't Dixie's place. It was one town over. Dixie would have chased that man away and likely called Armie on the guy. And I'm not alone. Every woman I know has a story like what happened today. But I got my discount and my flooring. I might have to rent a boat to get it all home, but it's mine." She pressed the bandage against him and got to her feet. "I think you will survive."

He'd dried himself off with a towel and there was no way to miss how good that man looked in nothing but a pair of boxers.

"Only because I had an excellent nurse." He stared at her for a moment as if he wanted to take her in, memorize her. He shook his head and took a long breath. "We should get you to bed. Did you see any extra blankets?"

Did he honestly think she would make him sleep on the floor? Now that she was in, she kind of wanted to be all in. She had no idea how long she would have with him. "It's a king-size bed. I think we can share it."

"Are you sure?"

She nodded and got in position to help him back to the bed. She liked him leaning on her, liked knowing he understood she was strong enough to help him. And she definitely liked that he hadn't fought her on it, hadn't pulled some masculine BS. "I am."

She settled him on the right side of the bed and wished

she were wearing something sexier than a way-too-big-for-her beer T-shirt. It hung to her knees and hid the one part of her she felt pretty confident in. Despite breastfeeding for almost a year, her boobs were still perky. Of course, he was a fairly careful man. He might have rules. "So if we're going to date, I need to ask you a question. How do you feel about fooling around?"

He went still. "Are you asking specifically how I feel about fooling around with you or in general?"

All the talking stuff made her anxious. Why couldn't he be one of those guys who took any shot he could with a woman? It would make it infinitely easier to get what she wanted if she didn't actually have to admit that she wanted it. Of course, then he wouldn't be Harry. Honest, upright, gorgeous Harry, who was going to make her admit everything. "I'm talking about you and me. I can't stop thinking about kissing you."

His hands came up to take hers. He pressed until they were palm to palm. "That's because I told you I'm the best kisser in the world."

He made her smile. She knew why he'd pulled that arrogant routine on her. He'd known how close she was to getting emotional, and he'd given her an out. This man always seemed to know what she needed. She threaded her fingers with his, loving how big his hands were. Harry's hands were calloused and warm and strong. "I don't know about that. I seem to have forgotten, and then of course, how could I be sure? I haven't kissed a ton of guys. Wouldn't I need to kiss, well, all the other guys?"

He pulled her in, his eyes going hot. "You're going to have to take my word for it because I don't want you kissing anyone else. Not now that I have you where I want you."

"In a motel room?"

He pulled her close and she suddenly found herself on

her back, him looming over her. "Right here. With me. No matter where that is, Seraphina. As for fooling around, I am all for it if you're willing to be with me. But it's not fooling around. I'm serious about you, and you need to understand that."

She let her arms go around his shoulders, her whole body softening under his. Her skin was starting to sing with anticipation. "You're serious about me and you would be upset if I used you for sex."

A shudder went through him. "You should understand that I would not take that well. I would be depressed and likely very vocal about how the gorgeous, smart blonde used me for my body."

He was ridiculous. "Yes, everyone would believe that the single mom ruthlessly used you for sex."

His face went serious. "I don't only want sex from you."

She cupped his face because her heart was already melting for him. "I don't just want sex from you, but I do want it. I want you, Harry. I want you like I haven't wanted anything in a long time. I want to be close to you. I want to be with you."

"I want to be with you." A hint of a smile crossed his face before he lowered his head to hers.

She could hear the rain beating against the window as the storm started up again, but it was mere background noise because Harry was kissing her. His lips brushed along hers, gentle at first, and then deeper, his tongue running along the seam of her mouth and coaxing her to open for him.

When she acquiesced, he took her mouth by storm, and Sera offered no resistance. What she had not been ready for before, she was eager for now. All of the problems and questions fell before this new, undeniable desire. Never in her whole life had she felt this way about a man. Her heart thudded, her breasts rubbing against his chest, legs restlessly entwining with his.

Harry's breath was ragged, but his tongue was hot and soft as he licked a path across her lips. He kissed her everywhere—her lips, her eyes, cheeks, and chin. She reveled in the rasp of his whiskers against her soft skin. It was something she'd learned about him. Harry started the day with his face baby smooth, but by the middle of the afternoon a sexy scruff would make an appearance. He nipped at her earlobe, and she was surprised to find out exactly how amazing that felt.

"Are you sure about this? I don't have to have this tonight," he whispered against her ear before running his tongue along the shell and making her shiver with desire. She'd never considered her ear to be an erogenous zone, but Harry was making her rethink that. Pretty much everywhere he touched seemed to flare to life, every inch of skin where they connected alive and aware of him.

"I do," she protested. She let her fingers find his hair, running through the soft gold and brown silk. "I do need this. It's been so long since I felt like this. Maybe never, Harry."

Because she'd never been with a man like him. Because she'd viewed sex as something she needed to get through to get to the part where her boyfriend would hold her. She'd gotten pleasure from sex before, but somehow she knew it would be different with him. It would be more, and now that she'd made the decision, she didn't want to wait, didn't want to take her time. She wanted to jump right over the edge with him and enjoy every moment they might have together because she knew damn well it could all come to an end.

One strong hand reached out to cup her cheek tenderly. "I want you, too. I've wanted you since the moment I saw you. When you tossed that blond hair and warned me not to listen when your momma inevitably tried to set us up, all I could think was how did I get you to change your mind about me."

He was staring down at her like she was something precious he needed to protect. He made her feel that way. "It wasn't that I thought you weren't attractive. But you're . . ."

"Not a Beaumont," he said, laying a kiss on her nose and proving he was pretty good at reading her mind. "Put that out of your head right now. I'm my own man and I want very, very much to be *your* man. My aunt does not make choices for me, and I don't want you to take this choice out of my hands. I want you. Trust me to know what I'm doing, and I will give you the same courtesy."

All in all, it was a deal she would be a fool to turn down. "Yes."

The sexiest smile tugged his lips up. "I like the way you say 'yes' to me." He turned serious. "But there's no going back after this. We're together. I'll take care of you."

"And I'll take care of you." She liked the idea of Harry needing her.

His kiss was light, and he stroked her body gently. The feel of his work-roughened hands on her skin was electric, and she found herself not only welcoming his touch but also seeking it. His tongue reached out to caress her lips. He whispered erotic words that sent a spark through her body. Gradually, relaxation gave way to excitement and the strongest ache in the center of her body. She began moving to the music he made with every touch.

"As gorgeous as you look in this, it has to come off," he whispered, tugging at the hem of her shirt.

It all had to come off because she didn't want anything between them. She wanted to be skin to skin with him, all her scars and imperfections exposed to his eyes. It was all right because Harry understood nothing perfect was real. She didn't have to pretend with him.

The way she'd loved taking care of his leg. There was nothing ugly about his scars. Each one proved he'd survived. She sat up and dragged the shirt off, leaving her in nothing but the cotton undies she'd dried with the hair dryer. "Have I told you how gorgeous you are, Harry?"

His eyes were on her breasts. "I think that's my line. I think you're lovely, and it's only partially about how good you look. I also adore how good you are with a jigsaw."

And she loved how easily he could make her laugh. Although she was getting good with saws of all kinds. She'd managed to keep all her fingers.

"Just one more thing," he said, his fingers going to the waistband of her undies. He eased them off and tossed them aside before taking her in his arms again. "That's what I want. You feel so good. So right."

There was nowhere his hands didn't stroke, nowhere his lips didn't caress.

When he bent down to take her nipple in his mouth, Sera nearly came off the bed. She had never been particularly sensitive there, but now she was on fire. Her fingers tangled in his hair, but he did nothing to hold her back. He sucked strongly on the nipple before turning his attention to the other.

He kissed his way down her body, lavishing her with affection.

"I'm ready now, Harry." This was lust. This terrible, wonderful excitement had to be lust. She wasn't thinking about how he would hold her afterward. She was thinking about how much she wanted him inside, to be surrounded by this magnificent man. "I want you so much."

His blue eyes darkened, and his muscled body was taut with restraint.

He shook his head. She could see the strain he was under, but he still refused. "Not yet."

"Please." She was begging and she didn't even care. All that mattered was this crazy connection she felt to him.

"Is this better, baby?" Harry spread her legs and slowly pushed a finger into her. When he had gently gone as far as he could, his thumb reached up to stroke her pleasure point. She gasped at the sensation. This was what she needed. He added a second finger and gently stretched her. In and out. In and out. Over and over and over again. All the while that lazy thumb made long, voluptuous circles that took her breath away and robbed her of her higher faculties. There was nothing but this man and this moment. Her hips came up, seeking more of him, more of this insane pleasure.

"I bet this will be even better, baby." He lowered his mouth, replacing his thumb with his tongue. "I knew you would taste sweet."

The firm, velvet stroke of his tongue caressing her sent her straight over an edge she had never imagined existed. It was the most magnificent wave, and it took over her body, leaving her crying out his name and shaking in its wake.

Just as the final ripple washed over her, she heard Harry groan. His hands were shaking as he reached over to the nightstand and fished a condom out of his wallet. "I have never been so happy my friends have a sense of humor. I swear I don't normally keep one of these in my wallet."

She didn't care. She watched Harry, watched him stroke himself before rolling the condom on. She was deliciously languid as he arranged her legs around his waist and positioned himself. She felt no trepidation as he slowly, carefully thrust into her. She could see by the strain on his face what his tenderness was costing him.

Sera wrapped her arms around him, welcoming him inside.

The rest of the world fell away. This was the way it was supposed to be. Just the two of them, warm and safe and happy. "It feels good. So good."

"Thank god," he rasped and then let himself go. He set a hard rhythm, and he grasped her hips to keep them close together. His head was thrown back, and the look on his face sent Sera reeling with joy. She was giving him that pleasure, the same glorious pleasure he had given to her. She pulled him close and kissed him with everything she had. She stroked him and urged him on with her hands and gave him back the erotic words that had aroused her to a fever pitch.

She hadn't expected the shuddering pleasure to start up again. She'd been more than content, but he seemed to find some magical place deep inside, and he knew exactly how to stroke her. It was happening again. She strained with him, bringing her hips up to meet his thrusts. For the second time that night, she went limp under his expert handling. Then Harry was groaning loudly, his big body shaking as he came inside her. He fell on her, gasping for air. She stroked his back and hair, loving the feel of his weight on top of her.

When she could finally speak again, she said the only word she could find to describe what she had found with Harry.

"Wow," she whispered.

Harry laughed and kissed her tenderly. "That goes double for me."

She settled in and knew there was no going back.

chapter eight

Celeste paced the floor as the rain kept coming down.

"Mom, I'm sure he's fine," Angie said from her place on the sofa. "He went to New Orleans to get the wood he ordered. He must have taken longer than he thought and he got caught in the storm."

"According to Annemarie, he left early this morning." She'd been surprised by the amount of anxiety she'd felt the minute she'd realized she couldn't get in touch with Harry. "There's no reason he couldn't have gotten back before the storm hit. Have you called Armie?"

"No," Angie replied. "I assume the sheriff is busy this evening. I heard he's already had to rescue a couple of people from the flash flood. And before you ask, none of those people was Harry."

The previous week had gone by in a whirl of activity. There had been plenty to do at the office, and she'd even had to make a trip into New Orleans to clean up some issues with human resources. Between dealing with that problem and handling the catering for the wedding, she'd almost been able to completely forget about the situation with Guidry Place.

Ninety days wasn't so long when she thought about it, and according to the rumors she'd heard, Irene had left explicit instructions on how the money she'd left Seraphina had to be spent. There was no way she would live there. The house was far too large for her, and even if Delphine and that wastrel of a brother of hers decided to move in, they likely couldn't afford the taxes and the upkeep.

It didn't make any sense for her to keep it, and Seraphina was a girl who knew how to survive. It might cost her a bit more, but Celeste would be able to buy the place, then Sera would have the money to leave Papillon and go to a city. She would be made to understand that was the absolute only way this ended.

Celeste had actually felt fairly calm until the moment she realized Harry hadn't come home from his errand.

It had been raining the night she found out about Wes. The officers who'd come to explain what had happened to her son had carried umbrellas, and the wind had been fierce.

She shook off the horrific memory. "He's not answering his cell phone. Shouldn't he have called?"

"I think Harry's used to being on his own," Angela said. "And he's been complaining about his cell losing charge. It's pretty old."

She would buy him a new one immediately.

The door came open and Cal rushed inside, handing his umbrella to the maid and shrugging out of his rain jacket. "I talked to LaTonya Nichols at the Feed Store. Harry rented the largest of their trucks and it's got a tracker on it. It's parked outside town. From what we could tell, it's in a motel parking lot."

She breathed a sigh of relief. He'd gotten caught in the storm. He'd probably taken the chance to enjoy New Orleans for the afternoon, and he'd tried to come back too late to get past the storm waters. The road into town often flooded this time of year and Harry was a sensible man. "Do you know the name of that motel? Surely they still have phones in the rooms, right?"

It had been decades since she'd stayed at anything but a luxury hotel.

Cal sighed and moved toward her. "Mom, stop. He's okay. I know you're worried about him, but he's a grown man."

"He should call his family," she insisted.

"I don't know that he considers us family just yet," Cal said quietly. "At least not the kind who he needs to call when he's staying out all night. Give Harry some space. I know you want him to stay here, and giving a grown man a curfew probably won't help your cause."

"I wasn't saying that."

He stared at her.

"I only gave you a curfew because it was starting to affect your performance." At least she'd tried to. Naturally Cal had told her if she didn't like how he performed, he could perform somewhere else. In another company. In another state, perhaps.

It had been so much easier when they were younger.

"All I'm saying is you should cut Harry some slack. He's been on his own for a long time," Cal explained. "He's fine. You don't have to worry about him. Now, I can't get back to New Orleans this evening. That's so sad. Well, I'll have to take a three-day weekend, I suppose."

"Or you can work from here." She loved her oldest, but he could be terribly lazy.

Harry was safe. She let herself relax. Perhaps a night at that terrible motel with no one but his dog for companionship would teach Harry to plan more carefully.

Cal groaned. "Maybe it'll be clear by morning."

Because of course he wouldn't want to work with her. She shook her head his way. "I'm going to check on supper. I'll be right back."

She walked out. She might have one glass of wine tonight. Though she was happy she knew where her nephew was, she wouldn't be satisfied until she'd seen him and ensured that he was truly all right.

"You know why she's worried," she heard Cal say.

"I do," Angie replied quietly. "She can't stand to not know where any of us are. I understand it but it can be suffocating. I'm going to lecture the hell out of Harry about keeping his damn cell phone charged."

"I don't know that would have helped this particular time," Cal said.

She knew she shouldn't eavesdrop, but she couldn't stop herself. She went still, not wanting to tip her kids off. Honestly, if she didn't eavesdrop, she would never know anything about their lives. She and her husband had done an excellent job of making them emotionally independent. With the exception of Wes.

"What do you mean?" Angie asked.

"Well, I happen to know that he's not alone."

Harry was seeing someone? She was definitely interested in that. She hoped the young woman was in New Orleans because she couldn't think of a local girl who would be right for him. And she'd tried.

"Who's he with?" Angie had that excited tone she got when she was talking about juicy gossip. No matter how many times she'd pointed out that gossip wasn't ladylike, Angie couldn't get past it. "Is it Deb? Or one of those waitresses? I heard they were all over him at Dixie's the other day."

There was a pause before Cal answered her. "LaTonya said he went to New Orleans with Seraphina."

Angie sighed. "Damn it. I hoped she would stay away from him. Mom will lose it if she finds out they've been sneaking around."

"Finds out? Are you telling me this is more than him helping her out?" Cal asked. "The way LaTonya told it, there was a mix-up and they had to use the same truck."

"Well, he's been spending most of his afternoons over there," Angie explained. "He's sly about it, but I run through there, too, and I've seen him working on the house. I was hoping he was just being a nice guy."

Cal snorted. "No guy is that nice around a woman with boobs like Sera. Trust me. If he's over there, he's looking to get in her panties. Hell, I would try to get into them if it wouldn't freak Mom out. She's hot."

Celeste moved back into the room, feeling ice come over her heart. "She's also the reason your brother is dead."

Cal turned, his eyes wide. "Mother, I'm sorry you heard me say that. I didn't realize you were listening."

But Angie stood up. "She's always listening, Cal. Always. And she's being utterly ridiculous about Sera. I have to wonder, Mother, if you would have blamed one of the many boys in high school and college who broke my heart if I'd gotten into a car accident and died. Would it have been their fault?"

She shook her head. "That's a ridiculous comparison."

"Why?" Cal asked, his jaw going mulish. "Wes basically died in a car accident. Sure, it was a Humvee and he wasn't joy riding, but Sera wasn't behind the wheel."

"She was the reason he was there in the first place," Celeste insisted.

Angie's hands were fists at her sides. "Really? Because honestly, I kind of think it was your fault he was there."

"What is that supposed to mean?"

Her daughter didn't back down. "It means you babied

him. It means you gave him everything and he couldn't handle it when he didn't get what he wanted. Don't get me wrong. I loved my brother, but he was an entitled brat."

How could she even say that? "Wes had problems fitting in. Problems you and your brother never had."

"That's so untrue, but we didn't run home to you every time we had a problem," Angie replied. "Probably because you were far too busy doting on Wes."

She'd had to dote on Wes. Ralph had been so hard on the children, and even from a young age she'd been able to see how sensitive Wes was. Cal was stronger. Angie was honestly in many ways beneath Ralph's notice since she was only a girl. Wes had been the one to take the brunt of Ralph's mean nature. "Not only was your father hard on him, the other children at school were cruel to him, too."

Cal shook his head and a weary expression crossed his face, making him look far older than his years. "Dad was an asshole to all of us. You just didn't see much past Wes. Dad was disappointed in me because I wasn't smart enough to run the company, upset with Wes because he wasn't manly enough. Upset with Angie because she wasn't pretty enough, even though she's beautiful and always was. There are bullies at every school, and we all dealt with them. Do you know who wasn't a bully? Seraphina Guidry. She was kind to Wes. She liked him even though it was obvious to everyone in the world he hung around her because he was trying to wear her down."

"She stayed close to him because she wanted his money," she argued.

"Then why the hell would she send him away?" Cal said with a sigh. "You know this argument never made a lick of sense to me."

"I've always wondered if he found out she was pregnant by another man." She'd thought about this far too much.

"By her married lover, and that was what did it. That was what made him run away."

"We'll never know," Angie said. "But what I do know is if Harry is determined to date Sera, he'll do it and he won't back down. If you ask him to choose, you won't like his choice."

"Well, I would think he'd choose his aunt," she replied. "I'm the one who took care of him."

"You wrote a couple of checks and went to visit him," Cal pointed out. "It's not the same, and I assure you Seraphina won't ask him to make a choice. If I know her at all, she's already tried to tell Harry it won't work and she won't come between him and his family."

"That's just a manipulation." The girl hadn't even learned from her mistakes. Sera was playing games with her family again. "She's trying to put herself in the better position, to make me look like the bad guy."

"You are the bad guy." Cal strode to the hall and picked up his umbrella. "You're going to drive Harry away. Hell, I think one of these days you're going to drive me away. No one is good enough for you, Momma."

"That's not true."

He pointed a finger her way. "Only because my last name is Beaumont. And if you want to know why you don't think anyone ever bullied me, it's because I didn't trust you or Dad enough to tell you. He would have blamed me, and you would have backed him up because you saved every bit of your influence for Wes."

Her heart threatened to break. "Cal. Oh, Calvin, sweetie, I love you."

"As much as you can love anyone," he said with a bitter shake of his head. "I'm going over to Rene's. I'll probably get drunk off my ass and spend the night."

The idea of him on the road scared the hell out of her.

"You can't drive. There's a storm. Don't you know how terrified that will make me?"

He simply shrugged. "Hey, at least I'll know you're actually thinking about me."

He strode out, slamming the door behind him.

He couldn't possibly think he wasn't important to her. It was utterly ridiculous, and the fact that he would walk away from her . . . She preferred to focus on righteous indignation. "He's going to get himself killed."

Angie's eyes rolled. "He'll be fine. Cal always is. I think I'll skip dinner tonight. After all, we don't want a fat bride. That would embarrass the family name."

It looked like all her children were ganging up on her tonight. "I didn't say that."

"Yes, you pretty much did," Angie replied as she made for the stairs. "Please remember that the gazebo is important to my reception. If you're going to dump Harry for his taste in women, try to find someone else who can do the job."

"How can you say that? He's family." She had no idea how the night had gone so wrong. She'd just been worried about them. Tears threatened and she couldn't let them fall. She had to be strong. Strength was the only thing she had left.

"Well, Mom, I've learned that when people disappoint me, I move on. After all, that's what you do, and you're going to let your hatred for a girl who only ever was a friend to your son kill your relationship with your nephew. I'm smart enough to know which side of the purse strings I need to be on. Good night."

Celeste was left standing in her living room, the storm outside picking up again.

But it was the storm inside that truly raged.

They had been perfectly fine. Her little family had been

happy, and Harry had been fitting in nicely. Then Seraphina had waltzed in and it had all gone to hell again.

It was Sera's fault, but Celeste could see the game wasn't the same this time. She would need to play differently.

"Ma'am, should I serve dinner?" Annemarie stood in the hallway, a concerned look on her face. "I can make you a plate."

Annemarie had been with the family for ten years, but Celeste knew nothing about the woman. It was obvious she'd heard what had happened. Servants who knew secrets should be immediately dismissed. That was what her mother-in-law had taught her.

Why should she turn out a woman who did her job simply because she might know she fought with her children? Annemarie was excellent at taking care of the house and the family. And actually Celeste did know a bit about her. Annemarie was a mother of four. They were all out in the world now, but she was a mom, too.

"Have you eaten?"

Annemarie's eyes widened. "No, ma'am."

"Cook left her excellent roast." If she sat there alone, she would brood. Perhaps it would be good to talk to someone. "Would you please join me? Unless you need to head home. I'm alone. It appears I've angered all my children today."

"I was actually trying to avoid the storm. I don't like driving in this rain," Annemarie explained.

"Then let's not let that roast go to waste." It felt good to have one person not hate her. "How are your children, by the way?"

Annemarie began talking about college and the grand-baby she was expecting soon.

If she wanted her own grandbabies to care about her at

all, she needed to find a way to be more than purse strings. Perhaps it was time to change her image.

And then she would change Seraphina's. She was going to win.

She had to.

Harry came awake to the feel of Seraphina rubbing her cheek on his chest. His arm was around her and the night before came back in a rush.

Yes, they were in a cheap motel and he'd screwed up, but she'd come to him so sweetly he could only be grateful that Sera was a forgiving woman. The drapes didn't quite cover the whole of the window, so a shaft of light illuminated the room. He was covered in her hair. It was spread all over his chest and across his arm, flowing out on the sheet. Yes, he was caught in her web and that seemed like a perfect thing to be.

Sera yawned and cuddled close. "What time is it?"

He glanced over at the clock. "Early. Did you sleep all right?"

He intended to sleep with her a lot. As often as he could. If the night before had taught him anything, it was that their connection was real. It might be the realest thing he'd ever felt.

That should have been a problem, given how his aunt felt about her, but he wasn't going to let that hold him back. Aunt Celeste was wrong about Seraphina. She was not merely a good person, she was a person he looked up to. She worked hard and made him want to be a better man. His mother would have adored Seraphina. If his aunt couldn't see that, it was her loss.

"Like a baby." She sat up in bed. "I have a baby."

He reached for her phone. His was a brick because he hadn't charged it before he'd left. Sera was far more responsible, but then she had a lot she was responsible for. "Call. I bet your mom's awake."

She took the phone, the blanket falling away and revealing her breast.

He lay back and watched her. She was the single most beautiful thing he'd ever seen, and he was going to have to get a new damn phone because he wanted her to be able to contact him anytime she needed him. If she got a flat, he would be there. If she needed someone to pick up Luc, he wanted to be that person for her. He wanted the responsibility so badly he ached with it.

"Hey, Momma. How is Luc?"

Harry closed his eyes and let a feeling of serenity flow over him. It felt like something had fallen into place the night before, something he'd been missing for a long time.

Purpose.

He'd been floating around, looking for something to ground him, and he thought he'd found it. Her. He'd found her.

"Seriously? That's so sweet. I'm glad to hear it. I promise we'll be . . . Really? Well, if you wouldn't mind. Yeah, I would like to have breakfast before we . . . Yes, I'm still with Harry."

He opened his eyes and felt a smile cross his face. "Damn straight you are."

She flushed the prettiest pink and shook her head his way before getting back to talking to her mom. "Yes, that's what I mean. We're . . . dating."

He reached out and put a hand on her leg, loving the fact that he had the right to touch her.

"Okay." Sera smiled down at him. "Send me that picture. See you soon, Mom. Yes, I'm happy, too. I am really happy, and I'll talk to you later this afternoon. Thank you for taking care of Luc. Yeah. I love you, too."

He'd put that smile on her face. That breathy, almost anticipatory sound was because of him, and it made him feel like he was the damn king of the world. She'd seen him in all his missing-limbed glory and she'd still wanted him. She'd still let him press her down into the bed and take her in the sweetest way possible. She'd accepted him.

"What picture?" He needed her to understand that he knew she was a package deal.

He was ready to spend real time with that kid. He was ready to see if they could work as a family. Damn but he was ready for a family.

She stared down at the phone, moving her finger across it and then turning it his way. "Luc got out of bed, but Shep took care of him. Oh, it's so sweet. Look at them."

He looked at the phone, and the picture there damn near melted his heart. It was of a little boy curled up on Shep. He'd pulled his blanket with him and had covered himself up. His head was resting on Shep's chest and the dog was curved around him protectively. The deep affection between the two was unmistakable.

They might be soulmates. Like him and Seraphina.

Should he even be thinking that way? It was far too early but he couldn't help it. He knew what was in his heart. She was.

He stared up at her and the moment held. She went still for a moment, her eyes on him and a heaviness in her gaze.

"Did you tell your mom you're with me?" He knew what she'd said, but they needed to acknowledge it. It was important.

"I did." She put her hand on his chest. "I told you. I'm in. I'm all in. I won't pretend or hide it. I know that's what you want."

"Why do I want it?"

She was quiet for a moment, and he worried he'd pushed her too far. But then her hand moved over his chest, stroking him. "Because you're serious about me."

He caught her hand and held it against his heart. "I am very serious about you."

Her eyes closed. "I'm serious about you, too."

"Then kiss me, because we can take a little time. Luc is safe. I'll get ready in a couple of minutes and then I'll grab some coffee for us before we head back into town. But right now, I want you to kiss me and drop the blanket because you're the prettiest thing I've ever seen."

She loomed over him, her hair creating a waterfall around her and framing that smile that got his heart going. "You're not so bad yourself, Jefferys."

She leaned over and brushed her lips against his. Once and then again.

It was all he needed. He sank his hands into her hair and dragged her down on top of him, his arms winding around her.

He kissed her over and over again. This was how every single day should start, but he knew it would be a while before they could do this again. Somehow he didn't think he would stay over at her house, and she definitely wouldn't be staying at Beaumont House.

He knew he was going to have to deal with his aunt, but in that moment he couldn't care. He would find a way to spend sweet time with Sera, and it wouldn't be some quickie.

He wouldn't be having one of those today, either. He sighed and lifted his head. "I should go and get that coffee because . . . well, you know why."

Because he'd been prepared for one encounter. Not two.

"Who would have guessed I would be the one who needed the box of condoms?" Sera asked with an impish grin.

He might pick some up when he grabbed their coffees. "Give me fifteen minutes."

She shook her head and pushed against his chest, staring down at him. "You don't need fifteen minutes. You didn't need anything last night to make me happy. Anything but your lips and tongue and that creative brain of yours."

His whole body went electric at her words. The night before he'd found himself unprepared for another round, but he hadn't wanted to stop. He'd wanted every second of pleasure and connection he could have with her, so he'd kissed his way down her body and worshipped her with his mouth. Nothing had ever made him feel as good as Sera crying out his name and clinging to him.

But the feel of her lips on his neck, kissing her way down his chest while her hands caressed his skin, came close.

She showed him absolutely no mercy. There wasn't an inch of skin she didn't lavish her affection on.

He reached for her, but her head came up, giving him a shake. "No. Do you remember what you told me last night?"

He did. When he'd realized he couldn't make love to her again because he'd run out of protection, he'd had her lie back and he'd spent a whole lot of time making sure she understood how much he could give her. "I told you it was my time."

She nodded with the wickedest grin on her face. "Yes, you did. This is my time, Harry."

She lowered her lips to his chest again and he relaxed back. It was beyond obvious that his lady believed in equal time, and he meant to give it to her. She seemed intent on exploring him with all the thoroughness he'd explored her with the night before.

Everywhere she touched him, his skin lit up, sensitizing places he'd never thought of as erotic before. When she kissed his elbow, he had to hold back a groan. The same with his knees. And when she laid a tender kiss where his right leg ended. It wasn't pretty. It was scarred and the skin around it oddly smooth. But she kissed his stump like it was utterly perfect.

She was the perfect one, and no scar could take that away from her. He'd kissed her surgical scar the night before, letting her know it didn't distract from how gorgeous she was. She was telling him the same thing. He was enough for her.

He was in so deep with this woman. Now he knew he'd never really been in love before. He'd liked women, felt a certain affection for his girlfriends, but it was nothing compared to the passion he had for Seraphina Guidry.

Then he wasn't thinking about anything at all because her mouth closed over him and pleasure made his eyes close so he could concentrate on how he felt. Desired. Wanted.

Over and over Sera worked her magic. It wasn't long before he couldn't hold out another moment.

"Baby, I'm going to . . ."

"Yes," she murmured, the words rumbling along his skin and making it harder and harder to stay in control. "That was my plan."

She settled back in and he let go, tangling his hands in her hair and giving her everything he had.

After the tremors had subsided, a glorious languor thrummed through his system. "Come here."

She slid up against him, cuddling down.

For a moment, all was right with the world.

Sera started at the knock on the door. She'd just finished cleaning up, but she hadn't expected Harry back so soon. He'd been planning on going to the nearest fast-food place to grab some breakfast sandwiches. She glanced at the clock. It had only been fifteen minutes, but he must be quick.

It had been fifteen minutes and she'd missed him.

She was in way too deep when she still wasn't even sure she could stay in town. But then wouldn't it be easier to start a new life somewhere else if she had Harry with her?

She shook off the questions because it was far too early to be thinking that way, especially since she knew Celeste would do her best to keep them apart. There would be a whole bunch of worries to deal with the minute they drove over the bridge this morning. Telling her mother she was dating Harry was the least of what she would have to deal with. She was taking the next hour or so to revel in the peace they had left before the storm. Because there was no doubt the storm was coming.

She threw open the door to let her boyfriend in and realized the storm was already here. Celeste Beaumont stood there dressed in a chic business suit, a Chanel necklace, shiny pumps, and a handbag to complete the feminine-power ensemble.

She had a frown on her perfectly made-up face as she glanced inside the cheap motel room. "Seraphina, is my nephew here?"

She shook her head, wondering if she could get out of this. She wasn't ready for this showdown. "No. Harry isn't here."

It wasn't a lie. He wasn't here. Now.

Celeste took her sunglasses off with a sigh and waltzed into the room like she owned it. "Then where is he? And don't tell me you don't know. If you're planning on dating him, you have to stop acting like a sad mouse every time I walk into a room. Stand up straight, child."

Her spine reacted to the words, her shoulders going back. "I'm not a child."

Celeste nodded her way. "Yes, that's a much better tone to take. You sound like a woman. Now, where is my nephew?"

She wished she were wearing something besides that dumb beer T-shirt, but she'd kind of planned on seducing Harry into taking a shower with her before they headed back home. So she was left standing in front of the dragon without a bit of armor. But the mouse insult kind of pissed her off. "He's getting breakfast. He should be back soon."

Celeste squared off with her. "But he's all right? I couldn't get in touch with him last night. I was worried about him being out in the storm. He's not from here. He doesn't know what our weather can be like. I hadn't even realized he'd left Papillon until Cal told me."

Sera forced herself to look Celeste in the eye. No matter how she felt about Harry's aunt, she understood the reasonable fear that would come from not knowing where he was. Celeste had already lost a son and a husband. Not being able to get in touch with Harry had to have been disconcerting. "I'm sorry he didn't call you. He's not good about charging his cell phone, but he could have used mine or the landline. It was inconsiderate of him to not let you know he wasn't coming home."

Celeste was quiet for a moment, as though deciding how to proceed. Or how to rake Sera over the coals. This was when the threats would start.

"I would appreciate it in the future if he's going to stay out all night that you would have him call me," Celeste said in a polite tone.

That was not what she'd expected. She'd been gearing up for a fight. Now all her insecurities came rushing back. "I don't know if that's my place."

Celeste sighed as though disappointed in her. "The

mouse is back. We should talk, Seraphina. It has recently come to my attention that you're sleeping with my nephew."

Since she'd only started sleeping with Harry last night, she was a little shocked it had already gotten around. Somehow she didn't think Harry had found a way to call his friends and giggle about his night out. "Who told you?"

Celeste glanced at the bed, which looked like someone— or a couple of someones—had been rolling all over it. "No one has to tell me. I have eyes. Unless you're going to lie and tell me he spent the night in another room."

The mouse thing was getting to her. "I don't need to lie to you, Mrs. Beau . . . Celeste." She wasn't a child, and Celeste hadn't done anything that would require a polite title. In fact, when she thought about it, she and Celeste should really be on a first-name basis. "It's none of your business."

"Much better. I believed you that time." Celeste managed a smile that didn't come close to her eyes. "And it is my business because he's my nephew and he can be a bit naive when it comes to women. I have to watch out for him."

Ah, now they were getting to the part she understood. She was far more comfortable with this Celeste than the one she had to understand and relate to. "Is this where you tell me I'm not good enough for your nephew?"

Celeste shrugged, an elegant gesture. "I don't particularly think anyone is good enough for him. Harry's practically a saint."

"No, I'm not." Harry stood in the doorway, a tray of coffee in one hand, a bag in the other. "Hello, Aunt Celeste. I'm surprised to see you. If I'd known you were coming, I would have gotten an extra sandwich."

"Oh, darling, you know I would never eat that," she said with a hint of a smile. "And neither should Seraphina. Do you know how many calories are in those things?"

Like she'd never been called fat before. Celeste would have to try again. And now that she thought about it, why *did* she always act like a mouse around this woman? In the beginning she'd done it out of shock at Wes's passing. There had been a part of herself that wondered if she truly hadn't been guilty of sending Wes to his death. Then there had been the guilt that came from keeping the secret of Luc's conception. Now it was simply a habit. It was one she was going to break because she wasn't going to be a doormat one second longer. "Well, I expended an enormous amount of energy between last night and this morning, so I think I can handle it."

Harry gasped but Celeste actually chuckled. "Yes, there you are. You're going to need that if you're going to survive."

"What exactly are you doing here, Aunt Celeste?" Harry asked, wariness in his gaze as he put the coffee and sandwiches on the small table that served as a desk. "How exactly did you find me?"

"She was worried about you," Sera said because now that she thought about it, she should have had him call his family. She'd been worried about her own, but Harry wasn't used to having to call home. He'd been on his own for a long time and he needed a reminder. No matter how she felt about Celeste, she didn't want the woman up all night worrying. "We should have called to let her know you were all right."

Harry's face flushed. "I didn't even think about it. I'm sorry. I'm not in the habit of calling home. I haven't had anyone who needed me to check in for a long time."

Which was why Sera should start training him now. "Well, I happen to know a couple of things about overly protective family members. I will give you some advice. If your cell had been working, your aunt might have been able to get a call or a text through and then she wouldn't have had to worry. You have to think about these things now."

Because I want to rely on you.

Harry seemed to hear her unspoken words. "I will. I promise." He looked back to his aunt. "I'm sorry I worried you. Sera and I went to New Orleans to pick up supplies. We had dinner in town and started back too late to get across the bridge. I didn't understand how bad the storm would get."

Celeste turned a pointed glare Sera's way. "You should have. You know what the weather is like here."

She shrugged. She'd decided to go for honesty. "I was way too busy staring at Harry to think about the weather. And he'd stolen my truck out from under me and wouldn't take me back home unless I had dinner with him."

"Which is precisely why you should give up on eating. I find life is far easier if men can't hold me hostage to my own physical needs," Celeste replied, her expression perfectly serious.

"Did you just tell me I would be better off if I starved myself?"

Celeste merely sighed. "We're all better off when we practice self-denial, dear. Now, since we've established that you and Harry have entered into a physical relationship, I need to know if this is going to go any further. Tell me you haven't decided to make this emotional as well."

She said the last with a hint of distaste.

"Aunt Celeste, perhaps we should talk about this later." Harry had moved to stand beside Sera as if he could stop whatever attack Celeste would send her way. "When we're at home."

"Why would we do that?" Celeste asked. "Are you or are you not emotionally involved with this . . . with Seraphina Guidry?"

Harry seemed to falter, but Sera knew a challenge when she saw one. She simply hadn't taken any challenge up in the last few years. Being with Harry the night before seemed to have changed something inside her. Or rather brought out a bit of the Sera she'd been before. Harry had been raised to be polite and deferential to the women in his life. A Southern gentleman. He might need some cover for this one. "Yes, he's emotionally involved with me. It wasn't a one-night stand, and you're going to have to deal with the fact that your precious nephew is dating a Guidry."

Celeste sighed. "Well, at least it isn't that scoundrel Zep."

"Aunt Celeste," Harry said with warning in his tone.

"Nah, babe, that's fair," Sera replied. "My brother is a hot mess. He's got his own cell at the sheriff's office. He really is the trashiest Guidry, and I've seen pictures of myself in short shorts and a tank top, so that's saying something."

She wasn't sure what Celeste was up to, but she got the feeling she wasn't about to start a fight. If it happened, if Celeste pointed out all the reasons Sera wasn't right for Harry, she rather thought Harry would shut his aunt down.

No, Celeste was playing at something else, and it kind of scared her because she had absolutely no idea where this was going.

"Your brother is a menace," Celeste said with a frown. "But that's neither here nor there. My Harry is a serious young man. Are you sure you wouldn't rather have Calvin? I've been told I can make that happen."

"Aunt Celeste," Harry practically growled.

Celeste simply sighed. "Well, Cal told me he finds Sera attractive, and he would be simpler."

"I'm not interested in Cal." She could growl a little, too.

"He's worth more than Harry," Celeste pointed out.

She stepped in front of Harry because she wasn't about to take that. "We have different versions of worth. Why don't you make yourself plain? What is this about? If you're going to try to buy me off or scare me away, you should know it's not going to work. I know we've had trouble in the past, but I'm not going to let you bully me anymore."

A brow rose over Celeste's eyes. "I was unaware I'd bullied you in the first place."

She was over pretending. "You're the reason I can't keep a job in this town."

"Or maybe it's that you're not very good at the jobs you've chosen."

That was sadly fair, too, though she was certain she would have had more of a chance without Celeste's influence. "Are you trying to tell me you didn't say anything about me, didn't influence people into not coming to the salon or shopping at places I worked at?"

Celeste's eyes closed briefly, and when they opened, there was a wariness in her gaze. "I'm trying, Seraphina. I will admit I did not understand your relationship with Wes and in my grief over his death I might have blamed you in a way I shouldn't have. I still don't know you, and I worry this relationship will hurt Harry. But I also know when I'm on thin ice and that sometimes we have to bend so we don't break. I don't want to lose my nephew over this."

Her heart softened, though she knew it was a stupid thing to do. It should be hard by now, shouldn't it? But did Luc need a mother with a hard heart? What was braver? To face adversity and protect herself? Or to face it all and still be able to open up? "I don't want that, either. I'm glad Harry has a family. He cares about you."

"Sera," Harry began.

"No," Celeste said. "This is between me and Seraphina."

"I think you need to clarify what we're talking about." She was getting frustrated.

"Harry isn't the kind of man to have a one-night stand. If he slept with you last night, he's serious about you," Celeste explained. "And that means I have to make a decision. I have to decide how to handle this. I can hold on to old grudges or I can try to move forward. I don't understand what was between you and Wes, and I don't want some therapy session about it. I want to move on. I want to look to the future because the past is dragging me down. I love my nephew. I don't want this to come between us, so I have to accept this relationship."

Was this really happening?

Harry's face had split into the sweetest grin. "I'm glad to hear that, because I care about both of you."

He moved in and hugged his aunt.

Celeste's arms went around him and Sera saw a version of the Beaumont matron she'd never seen before. Celeste held him so tenderly and the sight formed a connection. Sera understood that kind of love. Familial. Blood.

It was a strong bond and could overcome a lot of challenges. Celeste had played this perfectly.

Seraphina knew when she was on thin ice, too, and then Celeste had come in and melted what had seemed like solid ground.

Celeste put a hand on Harry's cheek and looked far softer than Sera could ever remember. "Such a handsome young man. I'm glad you're all right. Where's Shep? He's not at the house."

Celeste gave a damn about Shep? She'd thought dogs would be beneath the elegant woman who often wouldn't touch children at church because they might be grubby. But she looked like she was actually worried about Harry's dog.

"He's at Seraphina's," Harry replied. "The truck is big, but the cab is small for all three of us, and I really did rent it out from under her. I wanted to take her to dinner, and most of the restaurants in the Quarter don't cater to dogs. It's all right. Delphine watched him."

Celeste huffed slightly. "As if Delphine knows what to do with him. She probably fed him the wrong food and now he'll be gassy."

"He's always gassy," Harry replied.

Sera was still confused, but her mom could handle a dog. "He's fine. We always have food because Zep is constantly bringing home strays, and not just dogs."

Her brother had an affinity for animals.

"Well, the next time you have date night, he can certainly stay in his own home," Celeste said.

"I'm still confused at how you found me." Harry had moved to Sera's side and eased an arm over her shoulder.

"Cal knew you were going into town. He talked to La-Tonya and there's a tracking device on the truck. They traced the truck to here. As to how I figured out what room you were in, that was easy. I asked the man at the front desk and he told me," Celeste explained.

"Shouldn't he care about privacy?" It didn't seem right that anyone could ask where she was.

Celeste waved that off. "I asked quite forcefully. You don't get anywhere in life taking no for an answer. Now I will leave you two to your breakfast, but I expect to approve Seraphina's dress."

"I have a dress?"

"You better if you're coming to the wedding." Celeste strode to the door, sliding her sunglasses back on. "I assume Harry's bringing you. After all, people would talk if he didn't. Unless you were planning on making this a secret affair. I've heard those can be quite fun."

Harry shook his head. "Nah. I like things out in the open."

Celeste sighed as though she'd expected the answer but was still slightly disappointed. "I thought that was what you would say. Well, then it's expected she will be your date to the wedding, and there are several events before then that she will now be expected to attend."

Oh, she hadn't planned on that at all. "I'm good. I don't need to go to events. I'm sure you have enough to deal with."

"Yes, and I will have gossip to deal with if you don't attend." The sunglasses were back off and Celeste's eyes were like lasers threatening to pin her down. "If you are going to be Harry's girlfriend, you have to be around Harry's family. If you don't attend the wedding events, people will say I refused to invite you. Do you want to make me look like I am unwelcoming? Like I am not a gracious hostess and refuse to acknowledge my beloved nephew's choice of companion?"

The woman could turn the world to ice faster than Elsa. "No, ma'am."

She slid the sunglasses up again and settled her expensive handbag on her shoulder. "Excellent. There's a brunch next Saturday with Austin's family. I'll expect you to be there, and I'll need to approve your clothing. And do not do your own hair. I know you think I ran off your clients, but poor Lila LaVigne looked like a refugee from an eighties brothel after you got done with her. Now, I have to get to work and make sure Cal doesn't burn the place down because he's upset with me."

Celeste hadn't waited on an answer, merely assumed her

will would be done. The door to the motel room closed behind her, and Sera could hear her heels clacking along the sidewalk as she walked to her Benz.

Harry stood in front of her and cupped her cheeks, a smile on his face. "You don't have to do anything you don't want to. You don't have to go anywhere."

But it would be so much simpler if she did. Celeste was right about that. There would be gossip, and it would be on both sides. Celeste would be a snob for not inviting Sera. Sera would be perpetuating the feud for not going. Harry would be stuck in the middle, and it would be her fault because Celeste had decided to bend.

"I'll go." She was in a corner and she rather thought Celeste had meant to put her there.

Harry leaned over and kissed her. "See, I told you she wasn't all bad. This is going to be way easier than I thought it would. Hey, let's eat and then we can take a shower, because I stopped at the convenience store. I am once more a prepared man."

He winked her way and started talking about the day ahead, but her mind was still on Celeste.

Who might be far scarier than she'd ever been before . . .

chapter nine

Harry eased the sandpaper over the slat and eyed his work. It looked good. Despite the days he'd missed waiting for the custom wood to come in and spending a ton of time working on Guidry Place, he was confident the gazebo would be ready for the photographer in two weeks.

Two weeks until the pre-wedding pictures, and then another week to the wedding. He'd planned on pulling up stakes and heading to Houston because a friend of his had a job he needed help on.

He'd called his friend the night before and told him to hire someone else. He was staying here in Papillon for the time being. He might be staying here forever if he had his way.

It was a mere week into his relationship with Sera and he was already thinking long term, but then he'd done that from the moment he'd seen her. Even as he'd tried to be reasonable, there had been a part of him that had known Sera was the one.

You know when you know, Harry, his father had said. *I knew the minute I met your mom. It took her a lot longer, though. I think she thought I was a pleasant way to spend time, but I won her over.*

He was slowly winning Sera over, though they'd made a huge breakthrough thanks to his aunt. Sera was still on the cautious side when it came to Aunt Celeste, but they didn't have to sneak around or fight. In fact, when he'd stayed late with her the previous night, Sera had made him text his aunt to let her know he was all right.

It was crazy, but it seemed to be working.

Shep lay on the floor at his feet and his head came up, ears perking in a way that let him know they were no longer alone in the shop.

Sure enough, the door swung open and his cousin walked in. Angela had been in Sedona for the weekend with her bridesmaids at a girls' retreat. He'd been told that girls tended to retreat to places with massage therapists and lots of wine. But his cousin didn't look relaxed. There was a pinched look on her face.

"Hey, Angie. Welcome back. How was your getaway?"

She glanced around as though making sure they were alone. "It was nice. This doesn't look the way I thought it would."

She touched the unfinished latticework. As often when working with wood, there was an ugly duckling period before the swan was revealed.

"It's not done. I promise it'll match everything. It's coming along nicely. Are you all right?"

"I don't know. I get home and I hear that you have a date for my wedding."

He had not expected pushback from Angie. She seemed so nice. Did she have some sort of problem with Sera? "I was told I could bring a plus one."

"Yeah, I didn't imagine that would be Sera. You realize

Mom is up to something. She didn't do this out of the kindness of her heart. She's never liked Sera."

He'd been surprised, too, but his aunt seemed vaguely amused with Sera now. "I don't think she ever gave Sera a chance. Your mom has made it plain that she's not going to lock Sera out. I'm glad she made the decision to try to be friendly. I thought for sure I would have to fight her on it."

"Which is precisely why you shouldn't believe it."

She seemed so disturbed by the idea of her mother and Sera having any kind of relationship. "What's behind this? I thought you liked her. I know she speaks kindly of you."

Angie's mouth tightened and she was quiet for a moment. "Have you thought about that boy of hers?"

His girlfriend was a single mom, and he was serious about her. He thought about Luc a lot. He wanted to get closer to Luc, but he had to respect Sera's wishes. "He seems like a good kid. I've spent a little time with him, but Sera and I are getting to know each other. She doesn't want to confuse Luc. We'll deal with it as we move forward."

"You need to think long and hard about getting involved with a single mom," Angie insisted.

"You think single moms don't deserve to find happiness?" He was flat-out confused at why he was having this conversation with his cousin. Cal had slapped him on the back and congratulated him on getting Sera and his momma in the same room and surviving the experience.

"I think you're young and she's looking for more than a boyfriend. She's a walking, talking instant family. Are you really ready for that? Do you honestly want to give up partying and having fun to change diapers?"

"First off, Luc is three. He's totally potty trained, but I could change diapers if I needed to. I didn't have brothers and sisters growing up. If things work out between me and Sera, I would hope she wants more kids. I don't know if you've gotten to know me, cousin, but I don't party much, and I sure as hell am not some young stud out to get laid. I'm only three years older than Sera. I would think I should be getting a lecture about settling down since I'm rapidly approaching thirty. You're younger than me and you're getting married."

She shook her head. "That's different. Austin and I are starting our lives together."

"And Sera can't start a life because she has a kid? You know you're allowed to love children you had no part in creating." He sat back and studied his cousin. "If you don't want Sera at your wedding for some reason, we can make ourselves scarce that weekend."

"Do you honestly believe she can fit in here? That my mother will allow her to ever be a part of this family? How will that kid of hers feel when my mom rejects him?"

He felt like he'd been dropped into a bad soap opera. "I seriously doubt Aunt Celeste will reject Luc. He's kind of adorable. If you ask me, Luc is our secret weapon."

His aunt wasn't as cold as she seemed. Her acceptance of him and Shep proved it. Luc could win her over with that big smile of his.

Angie's eyes had gone wide. "She wouldn't. Sera wouldn't bring him here. She knows better than to trust my mom with . . ." She took a long breath and seemed to quell whatever had threatened to take her over. "All I'm saying is you might think long and hard about whether or not it's fair to bring a child into the middle of our family situation."

"What exactly is our family situation?"

"I don't care what games my mom is playing, but she's never going to forgive Sera for what happened with Wes," Angie said. "She might pretend because she knows you'll choose Sera over her, but she's counting on Sera selling that house and leaving town. She's counting on this being a short-term relationship, and that's why you should keep your distance from Luc. He's been through a lot, and he doesn't need to lose another father figure."

"Lose? I wasn't aware he'd lost one in the first place."

"You know what I'm saying. He's young. He needs stability, and this situation can't possibly give it to him." She turned to the door. "Bring Sera to the wedding. I like her. But please don't bring that innocent baby into our mess of a family."

He didn't understand her pessimistic attitude. "Has it ever occurred to you that messes can be cleaned up? Aunt Celeste seems to be trying. I know the last few years have been hard on you."

She shook her head. "You don't know anything, Harry. You think our family works like yours did, but you'll learn. I just hope you don't take Sera and her son down with you."

She let the door slam behind her, and Harry stared at it. Shep huffed and settled down as though glad to be getting back to the serious business of napping.

Maybe it was the stress of the wedding. He hoped that was all it was because something seemed to be simmering under Angie's surface, and it worried him.

Was he being fair to Luc by going so fast? He had no intention of hurting that kid. He wanted to know him better, wanted to be someone Luc could depend on, might even want to call Dad someday. That's what Angie didn't understand. He was serious about Sera and that meant he was serious about Luc, too.

His cell phone buzzed and a picture of Sera came on the screen. Angie was wrong about a lot of things. They could make this work. But she was right about one thing. If this was some kind of plot of his aunt's to break them up, she would find out they were far more solid than she imagined. He slid his finger across the screen to accept the call. "Hey, gorgeous. I was thinking about you."

"Were you?" Her husky voice sent a thrill through him. "Now just what were you thinking about?"

He let go of his worries. "I was thinking about how long it's been since I kissed you."

"Too long," she replied. "Maybe we should fix that. But first we have to talk about your aunt. She's making me crazy. What's her problem with jumpsuits? She's sending me a bunch of e-mails."

And then Sera was off and he had way more problems than his cousin's weirdness.

It was going to be okay. He wouldn't accept anything less.

To: Seraphina Guidry
From: Celeste Beaumont
Re: Scheduling

I have attached the following schedule of events Harry is expected to attend in anticipation of Angela's wedding. You should be appropriately dressed for each occasion. You will notice I've had my assistant include a symbol which will let you know the preferred dress length for each party or soiree. Please reply so I know you have received and understand the instructions.

To: Celeste Beaumont
From: Seraphina Guidry
Re: The royal wedding schedule

Celeste, I received your instructions and have noted each date in my planner. You seem to have forgotten that it is the twenty-first century and women can now wear pants. I've got the cutest jumpsuit with sequins I've been dying to show off.

Thank you sincerely for including me. I will try very hard not to embarrass you. I assure you that, having worked in the restaurant industry most of my life, I know which fork to use. I also know how to use a knife. In case you were wondering.

Sera

Your aunt just sent me a schedule for ten events I'm supposed to attend, including a reception at the Jaycees Club. I don't even know what that is. And why are we burying a perfectly good bottle of bourbon in the yard???? Help.

Harry

Baby, I know nothing about these wedding things. I've been told my only job is to make sure Cal doesn't drink too much, and to tackle your brother if he shows up to spike the punch with moonshine. Obviously, she's talking about Zep, not Remy. Oh, and my aunt lost her mind because she now wants to make Shep the ring bearer since Austin's two-year-old niece threw up on her Hermit handbag. Or Hermes. Or something. It was a thing. The long and short of it is I have to find a tuxedo for my dog.

To: Seraphina Guidry
From: Celeste Beaumont
Re: Proper Attire

I understand that we are living in a dying hellhole of a century where ripped-up denim is considered proper dinner attire. I know it is hard for young women to resist the peer pressure to attend special events decked out like a disco ball walking on two legs. Jumpsuits are for prison inmates. I'll make it easy for you. We'll go shopping together. I've made an appointment at a shop in New Orleans. The directions are attached. I will meet you there as I have business at corporate headquarters that day. You are representing the Beaumonts and you need a Beaumont-approved wardrobe.

To: Celeste Beaumont
From: Seraphina Guidry
Re: Proper Attire

Message received. I will report for my personal Beaumont prison garb at the proper time. I have a leopard-print belt bag that goes with everything so I will not need a handbag. I find it so much easier to simply carry everything I need around my waist. Also, I've got some sparkly flip-flops I picked up at the Shop Smart that would be great for the whole bridal party. How many should I get? It's totally on me. I've got a coupon.

To: Seraphina Guidry
From: Celeste Beaumont
Re: Proper Attire

I hope you can feel my judgmental stare.

Sera
We need to break up.

Harry
No can do. I'm on the hook for some of these too. I've been told if you're not my date, one will be found. I'm scared of who my aunt will think is proper. And

Sera . . . have I mentioned how crazy I am about you?

Sera
Fine. I'll go, but there better be a foot massage at the end of this because she's talking about shoes. I don't suppose she means comfy shoes.

Harry
Absolutely not. If I know her, you will be taller than me by the end of this. And you know I'm the best kisser in the world, but did I mention I won a prize once for my foot massages???

To: Seraphina Guidry
From: Celeste Beaumont
Re: Tips and practical advice

The brunch is coming up soon and I need to give you a few tips on how to handle my daughter's fiancé's family. Austin is a lovely young man and it's easy to think his family must also be as lovely. They are successful and well respected in society. They, like many respected members of our society, have done little to deserve this. Austin's father has cheated on his mother twelve times. I give you this number because Austin's mother likes to drink and complain about her cheating husband. Do not look shocked. Simply nod and agree with everything she says and try to switch out her gin with water. At some point she no longer notices the difference. The only safe topics to discuss are the weather and the Saints. Professional sports only. Wear something modest because the elderly aunt believes we're living in the eighteen hundreds and she will have a fit of the vapors if you present her with too much cleavage. Angela is insisting on wearing pink. Please choose a different color or our side of the party will look like the inside of a Pepto-Bismol bottle. Also, do not wear all black because you're an adult female and neither attending a funeral, nor are you a nineteen-year-old trying to rebel against your parents by playing at being a vampire. And please convince Harry to wear a collared shirt.

To: Celeste Beaumont
From: Seraphina Guidry
Re: Tips and practical advice

Harry is his own man. You know he needs to feel comfortable and I want to support him in being who he is. Of course, arrangements could be made . . .

To: Seraphina Guidry
From: Celeste Beaumont
Re: Tips and practical advice

If you can get Harry into a collared shirt, I'll accept kitten heels. Don't test me further. There will be no rhinestone-encrusted flip-flops.

Sera
Babe, you're wearing a dress shirt to the brunch and a tux to the wedding. The good news? I think we can get Shep one at the same place. Two for one deal!

Harry
We should talk about this . . .

chapter ten

❧

"What do you mean you're invited to brunch with the family?" Hallie asked, her voice hushed in deference to the class going on around them. "With whose family? The Beaumont family?"

Sera moved into downward dog. There was a reason she'd sprung the news on her besties before the class had begun. Every Wednesday morning a group of women gathered in Harte Park for a yoga class. If it was raining, they would move inside the rec center, but she loved the days when they could enjoy the outside. It was peaceful. It was one of the few things she did that was strictly for herself. She found it centered her and allowed her to breathe when it felt like the rest of the world was on fire.

Except not today because she had to meet Celeste in New Orleans. Without Harry. She'd gotten a text from him thirty minutes before that he had some sort of woodworking emergency, and now she had to go and meet his aunt all by herself. She needed the yoga to help center her today.

She was certain yoga would be one of those off-limits things at the Beaumont house. She'd already received several e-mails from Celeste about the brunch next Saturday that included helpful dos and don'ts of attendance.

"To the brunch at Beaumont House?" Sylvie slid in on Sera's other side. She'd been running late. "Why would you do that? I know you're dating Harry, but that doesn't mean you're a member of the family. Chrishelle Mills dated Cal for two years and never got invited to Beaumont House even once."

"I wouldn't call it dating," Hallie argued in a whisper. "It was more like he would pick her up after her shift at the strip club and they would screw for hours. It's not the same. Sera's a real girlfriend. Harry takes her out to the grocery store. A man is not truly committed to a woman until he's pushed a grocery cart full of actual food, and not beer and chips."

Harry had been the perfect boyfriend for the whole week they'd been dating. Not only did he come by to pick her up every morning to take her to Guidry Place, but he often sat down and had breakfast with the family. Her mom fawned over him and had taken to making pancakes or French toast every morning, much to Zep's chagrin since breakfast was his favorite meal of the day and his momma would toss a box of cereal his way. Not for Harry, though. Harry, she'd been told, did a man's work and needed a man's breakfast.

"That still doesn't explain why Celeste is having her sworn enemy over for a family event," Sylvie whispered. "You know how she is about family occasions."

"Unless she wants to lull her sworn enemy into a false sense of security before she thrusts the knife in," a new voice said.

Seraphina glanced back, and Lila Daley LaVigne was moving from downward dog into cobra pose with flawless grace. "You think Celeste is going to stab me?"

"I don't think Celeste would get her hands dirty," Hallie whispered. "She's always telling me my nails make me look like I'm the oil rigger instead of my husband. I don't have time to spend all day in a salon. I'm a young mother. We're lucky I took a shower three days ago."

Sylvie sent her a shake of her head. "I'm going to have to hose you down, girl."

"I will welcome it," Hallie admitted. "And if you put some wine in that hose, that would be even better. I definitely think Celeste is probably planning on poisoning you at the brunch. But it will be one of those poisons that kills you outright with no vomiting because I've heard those rugs of hers are worth more than Johnny makes in a year."

"She doesn't have to worry about the rugs," Sylvie argued as they all moved into a lunge. "She would definitely put down tarp."

"Yeah," Hallie agreed. "If you see tarp, do not step on it. Do not let Celeste trick you into stepping on it."

She brought her feet together, completing the sun salutation. If Celeste was going to do anything, it would likely be this afternoon. She still wasn't sure this meeting of hers wouldn't include the offer to write a fat check if she would stop dating Harry. "I don't think she's going to kill me, but she might be trying to make me run."

"I don't know. The tarp thing is solid advice," a masculine voice said.

"You're supposed to stay quiet," Lila whispered back at her husband.

Armie LaVigne sat on a bench a few feet away from his wife. The sheriff of Papillon was wearing sweats and a T-shirt, a book in his hand and a dog lounging at his feet. The big golden retriever mix was named Peanut and he was snoozing, his head resting on Armie's sneaker. "I'm supposed to be working undercover, but I also have a duty to the public. I absolutely believe Celeste Beaumont could kill a man. Now, I'm pretty sure she could do it with that stare of hers, but I wouldn't step on tarp around the woman, either."

"Armie's undercover?" Sylvie asked as they started another sun salutation.

Sera knew exactly what was going on. "Kenny White's in town again. He moved back in with his momma because he lost that job packing boxes in Houma. He showed up last Wednesday with a camera. He said he was taking pictures of birds. Not our butts in leggings."

"Yeah, I got the whole Audubon Society argument," Armie admitted. "I don't buy it. He's a pervert. Every town has a couple. I'm going to let Peanut attack and then I don't even have to write up an incident report."

She didn't think Peanut had enough energy to attack. He might lick the criminal to death, but he wasn't a police dog. Shep had been a working dog. She often sat with him and wondered at all the things that dog had seen and done. And then she gave him an extra treat. Like his owner, Shep was a warrior who could also be so tender it made her ache inside. The big German shepherd was sweet with Luc, following him everywhere like it was his job to ensure no harm came to the baby.

She'd brought Luc with her a couple of days when they were working on safe parts of the house. Luc was corralled in a playpen, and Shep made sure he stayed there. Every so often, they would take a break and go out to the yard and sit and have a snack in the sunshine. Luc would laugh and run around, Shep always behind him.

They had felt like a family.

She shook it off because it was far too soon to think that

way. As far as Luc knew, Harry was just another kind male authority figure, like Remy and Zep. She was careful not to show too much affection for Harry around Luc.

Celeste was another story entirely. Sera had decided never to even mention Luc's name around Celeste. The less she knew about Luc, the better.

Lila snorted as she moved into warrior pose. "Yeah, it will be Peanut who takes down our peeper. I told you, babe, I can handle Kenny. I think you should watch the Beaumont situation, though. I've always thought Celeste could blow. That woman's wound up tight."

"I'm supposed to go shopping with her," Sera explained. "I'm meeting her in New Orleans to find a dress for the wedding. Well, not really to find a dress. Celeste already picked out the dress. I have to go and try it on and let them tailor it for me. She's concerned with my boobs."

"That's where she'll do it," Hallie vowed. "She'll hire an assassin to sneak into the dressing room and it will be death by Chanel. You know my momma says everyone gets killed in New Orleans."

Hallie's mom believed big cities were the work of the devil, but then she felt the same about tank tops, push-up bras, artificial intelligence, and avocados.

"Hallie Rayburn, do you have something you want to share with the class?" Joy LeGrande was one of the two yoga instructors who ran sessions across the parish. She stared at the back of her class, her dark eyes hawkish. "You do understand that this is supposed to be quiet, contemplative time, right?"

Hallie's eyes went wide and she looked a lot like she had when they'd gotten caught passing notes in English class. "Yes, ma'am. I'm sorry, ma'am."

Hallie could be awfully deferential to anyone in a position of power.

"We were talking about the fact that Celeste is probably planning on killing Seraphina." Sylvie was not.

Every head turned, all eyes on Sera.

"They're joking," she said weakly. "We should definitely move on to some core work, right?"

"It's true. I thought it was another rumor," Joy said, putting a hand on her nonexistent hip. The woman was fit. "You caught that gorgeous hunk of man. All right, you need to dish because he's turned down every single woman in this town, and a whole lot of the married ones, too. Don't you give me that judgmental look, Mary Lou. I saw you looking at him."

Yoga was completely put on hold in favor of intense questioning that Sera had not expected. Women who hadn't given her the time of day in years were suddenly interested in what she was doing. *How is the house going? Is Harry working on it with you? Have you been to Beaumont House? Does Celeste really have a movie theater in that place?*

Lila rolled up her mat and joined her husband on the bench, obviously unimpressed with the impromptu press conference, but Sera's friends stayed at her side as she learned the only thing worse than being the town outcast was suddenly being its sweetheart.

"I want to know what you're doing with Sera. I pretended everything was all right with Harry, but I know you're up to something." Cal hadn't even knocked on the door to the office Celeste used while she was in New Orleans. It was across the hall from his office and much smaller. She'd always loved that other office, which was reserved for the CEO. Not for its horrible dated and masculine furnishings but for its view of the Mississippi River. The CEO's domain had floor-to-ceiling windows on two sides, and when she'd stood there waiting for her husband, she'd always felt like she was looking out over her kingdom.

Well, she had until Ralph inevitably walked in and put her in her place.

Lately, she'd started wondering what her place was.

She sat back, studying her son. Cal looked different in a suit. She'd never really thought about it, merely accepted that a suit was what the CEO wore to work, but Cal didn't wear them in his normal life. He dressed well, but much more casually. The suit seemed odd on her laid-back son, and yet he put it on every day according to the network of employees she had looking in on Cal when she couldn't.

"I'm not doing anything with her at all." Except sending her a couple of dozen e-mails about the rules for how to behave. She'd found herself actively enjoying writing the snarky missives and waiting for Sera to reply with equal sarcasm. The young woman had a wit she often hid in deference to camouflage. If there was one thing she'd learned about Seraphina Guidry in the days since she'd made the decision to change up her tactics, it was that Sera preferred to go unnoticed now. Sera dimmed her glow in order to stay out of the spotlight.

Celeste could understand that.

"You invited her to the brunch next Saturday." He said the words flatly, but they were an obvious accusation.

"I thought you would be happy that I'm not going to fight your cousin on his choice of romantic partner. I remember a whole argument about what a terrible person I was and how downtrodden poor Seraphina is. You were right about that. The poor girl doesn't even have the money to buy herself a nightie. She has to greet the day in an ill-fitting T-shirt with the words *Beauty is in the eye of the beer holder* on it."

Her son's eyes narrowed. "You know that's not what I meant."

"Well, Calvin, it's been implied by several young people lately that I don't understand anything at all, so you will have to be more specific." She'd expected she would get an earful from her children. Harry was the only one who seemed happy with the invitation for Sera to join them at family events.

Harry didn't know her as well as Cal and Angie.

"You invited Sera to brunch with Austin's family. What are you planning to do to humiliate her?"

Her heart clenched a bit at the accusation. She'd decided this was the best path because Harry would likely change his mind, or Sera would, and her getting in the way would only bond them further. She'd never purposefully humiliated anyone. She'd had more than enough of that from her mother-in-law. "I am not the one who put those rumors out about Seraphina. I am not the reason she can't keep a job. I've never in my life told someone they shouldn't go to Guidry's for any reason other than the heartburn their gumbo gives the world."

"You didn't tell your friends to stay away from the diner she worked at? Or the store? Or Marcelle's?"

He really didn't think much of her. Her mother-in-law might have had a point about keeping the relationship with one's children fairly emotionless. "No. I don't talk to my friends about Sera." She didn't actually have friends. She had cronies. She had women and men around town who did her bidding because they wanted to be associated with the Beaumont name. "I know everyone blames me because I said some things in my grief, but I said them inside this family."

"Everyone knows how you feel about her," Cal pointed out.

"I can't help that." She felt a bit weary about the whole thing. Seeing the way Harry had lit up when he realized she wasn't going to give him hell about being with that little blonde . . . She had to stop thinking that word. From what she could tell, Sera wasn't a tramp. She'd dated one young man in the years since Wes had died. Obviously she'd had an affair that went wrong and resulted in an unplanned pregnancy, but Celeste was getting far too old to judge someone for a mistake like that. Lately, she'd started thinking that judging anyone at all took far more energy than she was willing to expend. "I don't know what's going to happen between them, but I will not lose another family member because they see something in Sera Guidry that I don't."

Cal stared at her for a moment. "I almost believe you."

"Do I hope this doesn't go anywhere? Yes. I believe they are jumping into this relationship far too quickly, and I don't want Harry to get attached to her child when we don't even know who the father is or if he's going to come into the picture at some point. But I'm not going to say a thing about it. It doesn't work. Trying to control situations . . . All it's done is cost me my children."

Cal was quiet for a moment. "You haven't lost me. Or Angie."

"It felt like I had the other night." Sitting and talking to her maid over some excellent roast and a bottle of wine had caused something to shift inside her. Annemarie reminded her of her mother. And her sister. They'd talked about Annemarie's grandbabies.

Oh, she'd missed her sister in those moments. If her sister had lived, she would have moved her into Beaumont House along with Harry.

"Did you know when I first married your father, I asked him if your aunt could come and live in the guesthouse?"

Cal's shoulders relaxed, but his eyes had widened in surprise. "Are you talking about your sister?"

"Yes, this was before Harry was born, but our parents had passed on and I helped her out because she was in college." They'd lived in a tiny apartment and Janelle had gone to school while Celeste worked. "I couldn't imagine her living alone, and let's be honest, her degree was going to be social work, so she was going to starve. I thought she could transfer to a school close to here and live in the guesthouse and she could help with you."

"But obviously she didn't come here, and I don't think she finished college, right?"

"She did not because your father thought if she couldn't afford it herself, she shouldn't have an education. He told me I could give her everything I had in my account, but after we were married, she was on her own." She could still remember how trapped she'd felt. It had been that moment that she'd realized her happily ever after wasn't going to be as promised.

"That sounds like dear old dad."

"I had to choose between being a single mother and taking care of my sister, and I couldn't do it." Her heart still ached with that choice. "My sister didn't even blink. She told me to follow my heart and not to worry about her."

"Mom, he was wrong to force you to choose."

"But the choice was mine." She reached for a tissue. The tears that always seemed close now were an annoying side effect of all this self-reflection. "I didn't follow my heart. I followed my fear. I don't want to do that again. For four years Seraphina has been a face for all my troubles, and the idea that Harry could fall into the same trap as Wes frightens me."

"I don't think she was trying to set a trap. I know you think she's some kind of gold digger."

Celeste waved that off. "I don't anymore. A gold digger tends to know how to dress and present herself. And I offered up you. You're a much better catch since Harry doesn't actually have any money of his own, and he has terrible taste in everything from cars to that beer he drinks."

Cal's face lit up and he looked younger. This wasn't his usual arrogant smirk. It was a beaming smile. "You offered me up?"

It was good to know she could surprise him from time to time. "Absolutely, my darling boy. She turned you down flat and then drank some coffee from a fast-food place. And if that motel I found them in is any indication of her standards, well, I don't have to worry about her looting the family coffers. Though I will have to direct her in how to dress for the wedding events."

"You're really letting Harry bring her? This isn't some wild plan to humiliate her and force them apart?"

It was time to be honest. She was finding a crazy sort of freedom in being honest. So much of her life to this point had been about artifice and protecting the family name. But how could she come to a place of peace inside herself if she wasn't ever honest about who she was? "I thought about it at first. I thought I'll be the good guy in this situation and let it all blow apart. I'll set her up to show her how she doesn't belong."

"That sounds more like the mother I know."

It was a fair assessment, but he was forgetting about something. "But if Sera doesn't belong because she wasn't raised wealthy, then Harry doesn't belong, either. Then everything your father and grandmother said about my sister was right."

Cal stared at her for a long moment. "You're doing this for Harry."

"I think I might be doing this for me." It had taken days to admit it. Or maybe it had been the sassy e-mails Sera had sent back. She'd been surprised that she hadn't taken offense. Instead, she'd enjoyed sparring with the younger woman. "I've spent most of my adult life following a bunch of rules your grandmother laid down. I've started to wonder why I keep doing it even though she's gone. Is this still her family?"

Cal put his hands on her desk and his eyes had softened. "No, Mom. It's yours now. You get to do what you want. But don't forget that I have a life, too. So does Angie. The times have changed. So should the Beaumont family."

"But I'm still not letting Sera wear that hideous jumpsuit. And you're going to have to hold her down so I can get her in a proper pair of shoes." There would be no flats at the wedding. Some things would never change as long as she had breath in her body.

"See, you are trying to scare her away," Cal said, but there was a grin on his face.

"Well, she's not going to show up in flip-flops. Silly girl."

"You like her."

"I am amused by her. We'll have to see if that amusement translates to charming dinner banter," she allowed. "I'm supposed to meet her in an hour at Claudine's. And don't look at me that way. I called ahead and told them to expect my nephew's girlfriend. I know how snobby those clerks can be. I asked Patrice to meet her."

"Thank you. I don't think Harry understands what you've done for him," Cal said solemnly. "But Angie and I do. We appreciate that you're willing to keep an open mind. Speaking of open minds, I have a problem with the accounting this month and I'm not sure how to handle it."

"Well, we should fix that." Celeste gestured to the door. "Let's go to your office and we'll have some coffee and you can explain it to me."

"I hate accounting," Cal grumbled.

Everyone hated accounting, but it had to be done. She followed her son out, perfectly happy with the way the morning had gone.

chapter eleven

Sera stood outside the posh store and wished she'd taken the time to change her clothes. She'd thrown a T-shirt over her leggings, but she feared her athleisure wear and sneakers would stand out among the New Orleans elite.

She was really more comfortable in the Quarter, where no one cared what you wore. Or sometimes if you wore anything at all.

She stared up at the imposing building that housed the luxury boutique known as the House of Hanover. She wasn't sure where they got that name since the building obviously wasn't a house, and there was a smaller plaque with the name *Justine Reneaux, Designer*.

She glanced down at her watch. She was right on time, but she couldn't see Celeste inside.

Of course, that meant nothing. Celeste probably knew this Justine person and they were in the back somewhere sipping champagne and trying to find more material to cover Sera's boobs since they might give the elderly aunt a heart attack.

She pushed through the gilded doors and couldn't help

but gape a bit in wonder. This was an impeccably done space, styled to look like a grand Parisian apartment. She had to smile at the glamorous store. The colors were rich, baroque style. And the place smelled good, too. There were clothes along the walls, beautifully displayed near two grand staircases that rose up on either side of the room. There was a large lounge currently taken up by a man in a business suit. He looked to be in his late forties or early fifties. He was pacing and talking on a cell phone. A woman in a designer suit carried out a tray with champagne glasses and he took one.

"May I help you?" The woman carrying the tray crossed the space between them.

"I have an appointment with . . ." She couldn't remember the name Celeste had sent her. She was pretty sure it started with a P. Had she deleted the e-mail? She'd written down the address, but the e-mail might still be on her phone. If she could find it at the bottom of her tote bag. Yeah, she wished she hadn't dragged in her gym bag. The last thing she needed to do was dig through old socks, scrunchies, and her water bottle to find her phone. "Priscilla? Sorry, I can't remember the exact name."

The woman who looked completely flawless frowned. She stood tall in front of the lounge as though she was its guardian, sent to ensure only the worthy got through. "We don't have anyone here by that name."

"Well, I'm supposed to meet with someone. My name's Seraphina Guidry. I have a dress fitting for the Beaumont wedding." At least she was pretty sure it was for the actual wedding. She still had to find something to wear to the brunch coming up, and it had to be approved by Celeste. She was hoping Sylvie had something she could borrow. Sylvie had a very mayoral wardrobe.

"I'll see if you're on our schedule. Please stay here." The woman turned and walked toward the back of the store.

"Hello." The businessman seemed to have ended his call. He slid his cell phone into the pocket of his slacks as he approached her. "You are not the usual type at this place. It's all uptight socialites. What's your name, honey?"

"It's Nonya." She knew the type. No man called a woman he'd just met *honey* without having creepy intentions. Every middle-aged woman in the South called anyone she met *honey* or *hun* and meant nothing by it, but it was different when a man used the term while he let his eyes slide over a woman's body. "Last name Bidness."

She started to move down the steps. She could sit and wait patiently. Hopefully Celeste was somewhere in the back and they could get this over with as quickly as possible. She would love to study this place and maybe get some design ideas for the house, but she knew when she wasn't wanted. If she could get in and out with the least amount of humiliation possible, she would call it a win. Unfortunately, before she could get far, the man in the suit blocked her way.

"Now, that was rude," he said. "You don't look like a young lady who wants to be rude to a man who knows the owner of this place."

A sinking feeling hit the pit of her stomach. Celeste knew the owner, too. This man could twist the story any way he wanted to, and she would look like the one causing trouble. "I don't mean to be rude. I'm only trying to wait for my boyfriend's aunt. She should be here any minute. This place is doing the dresses for her daughter's wedding. Angela Beaumont. She's my boyfriend's cousin."

She would say the word *boyfriend* as many times as possible.

"That's funny since I know the Beaumont family and I've never met this nephew," the man said, looking her over from head to toe. "So I think you're here to con someone. I don't have a problem with it. Little things like you are always looking for a meal ticket. My wife is in the fitting room with our daughter. Her wedding's coming up. They're going to be back there for at least an hour or so. Why don't I take you across the street and buy you a cup of coffee and we can talk about whatever you want?"

There wasn't a coffee shop across the street, but there was a hotel. She turned and started to walk back up the steps. She would wait for Celeste outside. It would be infinitely easier not to haul off and slap this jerk if she wasn't in the same building as him.

She started to go and felt a hand on her arm.

"Hey, I was asking you politely," he said.

"Is there a problem?" A uniformed guard stepped away from his place at the front of the store.

"Yes, this man won't take no for an answer," Sera said, grateful someone was here. She pulled her arm away with a hard tug.

"Is this woman bothering you, Mr. Brewer?" The guard frowned her way.

Mr. Brewer smoothed down his suit. "I think she's here to cause trouble. She was asking me for money."

Sera felt her jaw drop. "I certainly did not."

The saleslady returned and sighed. "You're not on the list, whoever you are. Hank, could you please show this young woman the door?"

It was rapidly becoming clear that the whole situation was going to get out of hand. She wasn't sure what she'd done except walk into the place. "We have an appointment."

Had Celeste set her up? Was this all being done to show her she didn't belong in the Beaumont world? She wished

Harry had been able to come with her. Somehow she doubted Harry would get tossed out like the trash.

"And I told you you're not on my list," the saleslady insisted. "Even if you somehow magically got an appointment, I would still ask you to leave. We don't cater to your kind."

"I have a kind? What kind is that?" Humiliation swept over her, mingling with the anger that boiled inside. How many times had she been treated like a piece of trash? How many times had she left, not wanting to cause a scene?

She really wanted to cause one now, but it could hurt Harry.

What the hell would she tell Celeste? If Celeste hadn't set this up herself, how would she feel about her nephew's girlfriend getting kicked to the curb? She would probably shake her head like she'd known all along this was how things would end.

"Seraphina, what have you gotten yourself into now?" Celeste stood at the top of the steps, looking totally intimidating in her all-white suit, a wretchedly expensive bag tucked against her arm.

Sera wasn't at fault here. She needed to remember that.

"I'm sorry, Mrs. Beaumont." The saleslady rushed to greet her. "We're having trouble with some unwanted guests. Come with me and I'll get you set up in one of the private rooms. Hank is going to take care of our issue and we can get back to business. I have your favorite champagne waiting for you."

The guard put a hand on Sera's arm.

"Did you not hear me call her by her name?" Celeste really could bring out the death stare, but thankfully it wasn't directed at her. Celeste was staring right at the saleslady. "Do you believe I pull names out of thin air? That I go about guessing the names of people I do not know?"

The saleslady's eyes had gone wide and her jaw dropped slightly.

Celeste nodded. "Yes, make the right connections. I know you can do it."

"She's your guest," the saleslady stammered.

"Yes, and I'm disappointed in her," Celeste said, turning her way with a frown. "Seraphina, that man has a hand on you. Shouldn't you karate chop him, or whatever it is your brother learned in the Navy? Surely he taught you some self-defense. Don't you have a gun or something you can threaten him with? And you're crying. That's going to mess up your mascara and we won't be able to tell how you'll truly look in that dress."

"I don't have a gun." Sera pulled away from the guard. An odd relief had rushed over her the minute she'd realized Celeste hadn't set her up and seemed to be on her side. In a very Celeste way, of course. "But I do have a foot and I'm thinking about kicking a few of these people. That man hit on me and then told everyone I was begging him for money."

"You should have been begging him for some hair care products," Celeste said with a shake of her head.

Sera shrugged. She was getting used to Celeste commenting on her appearance. She did it to everyone in her life. In a weird way it almost felt affectionate since if Celeste didn't like a person, she simply did not speak to them. "I came from yoga."

"Then you should be well warmed up and ready to defend yourself." Celeste pulled out her phone. "Also, you're not actually wearing any pants, so that should have made it easy to do that kicking thing."

"I have on leggings." She attempted to defend the most comfortable of pants.

"Leggings are not pants. They are the cellophane of

the clothing world." Celeste glanced over at Mr. Brewer. "She was talking about kicking your masculine parts, you know, Brian."

"Mrs. Beaumont, you're telling me you know this person?" Brewer asked, staring at Celeste like he'd never seen her before.

"I told you." Sera moved to join Celeste because it appeared she wasn't getting in trouble the way she thought she would. Celeste seemed almost disappointed she hadn't caused a physical fight. "She's my boyfriend's aunt and she won't let me go to the wedding in a perfectly nice jumpsuit that is both comfortable and flattering."

"We have two different versions of flattering, Seraphina," Celeste said, her fingers moving across her phone.

"Mrs. Beaumont, I had no idea you were coming today. Patrice was taken ill and couldn't come in," the saleslady was saying. "I'm going to help you, and please accept my apologies for the mistake. If your friend had properly identified herself, we wouldn't have had the confusion."

"I told you exactly who I was," Sera replied. "And I told him who I was waiting for and he got all creepy and pervy, and I already had to deal with Kenny White trying to take pictures of me." She stopped because she really did have to think about Harry. "Is this one of those things where I'm supposed to be a lady and pretend like he didn't hit on me while his wife and daughter are in the other room? And pretend that saleslady didn't take one look at me and decide I'm trash?"

Celeste seemed to think about it for a moment. "My mother-in-law would say yes. This design house is one of the best in New Orleans. She would tell you every woman in the world has a Brian Brewer who behaves like an animal, and you should learn how to keep your mouth shut and deal with it. She had to. I had to. Why shouldn't you?"

"That doesn't seem like a nice thing to say. I wouldn't want my daughter to have to put up with it." If she ever had a daughter. She would teach Luc never to treat a woman like something he was entitled to, like she didn't exist unless some man wanted her.

"As it happens, my mother-in-law was a terrible person and I don't want any woman to have to deal with it, period. Brian, if you ever so much as look at a young lady under my charge, I will ensure that no one in your family can show their face in society again. Don't think I can't do it, and you should simply expect that every young lady you meet is in my charge. I'm taking on charity work, you see."

"Hey," Sera started and then decided to go with it. Besides, she'd learned that when Celeste got on one of her lectures, anything could happen.

"As for taking a load of humiliation in order to keep in good standing with the House of Hanover, I believe we shall forgo that as well." Celeste slid her phone back into her bag. "I just canceled my order for twenty dresses. I also let your boss know why. I believe until she changes her policy of allowing young ladies to be molested in her place of business, I will no longer be a client. I understand that she is dressed like she should be drinking it up on Bourbon Street, but that's the way most young women dress these days, and at least she's got a bra on. Seraphina, come. The car will pick us up and we'll find a dress somewhere else."

"Oh, I've got my car. I can drive us." She was parked in the garage down the street.

Celeste stared.

"Or we can go in yours." She knew when Celeste couldn't be moved. And honestly, the idea of Celeste in her broken-down Chevy was pretty humorous.

"Excellent. Say good-bye, Seraphina. You won't have to

see these people again," Celeste said. "Likely because they'll be fired or trying to save their marriages."

Sera gave them a jaunty wave and raced to keep up with Celeste. For a woman in five-inch heels, she could move.

And maybe Celeste had something to teach her.

"And then she took me to an even better store and the sales guy there was wonderful," Seraphina said as she practically bounced up the steps.

All in all, it was not the way Harry had expected her day to go. When he'd been forced to let her go meet his aunt alone, he'd worried it would all go to hell. It had run through his head that this might be what Angie had warned him about, that Celeste would use the time alone to scare off Sera, but she'd been all smiles when she'd driven up five minutes ago.

He hadn't even told her the good news yet, but she was bubbly and happy and bright. It hadn't taken long before he'd started judging his day by how big Seraphina's smile was at the end of it.

"She was nice to you?" He'd been thinking a lot about what Angie had said. He wasn't used to this world. He lived in a world where people said what they thought. Sure, a lot of it was dumb, but you could trust that most of the people he knew didn't have plans and machinations going on behind all their words.

"Absolutely not," Sera said with a grin. "After the first saleslady kicked me out and Celeste then canceled all her orders and threatened everyone like a boss, she complained about my leggings, my hair, thinks I need a sturdier brassiere, made fun of me because I didn't know that meant bra, and then she wouldn't let me walk back into the first store with all my shopping bags and yell '*Big mistake*,' like in *Pretty Woman*, because I shouldn't idolize prostitution. I kind of like her."

He was confused again. "She was mean to you? Wait, why did the first saleslady kick you out?"

"Because some jerk-faced business guy hit on me and then said I was panhandling because I wouldn't go to a hotel with him."

"Excuse me?'

She waved him off. "It happens all the time, but now I know how to handle it. I threaten him with confidence. See, that's what Celeste told me I was doing wrong. She said I was saying all the right things, but I need more confidence. Also, she told me I have to follow through on threats or people will know I'm a whining doormat with no hope of being anything more. So if I ever see that man again, I have to actually kick him in the balls. But it's cool because Celeste bought me these shoes with spikes on them."

"Who the hell asked you to go to a hotel room with him?"

She put her hands on his chest and tipped her head up. "It's not a big deal. It might have been, but your aunt handled it. It's okay. It's nothing I haven't had to deal with before. It's kind of the way a certain class of men treats women like me."

"Women like you?"

"Younger, considered pretty, obviously not wealthy."

It wasn't merely Papillon that had the problem. He knew he was often treated differently because he was a guy. Some of the best woodworkers he knew were women, but getting jobs in construction could be difficult because it was still a man's world. "It's not right."

"I know, but I still have to deal with it. A lot of people

tell me to go along with it and ease my way out of the situation so I don't cause trouble."

A little of the story she'd told was starting to seep in. "But my aunt didn't tell you that, did she?"

Sera shook her head. "We had lunch in the café at the store and she told me about the rules her mother-in-law put on her. She said she'd been thinking about it a lot and didn't like the idea of Angie having to follow the same ones. Or her granddaughter someday." Sera moved away, pacing across the porch. "She was different than what I thought she'd be. I guess I never considered that it would be hard to be Celeste Beaumont."

"She's lost a lot."

"I wasn't talking about that. No one gets out of life without loss. I was talking about the daily stuff. I have to put up with people thinking I'm less than I am, but she did, too. I think her mother-in-law was pretty hard on her."

"She didn't grow up wealthy. She grew up like my mom," he explained. "She grew up in a house where they lived paycheck to paycheck, and sometimes that paycheck wasn't quite enough. I think living in this world has been rough on her."

Sera was quiet for a moment. "It was rough on Wes, but I know how much he loved his mom."

"I'm sure Wes loved his whole family," he replied quietly. She almost never talked about Wes. The one time he'd asked about her relationship with him, she'd found a way to turn the conversation.

She stopped pacing and faced him. "He had a tough relationship with his father. When it was obvious Wes was highly gifted, his dad decided he should be the heir to the company, and Wes always said the only thing worse than his father ignoring him was his father paying attention to him." She shook her head. "But I don't want to talk about that now. I had a good day. And I have a nice outfit for Saturday's brunch. Do you want to see it? I've got about an hour before I need to get home. Zep's got a shift at Guidry's and it's Momma's book club night. Let me tell you, those ladies love their books, and by 'books,' I mean wine."

He let it go because he did want her happy. He'd worked damn hard to be able to give her this surprise. "First, come inside. I need to show you something."

He held out a hand and she took it, though she winced. "Did something fall apart? I was worried about the mirror in the guest bathroom. Was it too heavy?"

"It's perfect. I checked the work myself," he assured her as he led her inside. They were only a couple of weeks into the project, but the house was coming along nicely. Once they'd gotten rid of many of the old pieces of furniture, they'd discovered the place wasn't as bad as it seemed. The structure itself was solid. The roof needed some shingles replaced, but overall he felt pretty good about the budget Sera had and the timeline. She wouldn't get everything she wanted, but the house would be livable at the end of ninety days.

"I thought you had to spend the day on the gazebo." She let him lead her to the kitchen.

The kitchen was in the middle of renovation. It was a holy mess, but one thing about it was perfect and the proof was sitting right on the plywood bar that would soon be replaced with a pretty granite Sera had selected earlier in the week. "I lied about that."

She frowned his way and dropped his hand. "You lied."

He suspected more than one man in Sera's life had lied to her, but in this case, he'd done it for a good reason. "It was the only time this week Darnell could come out and inspect the plumbing." He picked up the paperwork and offered it to her. "I'm sorry. I know you wanted me to go to New Orleans with you, but I needed to bring Darnell out without you here. I didn't want to worry you if something went wrong."

She took the papers, glancing down at them. "We passed?"

This was what he'd wanted to give to her. Ever since she'd realized the inspector could shove roadblocks in her way, she'd been nervous. He needed her to understand they could handle this. "We passed. The whole house."

"But we only spent fifteen hundred on plumbing." She was staring down at the papers.

"We're going to have to replace the water heater in a year or so, but the rest of the plumbing is good. Now, the electrical is going to be different." He would have continued, but he found himself with an armful of happy blonde. Sera wrapped herself around him and kissed his cheek.

"I can't believe it. We passed something," she said with a laugh.

He whirled her around. "We passed. We're going to pass all of it. This house is going to shine when we're through."

Her head came back so she could look him in the eyes. "Harry, I'm starting to wonder if maybe I might keep it."

That was exactly what he was looking for. He wanted her to have choices. He was getting to like it around here, starting to think this could be a great place to settle down and raise a family. "I think that's a fine thing to consider."

"Thank you for this."

He set her on her feet and she stared up at him. He didn't want her to go but knew she took her time with Luc seriously. She'd been gone all day. She would need to spend time with him. "You're welcome. Why don't you show me that pretty dress and then you can get home? I'm going to stay here awhile and work on the bathroom. Now that we know the plumbing's good, we should think about what you want in the master."

"How about you take the night off and we go to dinner?"

He wanted that more than anything. He loved being out in the open with her, loved being able to show that they were together. The people around them were still openly gawking, but they would get used to them as a couple. But there was a problem. "Don't you need a sitter for Luc?"

"He likes to eat, too. Maybe we could all go out. We could go to Guidry's if you want to."

If they went to Guidry's, it wouldn't be long before Remy or Lisa came out and stole the baby away. No. He wanted the whole experience if she was going to let him. "I would love to take you to dinner. You and Luc. But I want to go somewhere else. Someplace your family doesn't own and my cousin doesn't frequent. He's getting back into Papillon this evening and he'll head straight for the bar."

"Agreed," she said. "Because you know my brother or sister-in-law will whisk Luc away, and I think it would be good for the two of you to get to know each other. If you want to. He's still a pretty messy eater."

That's what he wanted to hear. "I can handle it."

"And maybe if you want to, you could stay the night at my place. I know it seems weird because my mom is—"

"I would love that," he said before she could talk herself out of it. He seriously doubted Delphine would have a problem with it because she'd already started to treat him like free labor. Maybe not free exactly, but her incredibly delicious bacon and grits came with the price of unclogging sinks and making sure the back porch door didn't squeak. "How about I stop by Beaumont House to get Shep and an overnight bag and I'll pick you and Luc up in half an hour."

She stepped back and looked almost shy. "I think you'll like Luc."

He needed to make something plain to her. "I already like Luc. I'm thrilled to get to spend some real time with him. I know you think you need to wait six months to see if this is serious, but I promise you, it's serious. I'm serious about you and that means I'm serious about him, too."

"A lot of men are hesitant to take on a kid."

"I'm not a lot of men." He knew what he wanted and it was her.

"I'm starting to believe that." She went on her toes and brushed a kiss along his lips. "And I'm starting to believe this can work between us. Your aunt doesn't hate me."

He had a lot to thank his aunt for. "I don't see how anyone can hate you."

"I know at least one person who did at the end." She stepped back. "I'll see you in a little while. And you should expect to tell me how good I look in my new dress. And modest. Apparently modesty is very important to your family."

She turned and walked back toward the door, those papers in her hand.

Harry watched her, a smile on his face because everything he wanted was so close. All he had to do was reach out and grab it.

"Welcome home, Mrs. Beaumont." Annemarie held open the door as Celeste walked through.

It was good to be home. It was nice to have her housekeeper smile at her for once. Servants should be serious. That's what Ralph had always said.

Ralph had been . . . what would Sera have called him? No. She should find her own words. Wasn't that what being her age was about? She'd paid her dues and now she could be who she wanted to be. Ralph had been an ass.

"Thank you, Annemarie." She took a deep breath, letting the heavenly scent of something roasting wash over her. "What is Cook making for dinner? Because it smells delicious."

Servants also weren't supposed to be praised. She'd spent the hours driving back from New Orleans contemplating the day and much of her life, as she'd been inclined to do for the last several months. She was sure her mother-in-law would tell her that thinking was a waste of time. Of course, her mother-in-law wouldn't have spent a good portion of the afternoon with a woman like Seraphina Guidry.

Like so many other things, she would have been wrong. She should have done this years ago, when it was obvious Wes was infatuated with the girl. She still didn't believe Sera would have been right for Wes, but she might do well for Harry. The young woman had some rough edges, but nothing that time and patience wouldn't smooth out. It was obvious she was crazy about Harry and not at all eager to try to fit into the Beaumont family for any other reason than she wanted to please her boyfriend. It would have been far smarter for Sera to have gone out of her way to please Celeste.

She had not. It had been refreshing. Sera had a quick wit and didn't mind stating her opinion once she'd relaxed a bit and realized no one was going to murder her. Celeste could have sworn the young lady asked if there was tarp around. She'd been charming, and the truth was she'd reminded Celeste a lot of her sister.

"It's roast chicken, potatoes, and a salad, I believe." Annemarie closed the door. "Your daughter returned safely, though Harry left a note. I believe he is spending the evening out."

He'd called her moments before and told her not to expect him home. She'd told him to be discreet. He'd asked her what that word really meant. Silly boy, but then the times had changed and no one would think much about Harry and Sera spending the night together since she'd practically put her stamp of approval on the relationship.

It was odd how she'd softened. She'd gone into the whole thing with a mind to manipulate, but Harry was happy. Shouldn't he be allowed to be happy? She'd spent the last forty years of her life being terrified of making a mistake, of stepping slightly out of line and losing everything.

And then she'd stood in that design house where her mother-in-law had forced her to go twice a year for new clothes. Where her mother-in-law and the designer had consistently clucked about how she was overweight or underweight, how her skin was too sallow or she smiled too much. Where on more than one occasion she'd been forced to smile through one of her husband's "friends" talking down to her.

It had occurred to her when she'd seen that guard walking toward Sera that this could be the moment she broke the girl. She could manipulate the situation so Sera thought she'd caused it, or even though she'd been perfectly innocent, there would be no justice for her. Yes, that might have caused her to run away.

She'd known she could break Sera the way she'd been broken.

In that moment she'd wondered who would try to break Angela. She'd already cracked. Angela had lived under many of the same rules. Did she want that for her daughter? Did she want that for any woman?

"Mom?" Angie came down the stairs.

Her baby girl looked so pretty in her dress and cardigan. Celeste held her arms open. "Hello, my darling. How was Sedona? You look lovely. Doesn't my daughter look pretty, Annemarie?"

"She does, Mrs. Beaumont. That color suits her nicely," Annemarie said with a gracious smile.

Angie started to give her the air kiss she was used to, but Celeste wanted more. She drew her daughter in and hugged her like she hadn't in years. Angie was stiff for a moment, but then her arms wrapped around her and she laid her head on Celeste's shoulder. "It was good. The spa was beautiful. Did I say thank you for sending me and my friends?"

She kissed her baby girl's head and stepped back. "I was happy to do it. Was the plane okay?"

"It was wonderful." Angie glanced over at Annemarie. "Could I have a moment alone with my mother?"

Annemarie nodded. "Of course. I'll go and see if Cook needs any help. I believe dinner is in half an hour."

"Thank you so much," Celeste said, taking her daughter's hand and leading her into the study. "Would you like a glass of wine? I've told Annemarie I would like to have wine or a cocktail in the study every evening."

"I thought you said wine was only for special occasions."

"I've changed my mind on a couple of things," she said, crossing to where the bottle of Cab had been properly decanted and waiting to be poured. "I've decided I'm close enough to death that every day should be celebrated."

"Mom," Angie said, sounding shocked.

She poured two glasses of wine. "Well, it's true."

Angie took the drink like she needed it. "What is going on with you? I leave for a week, and when I come back, it appears the world has turned upside down. I got a frantic call from the House of Hanover. Justine said you canceled all the bridesmaids' dresses."

"Well, I'll probably change my mind if she apologizes and fires that uppity saleslady."

"And I got a call from Britney Brewer that you blamed her father for something a hooker did," Angie continued.

That man was going to pay. "Seraphina obviously isn't a hooker. Harry doesn't have two dimes to his name, and if Sera was making money off some other man, she would dress better than she does. Britney's father was being a massive ass and I dealt with him. The saleslady and security guard blamed Sera for Brian being a nasty lecher. Tell me something. Has that man ever hit on you?"

She shook her head. "No, but he does make me uncomfortable from time to time. Why on earth was Sera at House of Hanover? Tell me you're not getting her a dress for my wedding."

"Well, if I don't, she's promised me she'll show up in some sequin-encrusted jumpsuit that will make the entire wedding party look like a prison disco."

"I don't think that's a thing, Mom. I'm really confused. I thought you hated Sera. I talked to Harry about it earlier. I told him he shouldn't trust you, that you're playing some game."

She wasn't surprised that was what Angela thought. It was certainly what Cal had thought, but she was curious about Harry. He hadn't mentioned anything when they'd talked earlier. "And Harry said?"

"Harry said I was wrong and that even if I wasn't, once you got to know Sera, you would like her."

"I don't know if I would say I like her." She couldn't quite admit it yet. Not out loud. It still felt a bit like a betrayal of Wes. "But I think I should try to be tolerant if she's going to be around. Harry seems very taken with her. I would have thought you'd be all right with the situation. You're the one who argued I would lose Harry if I didn't change."

"You don't change."

"I assure you I have. I wasn't always the woman you know. I changed for your father, and now I'm thinking it wasn't for the better." She took a sip of the rich Cab. "Angie, I know I've told you in the past to not cause scenes, but you realize there's a place for them, right? Your grandmother was wrong about some things."

"My grandmother was a terrible person. She didn't care about anything but appearances. No, I don't tend to follow her rules. Dad wasn't much better."

"And I went along with it."

Angie frowned. "If you hadn't, Dad would have divorced you. Mom, what's brought this on? I don't understand what's happening. Did you cancel the dress order because someone wasn't nice to Seraphina?"

"They treated her like garbage," she explained. She'd been able to hear her mother-in-law's voice, clucking about how every woman in the world had to deal with a jerk like Brian Brewer, and Sera should have been gracious and found a way not to make a scene. "I know I say a lot about wearing the right clothes and presenting yourself properly, but I realized today that if my sister had walked into that store, they would have treated her the same way. Harry gets a pass because he's an attractive young man. He's white and handsome. My sister had her privileges, too, don't get me wrong. But she was poor, and in our world that means she could be preyed on."

"Did Sera slip something into your tea?" Angie asked. "You sound a little woke there, Mom."

"Well, of course I'm awake." She shook her head. "All I'm saying is I've been reminded lately that I came from humble beginnings. There were good things about that world. Sweet things. Things I miss, and I've started to wonder if I can't find some of that part of me again. I realized

I'm not actually offended by the sight of someone's toes as long as they're properly maintained. And I like dogs. I'm thinking about getting a dog. A small one, though. I think I might like a sweet companion."

"Who are you?" The question came from her daughter's mouth with a little bit of shock tingeing it.

Wasn't that the question? "I'm not sure. But I think I would like to find out. I definitely think I want a different life for my granddaughters, and maybe that starts with changing what I find tolerable. Your grandmother thought it was perfectly acceptable for a man like Brian Brewer to treat a woman like Seraphina as if he had the right to whatever he wanted from her because she was below his station, but god forbid I wore the wrong shade of lipstick or expressed a damn opinion. Or use the word 'damn' for that matter."

"I'm going to need more wine." Angie poured herself another drink. "Is now a good time to tell you Austin and I have decided to put off having kids for at least five years?"

Well, that was disappointing. And also encouraging. "You want to work on your career?"

"I know everyone on Austin's side of the family thinks I'm going to settle down and be a wife and mother, but I want something more. It's not that I don't—"

She held a hand up. "You do not have to explain yourself to me. Maybe I would have questioned you a few years back."

"It was Cal and Wes's places to make something of themselves," Angie said tightly. "Dad told me I had it easy. All I had to do was convince someone to marry me."

Sometimes she hated her husband. "You have a degree."

"I know the only reason Dad paid for college was you convinced him it would be a good place for me to find a husband. But then you didn't push me. I think you wanted me to have the degree because you didn't. Because you knew you didn't have any way to fight back if things went wrong. Dad controlled everything."

"And your grandmother made sure I understood that if I left, I left with nothing. I had to sign a prenuptial contract." There had been so many times she'd wanted to leave, wanted to find a way out, but she'd settled. "Your father never hit me. You should understand that. But he didn't love me."

"I don't think Dad loved anyone," Angie replied. "I think he had kids because it was expected. He did all the things a family of our station is supposed to do. Take good pictures. Go to church. Raise strong sons and obedient, marginalized daughters. I want a career, Mom. I want something to fall back on."

This was something she could do for her daughter. "I'm setting up a trust for you. It's exactly what your father set up for Cal, and would have set up for Wes on his twenty-fifth birthday."

Angie went still. "Are you serious? That was millions of dollars."

Millions of dollars that would keep her daughter safe from having to make the same hard decisions she had. "Yes. Sometimes I think your father's early passing was a miracle."

"I know Cal thinks that way. The idea of having everything dumped in his lap would have sent Cal running. I'm fairly certain if Dad had changed his will, Cal would have handed everything right back to you." She reached out, putting a hand on Celeste's shoulder. "Mom, I think all of this is great. I do. I'm just surprised."

"I think the last few years sent me reeling, but having Harry here, well, like I said, I've been reminded I wasn't always this woman."

"But I think we should be careful around Sera," Angie said, pulling away. "She's got a kid. I wouldn't want the child to get hurt."

"I don't think Sera's bringing the baby to the wedding events, if that's what you're worried about. Harry says she's been careful about introducing him to her son." Though it looked like the couple was taking a leap tonight. Unless they were going into New Orleans for the night, but that wasn't the impression she'd had.

"That's not what I meant. I meant it seems like it's far too early for anyone to get close to that child," Angie said, her tone going stubborn. "No one knows if it's going to work out between the two of them. They should wait to bring the kid into it until they're sure, and even then, I think it would be best if you didn't get close to him. You've been through a lot."

"Well, I didn't offer to babysit." She wasn't sure where this was coming from. She'd barely ever mentioned Sera's son. She wasn't sure she remembered the child's name. "I've already talked to Harry about the fact that the child's father could return at some point and cause trouble. He didn't seem to think that would be a problem."

Angie mumbled something under her breath about the least of their problems, but when she turned, there was a grim look on her face. "I'm only trying to think about that kid. I can't imagine what it must be like to get to know a bunch of men who disappear from his life. That's all I'm saying."

"Do you know something I don't? From what I've heard, Sera's only dated one man since she had her baby, and she never introduced them. I've heard the man is a roughneck, so she's probably better off. I don't know. Maybe that's a wonderful way to live. I know there were times I wished your father had spent months on an oil rig and not at home.

Honey, I don't think you should worry about this. Once we get through all the wedding craziness, I suspect she won't be around much. I've heard she's thinking of selling and moving to Houston."

She was starting to hope that wouldn't happen, especially if it meant losing Harry.

"That might be for the best. There's a lot of work in Houston." Angie nodded as though the idea pleased her.

Was her daughter getting jealous of Harry? Angie had spent so much of her childhood shoved to the side in favor of her brothers, and Celeste knew she was guilty of that, too. She slid an arm around her daughter's shoulders. "Come on. Cal should be here soon. Let's talk about your career. You know I wouldn't mind having you at Beaumont Oil."

The smile on her daughter's face was worth everything. She let her worries go as the door came open again and Cal walked in.

Her little family was all right. It was all she could hope for.

chapter twelve

Harry watched from the doorway to Luc's room as Sera kissed her son's head and placed him in his bed.

"Hey, is it okay if he stays in here?" He gestured down to Shep, who had been sitting quietly at her feet while she read Luc a bedtime story and sang a song to help him sleep. It had been a soft moment that he'd wanted to be a part of, but he'd hung back because she'd given him a lot tonight.

Shep had been patiently waiting at the door when they'd come back from dinner. Delphine had told them the dog had watched at the window until they'd returned.

"I don't think I can keep him away. These two are in love," she said with a smile.

Shep's tail thumped softly against the floor in agreement.

"'Night, buddy," Harry said, giving the dog a pat before he held out his hand. It was time to take Sera to bed, to wrap his arms around her and show her this could work.

She turned the light off, the room illuminated only by the small nightlight that cast a soft glow. She stepped up to him, and she was so lovely his heart seemed to tighten. "Did I thank you for dinner?"

It hadn't been a particularly romantic affair, but it had been one of the best nights he'd had in forever. Her hand slid into his and he tugged her out to the hallway. "I had the best company, so I think I should be the one thanking you."

She closed the door with her free hand and went up on her toes to brush her lips against his.

He backed her up against the wall, his hands going to her hips. "I loved our evening, Sera. I loved spending time with Luc. I loved seeing this side of you. You're a good mom."

She teared up slightly. "Sometimes it's nice to hear that. It can be hard. I get judged a lot. I always have to worry if I'm giving him what he needs."

"You're giving him everything he needs," he said, brushing his lips over her forehead. "He's a happy, healthy kid, and now he's got a sixty-pound furry ex-military body-guard who works for pets and kibble."

"Well, I kind of like having my own ex-military guy," she said with a hint of a smile.

There was a noise at the end of the hall and she started. Delphine walked by in a fluffy bathrobe, her hair up in a towel. "Don't mind me. I'm going down for some tea. 'Night, kids."

Sera had gone stiff. "'Night, Momma."

Maybe she wasn't ready for this. He backed up. "Hey, you know you don't actually owe me anything, right? I can go to my room at Beaumont House and be back here bright and early to pick up my dog and maybe have some breakfast with you. I'll bring the donuts. I had a wonderful time tonight and that's all I need."

Her shoulders relaxed again and she reached for his hand. "I want my sleepover. I'm sorry. It's weird. I live with my mom. I feel like you should be sneaking into my window. I've never had a man stay over."

Soon she would have other options. "You know when we get the electrical finished, it might be easier for you to move into Guidry Place. I think we can have the downstairs fixed up. You'll have a kitchen, and the master bedroom is attached to a study that could easily serve as Luc's room."

He would find a way to move himself in, and in a few weeks, she would wake up and wonder how that ring had gotten on her finger.

Because he was pretty sure he was going to marry her and stay here in Papillon and raise a family.

"I hadn't thought about that. It would be nice to be on my own," she said with a smile. "Even Zep has his own space, though it's an apartment over the garage. Don't get me wrong, I love my mom, but I've never lived in a place that was all mine."

She wanted to. It was easy to see she wanted a home where she was the queen. He could give her that. Oh, he couldn't afford to buy her a new house, but he could fix up the one she had. He could put all his talent and care into making that old space a wonderful home for her and Luc, and eventually for himself. She would see they could make it work and that Papillon was the place for them.

"I can have it ready in a few weeks, maybe less. Once the electrical is cleared, we can move you in and you can work on the house whenever you have time," he promised.

"It won't get condemned?"

He shook his head. "It was never going to be condemned. The house isn't nearly as bad as everyone around here thought. You'll have it gorgeous in no time."

"I don't think I've ever had anyone believe in me the way you do." She moved back toward him now, her arms drifting up around his neck. "I think you should take me to bed now, Harrison Jefferys."

He wanted nothing more than to do exactly that. He

leaned over and picked her up, carrying her the short distance to her room. It was next door to Luc's, though according to what she'd told him earlier in the evening, it hadn't been so long since she'd had his crib in her room.

She'd been a girl who'd had to grow up fast. Then she'd been a mom. He wanted to make sure that tonight she felt like a woman. His woman.

He eased into her small bedroom. It was pretty and feminine and made him think about what Sera could do with a space if she had serious cash to decorate. She had a great eye for design, for making a room both comfortable and stylish.

But she needed a bigger bed, though the good news was they would have to cuddle.

The even better news was he got to kiss her and be with her.

He tugged her shirt off before lowering his mouth to hers. Over the baby monitor, he heard a little huff and sigh.

Sera smiled. "It's okay. He's just turning over. He'll let us know if he needs us. Right now, I'm the one who needs you."

He wasn't about to ignore the invitation in her words. He let his hands find her hair and sank them in, reveling in how soft she was, how perfectly she fit against him. "I thought about you all day. I didn't like you going to New Orleans without me."

She tipped her head back, her palms running under his T-shirt. "I didn't, either, but I absolutely love that you took care of passing that first inspection for me. You're right. I would have obsessed over it, but next time I want to be there. I want to learn how to handle these things."

"I can teach you." He kissed her over and over again. He would love teaching her, standing beside her as she grew confident. With a twist of his hand, he eased her bra off and tossed it to the side.

"I can teach you, too," she said with a sexy smile. "I can teach you how to make me breakfast and how to babysit so I can have a girls' night."

He loved it when she was playful. The intimacy they'd found wrapped a warm blanket around him. He hadn't realized how cold he'd been before he met her. "If you're not careful, I'll think you're with me for my babysitting skills and not my fabulous body."

Her hands came up to pull his shirt over his head and it joined her clothes on the floor. Her hands brushed over his chest and he sighed at the feel. She looked at him like she could eat him up. "Well, it is a fabulous body. You're as pretty on the outside as you are on the inside, Harrison Jefferys."

He wasn't half as pretty as she was, but he wasn't about to argue with her. He would rather show her how much joy she brought him.

He leaned over and kissed her, letting his tongue play lazily with hers.

He undressed her and then let her ease him out of the rest of his clothes. They weren't hurried, rather enjoying the slow intimacy that kept growing between them. He sat on the edge of the bed and let her help him take off his prosthesis because she told him she wanted to learn how to do that, too. She treated his leg like it was a precious thing. Where she'd tossed his clothes, she was careful with the prosthesis, placing it where he could easily reach it.

He sat on the edge of her bed and put his hands on her hips, cupping them and exploring her curves. "You make me feel wanted, Sera. You don't ever look away from my scars."

She smoothed back his hair. "Because they're beautiful. Because they're this amazing part of you."

He let his hand find the beginning of the thin scar that curved slightly right above that spot he'd lavished affection on nights before. The scar that given her Luc. "This is beautiful. Just like the rest of you."

He drew her in and nuzzled her neck, breathing in the scent of her. It had been days since they'd been skin to skin and he realized how much he'd missed this. They'd had a few hurried encounters during the week, but nothing like this.

Her hands stroked up and down his back, and she cuddled close to him. Her breasts nestled against his chest. "Sometimes I forget I'm more than a mom. The days get so crazy and they seem to go by in a flash, but when you look at me, I feel like I can slow down."

Oh, he could make her feel like a woman. He kissed along her collarbone. "See, I felt like time dragged all week because I couldn't have this with you."

A little chuckle went through her. "Oh, I remember having this with you on my aunt's old sofa."

"Not the same," he whispered as he ran his hands down to her backside. "That was a quickie and that's not the way I like to make love to you. I want to take my time, make it last. I want to feel your body against mine, feel the way you sigh when I touch you. I want hours to spend on you."

A chuckle went through her. "Well, we didn't have hours. Someone's always showing up at Guidry Place."

Which was precisely why he needed to figure out a way to spend nights with her. All week long every time he figured out a way to get his hands on her, one of her brothers would show up to help. Or her friends would drop by with snacks. It was lovely, but deeply frustrating.

He cupped her luscious backside and turned his chin up to look at her. "Maybe after we get caught a couple of times, they'll know to knock before walking into your house."

She gasped as he turned and moved them onto the bed. He covered her with his body and finally had her exactly where he wanted her.

"Harry," she said with big wide eyes. "I don't think that's a good idea."

"I think it's the perfect idea." It wasn't. The perfect thing would be to spend every night and every morning with her, to tie himself so tightly to her that no one would expect she would be alone. He was fine with being known as the couple who couldn't keep their hands off each other. It was true. Anytime she was in a room, he wanted to touch her.

He lowered his lips to hers and felt that sigh he'd talked about. It softened her and made him feel welcome. Like he was coming home. Her arms wrapped around him and drew him in. He kissed her over and over again, doing exactly what he'd wanted to do all week long—take his time, explore every inch of her body.

He loved the way she gasped when he kissed her breasts and settled his lips on her nipples, pulling on them and lavishing them with affection. The feel of her hands tightening on his back, the bite of her nails digging in, made his whole body tighten with anticipation.

But he wasn't done with her yet. Not even close. He'd learned how good it could be to wait, to draw out the moment until he thought he couldn't wait a single second longer to have her.

He kissed his way down her body. He wouldn't make her wait at all. He would give her everything he had, and only when he thought she couldn't take it anymore would he give in and seek his own pleasure.

"You're going to drive me crazy, aren't you?" She whispered the words as her hands fisted in the soft comforter that covered her bed.

It was like she could read his mind. He simply kissed her belly button and moved lower. He slid down her body until he found that sweet part of her that needed so much.

He groaned as he let himself taste her. She was honey and sunshine and sweet arousal.

She cried out and immediately he heard a little whine from the baby monitor.

"Oh no," Sera said and started to move.

He pressed her legs back into the bed. "Give it a second, baby."

She relaxed back and they both waited for a moment. Blissful silence. He grinned up at her.

"You need to be a little more quiet, baby."

"But you're making me crazy," she whispered.

"And I'm going to make you even crazier." He settled back down and eased a finger inside, seeking that sweet spot that would send her over the edge.

She reached out and grabbed a pillow, putting it over her face as she moaned out her pleasure.

He rolled off her and grabbed the condom he'd left on the bedside table.

"Give it to me, Harry." She was on her knees, her hair wild around her shoulders.

She took his breath away. He handed her the condom and lay back. "You going to pay me back?"

Her lips curled up as she ripped open the condom. "I'm going to take what's mine, Harry. You're mine, aren't you?"

He'd always known she could be fierce when she wanted to be. "I'm all yours."

He was hers in a way he'd never belonged to anyone. She

fit with him. She completed something deep inside him he hadn't even known was lacking.

She reached down and took him in her hand, eliciting a groan from the back of his throat as she stroked him.

"You're going to have to be quiet," she said with a grin.

Yep, it was payback time. He bit back a groan as she rolled the condom on him. Now he was the one holding on to the comforter, trying his hardest not to lose control because she was a sexy goddess about to work her magic.

She took charge, straddling his body and leaning over to kiss him. He could feel the heat of her body as it skimmed against his skin. Everywhere she touched him seemed to heat and throb with the need for more. More touch. More connection. More her.

He flexed his hips, trying to find his way inside. She'd made him forget about anything but making love with her. She sat up and stared down at him for a moment, allowing him to memorize what she looked like, how gorgeous she was in the glowy light that came from the small lamp on her nightstand. He let his hands find her thighs and move up to her hips and waist.

"I'm all yours, Seraphina, and I don't want to be anything else," he promised her quietly.

She lowered herself down, taking him inside. His breath threatened to stop at the feel of her surrounding him. Warmth flooded his body and he had to grit his teeth in an attempt not to lose it then and there. He wanted this moment to last, wanted to watch her find her pleasure again.

She looked down at him, her eyes warm. "I'm crazy about you."

He let his hands stroke from her waist up to her breasts as she began to move over him. He watched her, studying and memorizing how gorgeous she was when she took over. He managed to last until she'd shuddered and moaned his name and then it was his time. He flipped her over and lost himself in her body.

He let himself go, giving her everything he had until he finally found his own bliss.

They lay tangled together. Somehow they'd managed to get under the covers, and he wrapped her up in his arms. Peace suffused him, his heart rate starting to come back down.

"I like having you here," she whispered. "I like not sleeping alone."

"Me, too." He liked knowing if she needed anything, he was right here, and Luc was next door. He liked being together. "I like waking up next to you even better."

"I hope I don't snore," she said with a yawn. "The only other man I ever spent all night with said I snored."

"He was obviously an ass."

"Wes could be a jerk when he didn't get what he . . ." Sera went still.

And he was suddenly perfectly awake again.

Sera sat straight up, utterly unable to believe she'd said the words. But she had. She held the sheet to her body and tried to think of a way out.

"Wes? My cousin Wes?" Harry's brow had furrowed as if he didn't quite understand the words she'd said. "Why would you wake up with Wes?"

"Oh, we were friends for such a long time." Now that the moment was here, she felt a pit of panic open inside her. She wasn't ready to tell him, but was she ready to lie?

His hand came out, tilting her head up. "Sera, did you sleep with Wes?"

She couldn't lie to him. She simply nodded.

"I thought you were only friends."

"We were. It was a mistake. I'd had a rough day. They were all kind of rough then. Everyone else had gone off to universities, and I couldn't get through community college. Remy had lost our part of the restaurant. He had to sell to our cousin when he got divorced. Then he left and joined the Navy and we kind of fell apart for a while."

Harry sat up, a blank look on his face. "So it was a one-time thing? You know my whole family thinks you and Wes were nothing more than friends."

This was why she never talked about it. Well, one of the reasons. It was complex, and she could still hear Wes screaming at her, telling her she'd lied to him, had led him on for years. She could feel tears pulse behind her eyes. "We were friends, but we'd drifted a little. He was in school and I was home. He called a couple of times a week and he invited me up to see him, but I knew he wanted more from me. I knew I should put some distance between us."

The old guilt came flooding back.

"But you didn't," Harry prompted. "So you were friends with him for years and one day you decided to sleep with him? I'm sorry. I'm not trying to be judgmental. I'm wrapping my head around it. It would be different if he wasn't my cousin."

"I honestly don't remember much of what happened." She hated this feeling. Loathed it. "I had just broken up with a guy I'd been seeing. He told me he had to get serious because he was about to graduate and I wasn't a serious girl. I was a fun time. Then I got fired from the diner I was working at. Wes called and asked if I would come up. Wes always made me feel good about myself. We kind of helped each other out all through school. So I went to see him. I didn't mean to stay, but he talked me into going to a party and I got drunk. I wanted to forget that I wasn't one of them. I wanted to pretend I was a college kid with a future ahead of me. It got out of hand."

"Did he . . ."

She shook her head. Her mother had the same questions. "I remember kissing him. I remember thinking maybe this could work. Maybe I had been wrong all along. But then I knew I'd made a mistake when I woke up the next morning and he talked about me moving in with him. It was way too much. I knew he'd had a puppy-love thing with me, but this was something more."

"Cal says he was obsessed with you."

"I told him that the night before had been a mistake and he got so angry with me." They'd rarely ever fought, but he'd been a different Wes that morning. "I left and I didn't see him again."

"He went into the Army after that night."

She nodded again. "He did, but I didn't tell him to do that. Not once did I say he should go away. I couldn't do what he wanted me to do. I couldn't love him the way he needed."

Harry's eyes came up, catching her own. "Is Wes Luc's father?"

She couldn't say it.

"Damn it, Sera, why didn't you tell him?"

She'd never heard Harry curse. "He left before I knew I was pregnant, and then I didn't want to admit it even to myself. Then he was gone."

"But his family wasn't." This was so complicated. It made his gut tighten with the implications.

"They never liked me. They didn't like Wes being my friend."

"That doesn't mean they wouldn't have cared about their grandchild," Harry argued. "How pregnant were you when Wes died?"

She hesitated but finally answered. "Four months."

"So you already knew you were going to have the baby, but you didn't write to him? You didn't tell him?"

This was what she'd wanted to avoid. "It wasn't like he could come home. He'd already been deployed at that point."

"Somehow I think he could have figured a way," Harry replied. "And none of that explains why you never told my uncle and aunt. My uncle was still alive when you had Luc. He could have had two years with his grandson."

"He could have taken his grandson away from me." It was what Angie had told her, and she'd believed every word she'd said. She'd believed it because she'd heard it all from Wes. Ralph Beaumont had been cold and distant and far more interested in his family name and reputation than his children's happiness.

"The state doesn't just go around taking children away from parents."

It was obvious he wasn't going to listen to her. What had she been thinking? She'd held the secret for so long, she'd thought it would never come out. She'd thought she could have Harry and keep her secret, too. She slid off the bed, wrapping the sheet around her because they were definitely not cuddling down for the night. "I was scared. The Beaumonts hated me. They blamed me for Wes leaving, and then they blamed me for Wes's death."

She needed to get dressed. She couldn't have this argument with him like this. She started for her bathroom.

"Where are you going? We're not done." Harry shifted to reach out and put a hand on her arm.

It was a lot like what Wes had done. He'd reached out and grabbed her, hauling her in and snarling at her. Telling her what a tease she was and how she'd wrecked his life.

She pulled away and closed the door between them.

Her hands were shaking.

"Sera, come out here and talk to me," Harry said.

She had a pair of PJ pants and a T-shirt hanging next to the shower. She pulled them on as her brain raced, looking for a way out. Harry didn't see his aunt the way she did. Despite the fact that she'd had a good day with Celeste, she didn't believe for a second there wouldn't be a fight if she found out about Luc.

He knocked on the door. "I'm not joking, Sera. You can't hide in there and expect me to go away. You understand that this means I'm actually related to Luc. I had a right to know that. I had a right to know I had more family."

She opened the door. He'd gotten dressed and stood tall and imposing. She couldn't let him intimidate her. "You had a right to nothing. He's my son. I am so sick of men telling me what their rights are. Wes acted like he had a right to me. He always did. Do you know what he told me that day? He told me he'd wasted years waiting on me to wake up and see how lucky I was he wanted to be with me."

"I don't see what that has to do with the fact that you've been lying to my family."

She wanted so badly to throw Angie at him. Angie had known exactly what her parents would do, and she'd saved Sera. But she couldn't put her friend in the line of fire like that. It hadn't been Angie who screwed up their secret. "Celeste tried to have my house condemned. She did it because she thinks that land should be hers, should belong to her family. Can you imagine what she would have done if she thought she had a grandson out there? Wes's child? I know she seems to have changed her mind about me, but she would have come after my son. I didn't have any money. Zep was just starting to get back on his feet after getting himself into a lot of trouble. Remy was gone. Do you honestly think I didn't want help? Do you believe I would have hidden this if I didn't feel like I had to? Of course I would have told Wes if he'd lived. I would have had to. But I listened to all his stories about being raised by Ralph and Celeste. I did not want that for my child, and I don't think he would have wanted it, either."

"You don't get to make that call," Harry said, a worried look on his face. "I don't want to have this fight, but I think you're wrong. I think you've been wrong about this all along. You should have told Wes the minute you knew. You should have let him help you."

"I should have married him." The tears slipped from her eyes now. "That's what you're really saying. I should have accepted that I screwed up and I owed the rest of my life to a man I didn't love. I know I don't look like I have much of a life right now, but it's mine. It's my choice. I chose to have Luc. I chose not to put myself in a position where I had to marry someone I didn't love, who I actively feared at the end of our relationship."

"If Wes had lived, you would have had to deal with him. He would have come home and then what would you have done? You say you would have told him eventually, but it sounds like you would have punished him. Did he scare you so much you would have kept his son from him?"

She should have known he would never understand. "You don't get to judge me. You don't get to decide what my fear felt like."

"You think I haven't been afraid?"

"It's a different kind of fear, and one you can't understand." She was suddenly weary. Harry wouldn't understand what it meant to be a woman in the room with a man who could hurt her, and there was nothing she could do about it. He would never feel the dread, the smallness that came from someone he loved threatening him with real violence. There was really only one question she had for him now. "Are you going to go home and tell Celeste?"

That seemed to stump him. He stood there for a moment, hands on his hips. "I don't think it's my secret to tell. I think you should tell her."

"I'll give it some consideration." She would need to prepare because she didn't think he would stay silent forever. He would give her a little time to come around to his way of thinking, but if Harry truly believed there was an injustice he could fix, he would do it. He might warn her or he might not.

He sighed. "Come on. Let's talk about this. You can't think you'll hide this forever."

It was obvious she'd been doing what she always did. Procrastinating and praying things would simply work out. It was what she'd done her whole life. She'd floated through high school because she'd been pretty and charming, and floundered afterward because pretty and charming didn't make a career. Now something good had fallen into her lap and she was letting the gorgeous man take over because it was easier than doing it herself.

"I think you should go."

Harry's brows rose in obvious surprise. "What? Hey, I know we're having a disagreement, but that's no reason to throw me out."

"This isn't a disagreement. This goes far beyond us arguing about where to eat for dinner."

"Yes, it's much more important. I'll help you. We can go to my aunt together."

There it was. He would insist. He would take over. He would make the decision for her. "No. You should go, and I would appreciate it if you would give me a few weeks before you tell her. I need to figure out how to pay for a lawyer. I need to prepare the rest of my family. Remy, Lisa, and my mom know, but Zep doesn't. Neither do my friends."

Harry seemed to understand things weren't going the

way he'd thought they would. "I told you I wouldn't tell her."

"And I don't believe you. I think you'll tell her when you realize I won't."

"Why would you want to keep your son from a loving grandparent?"

She huffed out a laugh that had nothing to do with humor. "Because at the time, I didn't think they were all that loving. I made that decision when Ralph Beaumont was alive. I kept the secret because Luc is my son and I make the decisions concerning him. I know I'll have to tell him one day and let him choose for himself, but that day is not today. I would like you to leave. I have to do some research because your aunt basically owns the only lawyer in town."

"You don't need a lawyer. You need to calm down," he said in a beseeching tone.

The words did absolutely nothing to help his case. "Don't you tell me to calm down. I am perfectly calm and I want you to leave."

Harry went still. "I want to help you."

She wanted that more than anything, but she couldn't give in on this. "You can't."

He stared at her for a moment. "Is this really what you want? You are so scared of my aunt that you'll throw away what we could have?"

Her heart was breaking because he was making her choose and there was only one choice. "Yes. I have to protect my son."

Harry sat down on the bed they'd recently shared and pulled on his boot, tying it with sharp gestures. "This is ridiculous."

"I agree. I should have realized it wouldn't work. I was dumb, but then I always seem to make the wrong choice. I need to stop hoping some white knight will race in and save me, and I have to start saving myself."

"Now you have to save yourself from me? How exactly did I become the bad guy?"

He wasn't bad. He simply wouldn't understand her. "You're not. You're probably right about everything, but you don't know your aunt the way I do. I had a nice day with her. But she won't forgive me. I walked into this relationship knowing it couldn't work. I don't even know what I was thinking. I wasn't thinking at all."

He stood in front of her. "You're kicking me out because I don't agree with you?"

"I'm asking you to leave because I need space and time to figure out what to do."

"I want to help you decide."

"No, you've already made your decision. You want to convince me to do something that could cost me my son because you don't understand what's at stake." It was obvious he was going to try to argue until he wore her down. If she didn't stand her ground, she would find herself walking into Beaumont House tomorrow and putting them all at Celeste's mercy. She wasn't so foolish to think one lunch truly changed things between them. "I've asked you for time, Harry. Are you going to give it to me?"

He was silent for a moment. "Yes. I don't want this, but if you insist, I'll give it to you."

"I insist."

He stared down at her, his eyes full of pain. "I think I could love you."

She'd wanted to hear those words, but now she knew they came with conditions. "If I'm honest with your family."

"I don't think anyone should start a life together with a lie," he said, his tone mournful. "I'll come by in the morning and pick up Shep. I don't want to disturb Luc."

But he did. He wanted to disturb Luc's whole life, wanted to shake it to the core and pray everything came out right on the other side.

She watched as he walked out. She managed to follow him down the stairs, lock the door behind him, and walk back up to her room. She managed to close the bedroom door before she let herself fall apart. It was okay because in the morning she would put herself back together and she would prepare for war.

chapter thirteen

Sera strode into Guidry's the next day, looking for her brother. Remy was the one she needed to talk to. He was the one who knew people outside of Papillon. She made her way into the kitchen and found him stirring a big pot of gumbo. It was midmorning, before the lunch rush, but Remy would have already been awake and working for hours. Her brother and sister-in-law were dedicated to their business, to growing it and positioning it for the future.

It made her wish she could find something in her work life she could be as passionate about. Not that she had much of a work life. She had an asset she needed to sell, and now it looked like that money might have to go to ensure she kept custody of her son.

Her big brother looked up and flashed a grin. "Hey, sis. I didn't expect to see you. You need a shift?"

It was what she did. When she was in between jobs, she took shifts here to ease the way to the next thing she would try, and her brother would make it simple for her. She couldn't float through life anymore, depending on her brother to give her a safe place. "No. I'm going to work on the house this afternoon. I have a crew coming in to fix the bathroom tile."

"Which bathroom?"

"Pretty much all of them," she admitted. She'd been ready to work on the bathrooms while Harry dealt with the stairs to the second floor of the house. She would need to ask Herve if his cousin was still available. "I need to ask a favor. Do you know any lawyers?"

A brow rose above her brother's eyes. "Sure. Lisa's brother-in-law is a lawyer. I'm pretty sure he's licensed to practice in Louisiana. But what's wrong with Quaid? If there's something you need with the house, he knows Louisiana property laws like the back of his hand. He also owes me twenty bucks from poker the other night."

If only it were that easy. "I need someone who can represent me in custody matters, and it can't be Quaid because he'll likely be on the other side of it."

Remy stopped stirring and turned to her. "Michel, I'm going to need you to take over."

The chef strode in from the back and eased into the place her brother had occupied.

Remy nodded toward his office. "All right, what's going on?"

She followed him in. This had once been her grandfather's office. It would have been her dad's if he'd lived. Now it was Remy's. He was carrying on the family tradition. So much of her trouble right now came down to family and how tightly knit they could be. So tight they sometimes frayed. "Celeste is going to find out about Luc."

Remy sank to his seat. "How? Have you decided to tell her? I thought you didn't want her to know."

When her brother had come home after years away, she'd told Remy everything, including the fact that Angela had been the one to convince her to keep the secret about Luc from her family. "Harry found out."

"And Harry can't keep his mouth closed, why?"

She fought back tears at the thought of Harry. The night before had been perfect, right up until that fight. "He's got a black-and-white view of the world. I'm afraid he believes in his aunt in a way I can't. The funny thing is, she's started to loosen up. When I began dating Harry, she decided not to fight it, and we've gotten fairly tolerant of each other."

"But she doesn't know about Luc. I think she's going to be far less tolerant of you once she realizes you never told her you had her precious baby boy's child," Remy reasoned. "He doesn't know what Celeste was like back when Wes was alive."

"I do," a masculine voice said.

She sighed because she hadn't meant for him to find out this way. She turned and Zep was standing in the doorway, already dressed for his shift in jeans, a Guidry's T-shirt, and boots. Her younger brother would have done well if he'd gone out to Hollywood. He had the looks and he knew how to make an entrance. "I should talk to you, Zep. There's something you should know."

"That Wes is Luc's biological father?" Zep asked, taking the seat next to hers. "I've known that since before he was born."

"How would you know?" Remy asked. "She didn't tell me for years. I thought only Mom knew."

"I know because I know my sister," Zep replied. "There's no way Sera fools around with some married man, and if it had been anyone else, she would have demanded the man support his kid. Also, I remember what happened in the weeks before Wes lost his damn mind and joined the Army. No offense, brother."

Remy waved that off. "Hey, I went into the Navy because I didn't have anywhere else to go. I would have been perfectly happy with running Beaumont Oil if I'd been that kid. I understand what it means to be expected to continue a family business."

"I think the situations are pretty different. You always loved this place. You always wanted to run it, and you had a great relationship with Pop-Pop." Zep looked over at her. "Wes had some serious issues with his dad. So did Angie and Cal. Cal still hates the old man and he's been dead a couple of years, so I don't see time changing his feelings. Anyway, I remember Wes tried to come back and see Sera, but she asked Mom to tell him she wasn't there. So I knew something had happened. Then Wes up and left town like he couldn't stand the thought of being here. I know I'm more famous for my good looks than my brains, but I can put two and two together."

All these years he'd known and kept her secret. "Why didn't you say anything?"

"I figured if you wanted to talk to me, you would," Zep admitted. "If Wes had lived, he would have come home to an ass kicking, but he didn't, and it was obvious you decided to raise Luc on your own. So I supported you. I don't need to know everything to know I love you, sister. I don't need to be in on the secret to help you keep it. And now I think I might have to fight Harry. Remy, I'm going to need some help. He's way bigger than Wes was."

She brushed away tears. She had her family. Luc had them, too. They could get through anything if they were together, and she needed to start trusting that. Her mom was crazy sometimes, but she would do anything for her kids. "I don't want you to go after Harry. He's just being Harry."

"Can he be someone else for a little while?" Zep asked. "Someone with less training and muscle?"

Her brother always made her smile. "Don't worry about

Harry. It's Celeste we need to prepare for. She'll be the one who comes after me."

"Are we sure about that?" Zep asked. "I'm not saying she won't want to see Luc, but is it all that bad to have a rich-assin grandparent? Celeste isn't Ralph. I know she's been nasty to Sera from time to time, but she loved her kids."

That was a big part of the problem. "Yes, I'm worried she'll love Luc so much she'll decide she can raise him better than me."

Zep's eyes flared. "You honestly believe she'll come after you for custody?"

"I think it's a possibility I should be prepared for. The truth of the matter is this is one hundred percent my fault and I need to deal with it. I should never have gotten involved with Harry knowing who his family is. I was crazy about him and I convinced myself it wouldn't be a problem. No one's ever connected Luc to Wes. Well, no one who mentioned it to me." She was thankful her younger brother knew how to keep a secret. "I should have gone with my first instinct and stayed away from him altogether. I should have fixed up the house and sold it and moved."

That had Zep sitting up in his chair. "Moved? Why are we even talking about you moving?"

Remy looked to their brother. "What did you expect her to do? I've always worried that the situation would come to this. Luc is growing up and he's going to ask questions at some point. He'll go to school and hear the rumors."

"Kids can be mean." She knew she couldn't keep him from all pain, but she had a choice in this. "And we don't know that he'll continue to look like our side of the family. I think he already has Wes's eyes. It was always a matter of time before I had to make this decision. It looks like my time is up."

"You do not have to move," Zep insisted. "I'm not going to allow freaking Celeste Beaumont to run my sister off."

"What are you going to do about it?" Zep had even less money than she did since he spent it all on beer.

"I could seduce Celeste, make a tape of it, and then we blackmail her," Zep announced triumphantly.

Remy's eyes rolled. "You're going to seduce Celeste Beaumont?"

Zep gave him a shrug. "Haven't found a woman yet I couldn't seduce. Maybe we should get Momma in on this. And Miss Marcelle. Those two always have a plan, and it's never bad to have the mayor on our side. Can't Sylvie make a law or something?"

Her brother hadn't paid attention in government class, and bringing her mother into it would turn the whole thing into some sort of long con. She couldn't hide behind them anymore. "The best thing I can do now is make sure I'm ready for when Harry tells his aunt."

"Why does Harry have to tell her at all?" Remy asked. "Did you ask him not to?"

"Of course I did, and he said he wouldn't, but I know him. He's not going to be quiet forever. At some point he'll decide it's for the best and he'll say something." Had she kicked him out too quickly? Should she have talked to him longer? Tried to make him understand? "I'm hoping he holds off long enough for me to get Guidry Place finished and ready to sell."

"I wanted you to keep it," Zep said with obvious regret. "I really thought you would like running a B and B. Of course, I kind of thought Harry would be there with you."

She had, too, and that had been the most foolish thing of all. "Well, I've got to grow up."

"This didn't happen because you're not a grown-up,"

Remy corrected. "You love him, don't you? We can't help who we love."

"And he can't help who his family is, which is why I should have stayed away." She stood up. "If you don't mind setting up a call with Lisa's brother-in-law, I would appreciate it. I know this probably isn't his area of expertise, but he might be able to give me some pointers. And tell me how much it's going to cost."

"Don't worry about that." Remy stood and she was enveloped in a bear hug. "We'll make it work. You don't have to do anything you don't want to, and that includes selling the house. I know you're panicked right now and it feels like you don't have choices, but you do."

"I could choose to kill Harry." Zep was still frowning. "I feel responsible because I talked to him about asking you out. I might have been pulling some strings like the ruthless manipulator I am."

She rubbed a hand over her younger brother's shoulder. "I always knew your plots would get me in trouble."

A forlorn expression crossed her brother's face. "I thought he would be good for you."

The sad part was he had been. Harry had been good to her, good for her. He would have been good to Luc, but she couldn't expect him to choose her over his family. She wouldn't even want him to. Remy was going on about how they couldn't kill Harry, and Zep argued that he could take them all out if it meant protecting their sister.

At least she wouldn't lose them. Her family would have to be enough. Now she had to see Harry one last time and let Celeste know she'd been right all along. She didn't belong anywhere near the Beaumont clan.

* * *

Harry stared at the gazebo. It was almost done and it looked perfectly lovely, ready for the wedding reception. Picture perfect, but then looks could be deceiving. He'd figured that out.

After all, he'd firmly believed he and Sera would make a perfect couple, and it turned out he was very wrong.

She hadn't been available when he'd gone to pick up Shep. He'd gone to her house ready to sit down and have a long talk about what had happened. He'd spent the entire night working in the shop because he couldn't sleep. He'd done what he always did when he was restless—he'd worked and let the problem run through his head. But instead of getting to talk to Sera, he'd been left with Delphine, who'd had a whole lot of questions about why he hadn't stayed the night. Sera hadn't told her anything, merely left saying she needed to talk to Remy and had to get to the restaurant before the rush.

He'd gotten to see Luc, who'd been toddling around behind Delphine. The little boy had hugged Shep before letting the dog go. Luc had asked him if he was staying and if he wanted to play, and it had taken everything he had to tell the kid he had to go.

What the hell was he going to do if Sera wouldn't even talk to him? How had things gone so wrong?

"You finished." His cousin walked out, a smile on her face. "I can't believe how good it looks. I've seen it in old pictures, but this is amazing. It's everything you promised. You do good work, Harry."

Yes, he could put this old gazebo back together again, but a relationship was a different thing. He couldn't patch up what had happened with Sera unless he agreed never to tell his aunt her secret. He wasn't sure he could do that. And now that he was done, he had no idea how he would pass the time. He could sneak over to Sera's at night and be her construction elf. "I'm glad you think so."

Angie ran her manicured fingers over the smoothed and finished wood. "You also work fast. I was a little worried when I found out Sera put you to work on Guidry Place. I thought you might neglect this job in favor of hers. Not that I would blame you. When I first met Austin, I neglected a lot of things. Luckily my fiancé is an excellent tutor or I wouldn't have graduated, and then I doubt my mom would have offered me a job at Beaumont Oil."

That was a surprise. He hadn't heard anything about Angie working with the company. "I thought you were going to take some time before figuring out what you want to do."

She shrugged, walking up the steps and glancing out the back, which looked over the rose garden. "That's just a way of saying I got a fancy degree and now I'm going to get pregnant and never use it again. Austin and I talked about it and we want to put off starting a family for a while. I want to work. I want to learn."

He could still hear Sera telling him the same thing. She wanted to learn. She wanted to be the one to handle code enforcement. She wanted to be a good partner.

Was he making the wrong decision? Had he handled her all wrong? At the time, it had seemed clear-cut, but he'd spent the whole night thinking about Sera's position and why she would have done what she did. It was more complicated than he'd made it in that moment.

And he'd been blindingly jealous of his cousin. His dead cousin. He couldn't pretend. He'd thought about the fact that Wes had been the one to give her Luc. He'd then turned around and been volcanically angry because it was apparent that Wes had taken advantage of her.

He'd been overly emotional, and it might have cost him the woman he loved.

"I think that's great," he replied, putting his tools up. He closed the box and started back to the shop. He needed some more time alone, needed to think about how he could convince Sera to give him a second chance. "Though you should know Cal hates it there."

"Cal only hates it because he hates managing people. He likes marketing and design." Angie strode beside him, not at all picking up his hints that he wasn't in the mood for company. "He's not the right person to be CEO, but Mom can't see it."

He stopped because this was the most open he'd heard Angie be about everything that was going on at Beaumont Oil. "You think you are?"

"One day I will be. Not now. I don't have any experience because I didn't work there the way Cal and Wes did during the summers. My father thought I should be learning more feminine things like how to dance ridiculous old dances that haven't been popular in years. I can fox-trot with the best of them. No, I'm not the person who can keep things running. My mother is. She should take the CEO position. She's got the votes for it. Right after my father died, she bought back some of the stock he'd sold off. We have a fifty-two percent stake in the company because Mom said you should never cut it too close."

He hadn't known his aunt had made a move like that. "I thought the family always owned the majority share."

"Dad sold some stock off to cover a couple of bad investments he'd made," Angie admitted. "It wasn't much. Four percent, but it took us under the majority vote threshold, and my mother doesn't like to take chances. That's one of the reasons I think the company would be safe in her hands. I'm hoping she'll finally see that I'm the one who should eventually take over. Cal will be far happier if he can have some freedom. He's actually quite a good artist, but he wasn't allowed to study it. The only reason Dad let him major in marketing was he'd decided Wes was his real heir."

"Well, I hope you get what you want." He stood outside the door of the shop. Now that he was done with the gazebo, he would have absolutely nothing to do if he wasn't working with Sera. He had to find a way to make her understand it was okay to tell his family about Luc.

Or he had to take the chance that she would never want to tell and live with it.

One way or another, he couldn't let her go. Not without a fight. He was in love with her.

Angie started to turn but faced him again. "I know that you think you want Sera, but I hope you've given some consideration to what we talked about the other day."

When she'd tried to warn him off. "I assure you, I've thought about very little except Sera. I was up most of the night thinking about whether or not we can work it out. We had an argument. You might get your wish."

"It wasn't my wish." Angie's shoe tapped on the concrete drive. "What did you fight about?"

He couldn't tell her. He'd promised Sera and he meant to keep that promise. This wasn't his secret to tell. "It doesn't matter. I've got to find a way to make it up to her."

He didn't even really understand what he was making up, and that was the problem. He hadn't listened enough the night before. He should have been patient and listened to her.

"Or you can understand that there are some things that aren't meant to be. I know it seems like Mom is coming around on Sera, but at some point we'll all find out this has been a major manipulation," Angie said with a sigh. "I love her, but she's never going to accept someone like Sera in our family. She would have done anything for Wes. Anything but accept Sera. He tried to date her for years."

"She wasn't interested in him that way." Now that he was thinking about it from her perspective, of course she'd been scared. He still wasn't sure it was right never to let Luc know a part of his family, but he could see how she'd been in a corner and hadn't known how to get out.

"She had to have been at least once," Angie said under her breath.

He stopped because that had been said with a fine edge of distaste. "What did you say?"

She shook her head. "Nothing. I'm sad you got hurt. It's exactly what I was trying to avoid. It's why I talked to you about it when I realized you were getting serious."

But that wasn't what she'd said. Her arguments against his relationship with Sera hadn't been about him getting his heart broken. No. They'd been about Luc. And that vaguely disgusted comment about Sera and Wes had been about Luc, too. He felt his eyes narrow. "You know."

"Know? Know what? I'm afraid I didn't know you'd broken up. It hasn't made the rounds yet, but it will. Everything does around here."

"No. Not everything. Some of you are good at keeping secrets." He should have known there was something more behind Angie's reaction.

Angie's face flushed and she turned, moving toward the house. "I don't know what you're talking about."

He dropped his tool kit and followed her. "I think you know exactly what I'm talking about."

She moved into the house, opening the kitchen door. "Let it go, Harry."

He couldn't. This secret was costing him the best relationship he'd ever had, and he wanted to know why it wasn't as secret as Sera seemed to think it was. If Angela knew, perhaps his aunt knew as well and didn't care. Sera had told him Celeste looked down on her. What if they all knew and he'd blown up his relationship for no reason? What if Sera had been scared for nothing?

"I'm not going to let it go," he said, pushing through the door despite the fact that Angie had let it close. "You know about Luc. It's the only reason you would have spent all that time trying to convince me to stay away from the kid. Why else would you care? You know who Luc's father is."

Angie gasped and her whole body went stiff as Celeste walked in from the dining room.

"Why would Angie know about Seraphina's child's father?" Aunt Celeste set her purse on the kitchen table and took them both in. "They're not close. And I assure you if my daughter knew some gossip, she would tell. Despite the angelic looks, she's not perfect."

"I thought you were going into the office," Angie said, a flush staining her cheeks.

He saw the moment Celeste decided something serious was going on. Her gaze sharpened and he knew it was all about to go wrong.

"I was joking with Angie," he said, forcing the lie from his mouth.

Unfortunately, he was a terrible liar.

"No, you weren't, and Angie isn't joking about anything. She's gotten caught. You think I don't know that look, my darling girl?" Celeste said. "What's going on and what does it have to do with the boy? It's a boy, right?"

"It's nothing." His stomach took a deep dive but he tried to smile. "She was ragging me because it turns out Sera broke up with me last night."

That got Celeste's brow rising. "Why would she break up with you?"

He shrugged, trying to play it off. "She decided I wasn't a good bet."

"You're an excellent bet and she knows it," his aunt countered. "I was with her yesterday. She didn't show a single sign of breaking up with you."

"Maybe that's why she did it." Angie seemed to find her spark again. She squared off with her mother. "Maybe you scared her away."

Celeste snorted, a sound she managed to make elegant. "If it was easy to scare that girl away, I would have done it years ago. No, she was perfectly fine when I dropped her off at that old jalopy of hers. She was happy we found a dress we could agree upon. She's got too much love for glitter, that one. I'm not having everyone at your wedding infected with glitter. Now, what's this about Luc's father, and if someone tells me it's Darth Vader, I'm going to get really angry. Yes, I know about movies, and you weren't talking about one."

"She doesn't think I would be a good dad." He had to make this right, had to throw his aunt off the scent.

"That's not what you said. You said Angie knew who Luc's father is. Is he coming back to make trouble?" Celeste sighed. "Because you'll have to deal with that."

"He can't . . . That's not the problem," Angie said with a frustrated huff. "Mom, it's Sera's problem, and now that she's broken up with Harry, we should stay out of it. Why don't you come out and see the gazebo? Harry finished it and it's beautiful."

"No." Celeste seemed to be thinking the problem through. "I think one of you can tell me what's going on or I'll call Seraphina myself. Maybe that's the best way to do this. Something's wrong and you two are lying to me. Why would Sera break up with you over Luc?"

The situation was getting out of control. He heard the doorbell ring but ignored it because everything was falling apart. "Aunt Celeste, I need you to let me handle this. It's my relationship on the line, and it's a private thing between Sera and I."

"How old is Sera's son?" Celeste asked, her face going stony. "When was he born? I want the date."

The door to the kitchen swung open and Annemarie walked in followed by the one person he didn't want to see. Seraphina had a garment bag over her arm along with the shopping tote she'd brought in the day before. She looked weary but resolute.

"Mrs. Beaumont," Annemarie said. "You have a guest."

Sera seemed startled. She obviously hadn't expected a crowd. "I'm sorry to interrupt. I was going to drop this off with a note. I didn't think anyone would be home except Harry." She turned to Celeste with a long breath. "Mrs. Beaumont, I want to thank you for the kindness you showed me yesterday, but I've decided it's best I don't attend any of the festivities. I'm going to finish my house and then perhaps we can talk about what a fair price would be. I'm probably leaving Papillon."

She was leaving? He stepped up. "Sera, we need to talk."

"No," Celeste interrupted. "She needs to tell me when her son was born. I want the truth and I want it now. If she doesn't tell me the truth, I can get legal."

The bag dropped from Sera's hand as quickly as the color left her cheeks. She turned his way. "What did you do?"

Lost it all. That's what he'd done.

chapter fourteen

Sera felt a fine tremor in her hands. Celeste's face was perfectly blank, but her eyes stared right through her.

"Sera, I'm so sorry," Harry was saying.

She ignored him. It didn't matter. She was here and it was everything she'd feared. Since the day she'd realized she was pregnant, she'd known she would have to deal with the Beaumont family one way or another. If Wes had come home, he probably would have used Luc to convince her to marry him, and that would have been a whole other fight. When he'd died, she'd put this off and hoped for the best, but deep down she'd always known she would have to stand alone. Oh, her family would be behind her, but she had to do this on her own. "Luc is my son. I don't have to tell you a thing about him."

"Is Luc my grandson?" Celeste's words came out measured, but Sera had learned that sometimes a snake was perfectly still right before it struck.

"Luc is my son and he has my name. I had him by myself and I'm raising him by myself."

"Only because his father died," Celeste said between clenched teeth. "Tell me I'm wrong."

There was a bit of sympathy for Celeste inside Sera's heart. She had no idea how she would handle it if anything ever happened to Luc. Devastation. It was what Celeste had to be feeling. The poor woman was a tidal wave of grief and rage, but Sera wasn't going to let herself drown in it no matter how much sympathy she felt. "I don't know what would have happened if Wes had lived, but I do know Luc is my son and I get to make the decisions concerning him. Now that Harry has made one of those decisions for me, I suppose we should talk."

She could be calm and rational.

"It wasn't Harry's fault," Angie said.

He might not have said the words out loud, but Celeste had figured it out because he knew. All this time she and Angie had managed to keep the secret. Harry had known for one day and it was already out.

"We'll do more than talk," Celeste commanded, ignoring Angie completely. "You'll bring that child to me. You've had years with him. You took him from me. You stole years of my grandson's life."

"And what would you have done if I'd come to you?" Sera asked, surprised at how steady her tone was. The time she'd spent with Celeste had made her understand the woman wasn't all bad. And Wes had truly loved her.

"I would have done what I'm going to do now. I would have called a lawyer and asserted my rights." Celeste proved she could revert to her normal, controlling, arrogant self with ease. "You should leave my house now and get ready because I'm coming for you, Seraphina. You need to think seriously about every move you make because I will have private investigators watching you twenty-four-seven."

Sera felt her stomach clench. She'd known there would be lawyers, but she hadn't thought about investigators.

They would be tracking her, trying to find ways to make her look bad.

"Aunt Celeste." Harry started to move in front of Sera, as if he could protect her.

He couldn't. He'd gotten her into this mess, but he was going to find out he couldn't do a damn thing to get her out.

Celeste simply moved around him. "They'll watch your every move and document it until I can prove you're an unfit mother."

She heard Harry gasp in shock.

Poor Harry. He was going to lose a lot today and she felt for him, but she couldn't ease his soul now.

"I'm not. I'm a good mother," she replied, holding her ground. "And I assure you my son loves me. I'm willing to talk about letting you get to know him if you can be reasonable, but if you think I'm giving you control over anything concerning him, you're insane."

Celeste's lips curled into a smile, but it was a hateful thing. "You might be a good mother, but you can't keep a job. You're aimless and without means. And how about the people you surround your son with? Your momma is half crazy and everyone knows she's practically a criminal. And your younger brother is a menace."

"Zep is all right," Harry argued. "He's actually a pretty good guy. Cal likes him, too. And Delphine is a good grandmother, a good person."

"She's not the kind of person who should be influencing my grandson," Celeste insisted.

"And you wonder why I kept this secret?" Sera shook her head. "I didn't tell you before because I knew this would happen. I knew you would come after Luc, and I know how Wes felt about his father."

Celeste pointed her way. "Don't you tell me a thing about Wes. You don't know any of us."

Sera was calmer than Celeste, and that seemed to give her the upper hand. "But I do. I know you far better than you can imagine because I was the one who listened to Wes talk about never being able to please his father. I was Wes's friend, sometimes his only friend, for years. Most of our childhood. Even after you shipped him off to private school, he would always call me. Wes talked about how scared he was of his dad and how he would smack him every now and then to toughen him up."

"How dare you say that. That is a vicious lie."

"Then it's a lie your son told," Sera replied.

Celeste raised her hand, but Harry stepped in between them.

"Don't you dare hit her," Harry growled. "I don't even know who you are right now. Sera, I think we should leave."

Celeste seemed to get control of herself. "Harry, you can't possibly think of taking her side. Do you understand what she cost this family? She lied to all of us."

"She didn't lie to your daughter. Angie knew," Harry pointed out.

Harry seemed determined to betray every single one of her secrets today. Angie had backed against the wall as though she could hide from the truth.

Celeste turned to her daughter but simply shook her head. "I will deal with that later. Seraphina, get out of my house before I call the sheriff in to haul you out. The next time I see your face will be in court. You broke my Wesley's heart. I won't let you break his son."

"You know what, Celeste, I just realized something. I'm not afraid of you." It came to her in a great rush. Being around Harry had changed something inside her. He'd gone through so much and had let go of his bitterness. He'd moved on. Yes, he'd proven he couldn't love her the way she needed him to, but loving him had finally convinced her she wasn't broken at all. "I've been stuck in a moment for years. I hid because I didn't know myself anymore. Maybe I never did. Maybe I spent my whole life allowing my existence to be defined by relationships. I was a daughter, a sister, a friend. To Wes I was an aspiration, an escape. Then I was a mother and a rumor and a joke. I'm more. I don't know exactly who that is, but I know one thing. I'm not hiding anymore. You want a fight, I'll give it to you."

She turned and started for the door. The funny thing was, it had been Celeste who pointed out that she acted like a mouse. She needed to be a lion now. Her son and her family needed her to be fierce. She had options and Remy was right. She didn't have to go out quietly.

"Sera, I didn't know she would react that way." Harry came through the door behind her, rushing to keep up as she made it to the front of the house.

She rounded on him. At least they were alone now and she could speak freely. "I told you she would."

He started to reach for her but pulled his hands back. "I should have listened to you. I'm sorry."

There was nothing she wanted more than to go into his arms and throw the whole situation at him, to beg him to fix things for her. She'd done it all her life, but it was time to stand on her own. "I'm sorry, too. I think we could have been good together."

He stood in front of her, his shoulders so broad and that face of his beautiful in a way that had more to do with his soul than his appearance. Harry's goodness was stamped on his face. "We still can be. I choose you. I would always have chosen you."

His words were sweet, but he was rewriting history. "No, you wouldn't have. You didn't. Do you think I could trust you again after this? I even know why you did it. I knew you would do it. I went to Remy's to plan how I would handle Celeste after you told her. I just thought I would have more time."

"It was a mistake."

"And now I've got to deal with it. You heard her. She will do everything she promised. She will have private investigators looking for every misstep I can possibly make. Hell, they'll probably make up a few. I bet she can pay for that. I've got to be perfect, and that means no dating. I'm sure she's already trying to come up with a way to use you to make me look bad."

"I won't ever let her do that," he promised. "In fact, I'll do something that will prove I'm on your side. Marry me. Let me adopt Luc. She won't be able to break up a family."

Here he was again, trying to be Captain America and save the day. He felt bad that he'd put her in this position, and he would do anything to fix it. It wasn't a feeling that would last forever. "But, Harry, we're already a family. We don't need a man to complete us. It would have been nice for Luc to have a dad, but he's surrounded by love no matter what your aunt says. I think I loved you, but I have to focus on me now. I can't marry someone out of obligation or guilt. Your family should know that by now."

It was precisely why she wouldn't date Wes.

"I love you. That has to mean something."

It meant everything to her, but she couldn't trust him. What happened when he decided his aunt was right? And how could she trust that he truly loved her? He was feeling guilty, and that would be powerful to a man like Harry. "I'm sorry. I have to go. I've got to find a lawyer."

And hold her son. It was time to protect her family.

A volcanic rage threatened to boil up from deep inside Celeste.

How dare she. How dare that little tramp keep her grandson from her? How dare she steal that last piece of Wesley.

Wesley. God, what had he been hiding from her?

"Mom?"

Her daughter's voice broke through the roiling anger. Her daughter. Angela. She remembered holding her and cuddling her close. How she'd looked up at her like she was the most important thing in the world.

Her daughter had known. "Why?"

She couldn't look at her yet. She had to find some control. It had been a near thing when Sera had stood in front of her, telling her lies. She'd felt the need to strike out, to create a physical manifestation of her rage. She'd wanted to smack that smirk off her face.

Except there hadn't been a smirk there. Sera had stood up for herself, and if she wasn't wrong, there had been a hint of pity in her enemy's gaze.

Yes, that was what she'd truly wanted to erase.

"It's complicated," Angie replied quietly.

Now Celeste turned and took in her daughter's face, how pale it was. Well, it was good she at least felt some guilt at what she'd done. "I don't care how complicated it was. You lied. You betrayed this family and I want you out."

Angie's eyes flared. "What?"

"You heard me." She didn't care. It was time to call on the numbness she was so used to. It had been cracking through the ice she'd built up—that was the trouble. She'd found a place where she didn't have to feel, and that had saved her. Wes's death had broken it all apart, and she'd only recently begun to come out of it. She'd thought it was safe, but it wasn't. "You have a fiancé. You can go to him, but you should tell him you won't get a dime out of me. And you can certainly not expect me to pay for your wedding after what you've done."

The door swung open and Harry strode in.

"How could you do that?" Harry asked. "How could you stand there and tell Sera you're going to take her son away from her? That was horrible. Do you know what you did to her?"

"She doesn't care," Angie said, her voice weary. "She's got a piece of Wes back. None of the rest of us matter now. You should know that she's disinherited me, and I'm homeless. I'm sure she'll move Luc right in and go back to having a child she can worship. Oh, and my wedding's off."

"You betrayed me. You betrayed this whole family," Celeste accused her before turning to her nephew. "And you . . . I brought you in. I treated you like family, and this is what I get?"

He simply shook his head. "If this is the way you treat family, I don't want any part of it. I always wondered why you never brought us here to meet you. I think my mom thought you were ashamed of us. But I know the truth now. You were ashamed of you. At least you should have been. How proud your own parents must be of you. You got the money, Aunt Celeste, but you damn well sold your soul for it. Angie, I'll help you pack up what you need. I'm not staying here, either. I wouldn't want to taint my aunt's perfect household."

"Her empty household," Angie added. "She should know that when Sera needs a character witness, I'll give it to her. I'll get on that stand and explain why I think Luc is better off not setting foot in this house."

"How can you say that? After everything I've done for you?" It defied imagination.

Angie's eyes rolled but there were tears in them. "What have you done, Mom? You were far too busy worrying about Wes to give a damn about the rest of us."

"Wes needed more than the rest of you. He was sick." Why couldn't anyone seem to remember how close they'd come to losing him? Yes, she'd paid more attention to Wesley, but he'd needed her in a way the others didn't. He'd been so frail. She'd sat by his bedside and prayed to anyone who could hear to save her little boy. Then she'd spent years waiting for it to come back like a shadow she couldn't outrun. That fear had attached itself to her and darkened everything else.

"And he got better but you never did. You never once forgot that you could lose him. I understand that. I just wished you'd given a damn about the fact that I was alive," Angie argued.

"So you kept Wes's son from me because you wanted attention?"

Angie took a long breath before she replied. "No, I kept him from Dad. When Sera first came to me, she was planning on telling you that she was pregnant and Wes was the father. I told her not to. I did it because I knew Wes wouldn't have wanted his son raised anywhere close to our dad."

"I know Ralph was hard on you." She wasn't a complete fool. She'd known how ruthlessly belligerent her husband could be. "I tried to intercede where I could, but I didn't have much sway with him. If I'd divorced him, we would have had nothing. My mother-in-law would have made sure I didn't get custody. I would never have seen you."

"I think I heard you threaten Sera with the very same thing." Harry looked at her like he couldn't stand to be in the same room. "Guess you learned a lot from your mother-in-law."

She felt her hands clench, her whole body tensing at the accusation. "I am not her. She was a monster."

"From where I'm standing, you've got the claws and fangs for it. Good-bye, Aunt Celeste." Harry turned and walked out.

Angela stared at her for a moment. "If you're wondering why I didn't tell you after Dad died, it was a combination of fear and longing. Fear that you would behave exactly like this. Longing because for once in my life, you saw me. For once I had a real mom, and I loved it. Even when you hated my clothes and my shoes and my posture, I thought you still loved me. I was wrong. Good-bye, Mother. I'll get a ride with Harry since technically you own my car. You can have all the clothes, too. I think it's time I started dressing to please myself."

Maybe Celeste had been hasty. Her daughter's words sliced through her. She'd never meant to make Angie feel unloved. It was just that Wes needed so much. Angie had always seemed strong. Cal had been handsome and on the right path. Wes had a brilliant mind, but his body had almost failed him once. She had to be vigilant because he was supposed to be the one to lead the company—therefore the family—into the future.

But that didn't mean she hadn't loved her other children.

They were wrong and she was right. They would come to see it her way. They had to.

She heard the door close and was left alone in the magnificent house she'd given up everything to have.

chapter fifteen

❧

Harry looked around the sad motel room and sighed. It had only been a week or so since he'd stayed in a room much like this one with Sera. Even at the time he'd known how pathetic and run-down the place was, but somehow she'd made it seem cozy. He'd held her all night in that motel and he'd been at home.

But without her, this place was completely different. Without her, everything seemed dull.

Still, at least the desk clerk hadn't blinked when he'd asked about his dog staying with him. The man had asked for a pet deposit, gave him the key to Room 4, and sent him on his way.

Shep stared up at him with accusatory doggie eyes, like he knew something had gone wrong with his world and exactly where to put the blame.

"I'm sorry." He was even apologizing to the dog now. Those words didn't seem to mean much. He might be saying them for the rest of his life. He hoped he had someone to say them to.

He checked his phone for the four hundredth time in the last couple of hours. Nothing. She hadn't answered his texts or voice mails. If he didn't give her some space, she might put a restraining order on him.

He dialed her number one last time. It immediately went to voice mail. "Hey, Sera. I know you don't want to talk to me right now, but I need you to know that I'm here. I want to help you in any way I can, and if that means leaving you alone for a while, I'll do that, too. Just know that I promise to keep my phone charged in case you need me." He took a long breath because these might be the last words he ever said to her. "I love you, Seraphina."

He disconnected the call and sat on the bed, utterly at a loss for what to do.

There was a knock on his door and he opened it, praying it was Sera since one of his many messages had left her instructions on where he was in case she wanted to talk to him.

Instead it was Angie. She had been true to her word, going up to her room only to grab the bag she hadn't un-packed from her girls' trip. She'd left everything but that one bag and her laptop behind. She was still dressed in the slacks and blouse she'd been wearing earlier, looking very much like the wealthy young lady she was . . . had been. She looked totally out of place with the singular exception of the six-pack of beer dangling from her hand. That beer was cheap, and she'd probably gotten it from the run-down convenience store across the street. "Hey, cos. You want to drown your sorrows with me? I got us a sweet spot right by the pool."

"Ang, that pool is green," he pointed out.

She shrugged and turned toward the tiny, filthy pool that sat in the middle of the concrete parking lot. "It's said that when the fading light of day hits it just right, it's a little like the aurora borealis of Southern Louisiana. I don't think many of our citizenry know what that really is."

He followed her because she was not in a place to make the best decisions. Three beers in and he might have to haul her out of said pool, and that would take a biohazard suit.

This town did need a nice B and B.

Angie lowered herself onto the rickety poolside chair and popped the top off the beer, holding it his way. He took it because he could use one, and no matter how upset he was, he couldn't leave his cousin alone. She'd lost everything.

He'd lost everything.

"Why didn't you fight harder?" Angie asked. "You know you didn't willfully tell my mother a thing. She overheard us and made a calculated guess. You didn't mean for that to happen."

He'd gone over and over it in his head and come to one conclusion. "It doesn't matter if I meant for it to happen. It doesn't matter that I thought Aunt Celeste wasn't in the house. I chose to follow you inside and continue the argument. It was my fault. If I'd backed off, she wouldn't know."

Angie sighed. "Or if I'd answered you instead of running. I guess it doesn't matter now."

"Have you called Austin?" Harry asked after she went silent. "You don't have to stay here. I could drive you into New Orleans. It would give him something to do.

Angie shook her head. "No, I don't want to interrupt him. He's having a boys' night with some of his friends. I'm not dropping this on his lap when he could be having fun. Let him have one more night before he realizes how screwed up my family is."

"Are you worried he'll be upset?" After all, Austin had thought he was marrying a woman with a powerful family and access to the Beaumont money. He seemed like a nice guy, but appearances could deceive.

"About the money? No. We'll have to adjust some of our

plans, but he really does love me. He'll be angry with my mom. I don't know how he'll feel about me keeping that secret, though."

"You didn't tell him?"

"Nope. I didn't tell anyone at all."

Shep walked up to the water's edge, sniffing and then running back like something would come up and bite him. The creature from the unchlorinated lagoon. He'd been thinking of talking to Sera about how nice it would be to put a pool in at Guidry Place. If she was going to keep it and run it as a B and B. There was a perfect place to put a pool and outdoor kitchen.

"I'm sorry, you know," Angie was saying.

"About lying to your mother?" His opinion on the subject had changed quite suddenly. He was incredibly grateful this hadn't happened when Sera was pregnant. "I'm glad you did now. Sera told me what would happen and I didn't believe her."

"No, I'm not sorry about that. I did what was right at the time. I genuinely believe if she'd told them when she was pregnant, it could have been a tragedy. No, I'm sorry for lying to you, and that it ended up the way it did. I was actually surprised Sera was willing to date you. She's been so careful. She must have really cared about you."

It had felt like more than caring. It had felt like love. "Will your mom do it? Will she go after Sera?"

"I suspect she will," Angie said before taking a long swig of beer. "You have to understand Wesley was her chief concern in life. He was sick for a long time. Then he proved to be the smartest of all of us, and Dad decided to hand him the keys to the kingdom because Cal wasn't serious enough and I was born with ovaries. And I think in some ways you were right about what you said to her. She can tell herself she wasn't close to her sister because her Texas relatives were poor and that they might embarrass her, but I think she was ashamed of what she'd become. She complains about losing a few years with Luc. I got to meet my aunt and uncle once. Once. Isn't it funny how the things we're most outraged by are the things we do ourselves? We are born into a state of hypocrisy in this family."

"So Sera wanted to tell them?" He tried to put himself in her shoes. She'd been young and alone and scared.

"She didn't realize how bad it would be. Wes had talked to her about how our dad treated us all. He never hit me, but he would slap Cal and Wes from time to time when they annoyed him or he thought they needed to toughen up. We never told Mom."

"Why?"

"What would she have done?" Angie asked, sounding weary. "That's the sad part. I do understand her position. She was right about one thing. Dad would never have allowed her to have custody, and Mom couldn't trust anyone at the time. Armie is a great sheriff, but he's only been here the last couple of years. The sheriff before would have told my mom that it was a family matter and she should deal with it herself. I do understand her. I also know I should have told her after Dad died, but I didn't. I didn't because I knew what would happen. If I'm honest, part of it was selfish of me."

"You wanted her attention." It wasn't a question. Everything he'd learned about his family in the last few weeks had taught him how hungry Angie was for someone to see her. But then he thought Cal had some issues with that, too. Being a Beaumont, he'd discovered, wasn't as easy as it seemed.

"Like I told her, it was good to have her with me. I know she loves me. Honestly, I know this whole 'I'm disinherited' thing won't last all that long. My mother shoves all her anger down. It was what she was taught to do. But she never, ever vents it, so every now and then it explodes. That's what you saw today."

"You think she'll forgive you soon?" He hated the thought of them feuding. "The real question is, can you forgive her?"

"I don't think she'll frame it as forgiveness. She'll wake up tomorrow and realize what she's done and then she'll call me. She'll tell me she's going to let the wedding go through because there would be a lot of talk if we didn't. And everyone knows she doesn't like talk." Angie sighed. "I understand that, too. I remember hearing my grandmother tell me I had to be better since half my DNA wasn't up to snuff, as she would put it. Anything my mom did was criticized. She's got her reasons."

"There's no reason for her to threaten Sera like she did." He wouldn't listen to any excuses about that.

Angie reached out and put a hand on his. "I know."

There was the sound of a car pulling into the lot and slamming into a parking spot. He recognized his cousin's Benz, though Cal wasn't the only one who got out of the car. Zep Guidry was with him, and his stare went right to Harry as he slammed the car door.

"Angie, is what Zep is telling me true? I got a call from Quaid Havery asking me to talk to Mom." Cal was still in his suit, as though he'd driven straight back from New Orleans. "Has she lost her damn mind? Should I call a doctor? Quaid said she was suing Sera for custody of Luc and that you're not welcome in the house anymore. I stopped by to talk to Sera but got him instead. Zep says it's true. Luc is Wes's kid."

Angie offered him a beer. "Yes, it's true, and it's true that I've known all this time and I kept it a secret. Even from you." She turned her eyes to Zep. "Is Sera okay?"

Zep's hands went to his hips, his whole stance aggressive. "She's crying her eyes out."

His stomach clenched. "I would like to talk to her."

Zep shook his head. "Talk to your aunt. Get her to back the hell off. That's all you can do for Sera now. I thought I would beat up Cal here when he called me. He's way smaller than you, and honestly, he's got a soft middle."

"Hey," Cal began.

Zep ignored him. "But now I think I'll do what I should have done in the first place and give you the ass kicking you deserve."

He should have known Zep would come out swinging. "Come on, man."

"Don't you think I can't do it. I've been in many bar fights." Zep's fists were clenched, his jaw tight. "I might be smaller than you, but I won't play fair, and if I can kick that leg off you, I will use it to beat you."

Zep understood neither how a C-Leg worked nor how Harry himself worked. He glanced down to make sure Shep wasn't about to defend him. Nope. Shep was on his belly, his eyes closed as if to tell the human he was on his own. "I'm not going to fight you. That's the last thing Sera needs. I love your sister. I would do anything to help her."

"Then why would you betray her like this?" Zep asked.

"I didn't mean to. I didn't mean to tell my aunt anything at all." But he'd walked into that house and asked the question. He hadn't thought Celeste would be home, but it was still his responsibility.

"He found out I knew." Angie settled back in the chair. "Sera hadn't told him that part. He also didn't know Mom was home. It was a weird situation. Then Sera showed up and Mom went nuclear. I'm disinherited and my wedding will now be held here. At the No Tell Motel. Can't they change the name? It's going to look really bad on the in-vites." She glanced up at Harry. "See, that's what I mean. The minute I tell Mom I've moved the wedding here, she'll cave."

"You're not getting married here," Cal said.

"No, I know exactly what will happen. Now I have to decide if I let it happen. She'll try to walk this back without ever acknowledging what the problem is."

"That sounds about right. She's going to come around. She doesn't understand why you did it." Cal took the seat by his sister. "I do. I would have done the same thing. I wouldn't have let my father raise another child. I can fix this."

"You shouldn't even try. It's too soon. If you go talk to her tonight, you'll be the next one cut off." Angie's lips curled up slightly.

Harry moved toward Zep. If he threw a punch, Harry would take it. "I'm serious. I didn't mean to hurt her. I love her. I offered to marry her."

"Excellent. We can have a double wedding right here. Split the cost," Angie announced.

He ignored her. "I'll do anything it takes to make this right."

Zep's anger seemed to deflate. "So you're just a dumbass? You didn't pick your rich family over my sister?"

"I walked out on my rich family. I was never looking to make money off my relationships," he explained.

"He's serious about that," Cal chimed in. "Mom offered him a cushy job with the company and he turned her down."

Like he wanted to be at a desk all day. He couldn't stand the thought of it. He wanted to be working on something he cared about. Like Sera's house. Like building a family with the woman he loved. "What can I do?"

Zep sighed and shook his head. "I don't know. She's so

upset, and she's scared about money. If Celeste is already talking to a lawyer, we've got to find one for Sera. Everything Remy has is in the restaurant. Momma has the house we live in. It's worth something. I've got a couple of thousand saved up, but that won't go far. I'll see what I can get for my truck."

"You don't have to sell your truck." Cal looked to his friend. "I'm going to figure this thing out."

"I can't wait for that," Zep replied. "We can't take the chance that things don't work out. Your mother has a lot of pull with people in this parish. She knows judges. We know shrimpers. Who do you think is coming out on top of that argument? No, we need a lawyer and we need a good one."

"So what she needs now is cash?" Harry didn't know any lawyers. Every word out of Zep's mouth threatened to make him sick. Sera was somewhere terrified that she could lose her child and he was sitting in a motel parking lot drinking beer and being useless.

"I thought she recently came into a bunch of money," Angie pointed out. "And I'm not with Cal on this one. I don't think Mom will change her mind about the kid."

Zep stepped up to the pool, staring down into it as though there were some answers there. "Sera can't use the money Irene left her, and she can't sell the place until it's ready. It's all written into the will. If she doesn't follow the rules, she loses the whole thing. She's in a bind."

There might be something he could do about that. Sera had been moving slowly because she was trying to do as much of the work herself as she could. It would go much faster if she hired crews.

Or found a couple who owed a man who loved her.

"She's not going to need anything because I'm going to talk to my mother," Cal promised. "I have to go back to my place in New Orleans. There's something I need to get. But I'll fix this. I promise."

"What do you have that could possibly fix this?" Angie asked.

"You're not the only one who has secrets, sister." Cal pulled his keys out of his pocket. "Come on, Zep. I'll drop you back at home."

He watched as Cal and Zep walked away and then got on the phone. It was time to do some work.

Celeste looked up at the clock and realized it was long past her bedtime. Not that she would sleep. The house was far too quiet.

Where was her daughter? Had she called her fiancé? Had Austin come to get her?

She'd been hasty. If what she'd said was true, Angie might have truly feared that Ralph could be bad for the child.

But why hadn't Angie told her? Did her own daughter think she was such a terrible mother that she didn't even deserve to know her grandchild?

Luc. It was not what she would have named him. Beaumonts had a set of names that were acceptable. They didn't have Cajun names.

It was cute. What would Wesley have wanted? Wesley probably would have given in to whatever Seraphina demanded. Foolish girl.

But not a damn gold digger. No. She couldn't even comfort herself with that. Sera hadn't used her leverage to try to force Wes to marry her.

What had happened between them? What had gone so wrong that Wes had needed to put half a world between him and Sera Guidry?

It didn't matter. Nothing mattered except making sure that Luc Beaumont had everything he deserved, and it certainly wasn't growing up in a family whose only asset was a bar.

She heard the security alarm go off and then someone put in the code to silence it. She stood because it was late and she wasn't expecting anyone. Had Angie come to plead her case? Had she realized how hard the world could be?

If she had, then they would talk like adults. She'd had time to think about it and calling off the wedding would simply cause a scandal, and that wasn't good for anyone. She would pay for the wedding and it could proceed. They had a lot to work out, but Angie was her daughter. She couldn't simply cancel her daughter's wedding at this point.

Perhaps Harry would still come to the wedding and she would have a chance to talk to him again.

"Hello, Mom." Cal walked into the room, tossing his jacket over the back of the couch. "I thought you would likely be up plotting."

Well, of course Cal was upset with her, too. He'd made it plain on the phone earlier that he'd thought she'd lost her mind.

"If you've come to talk sense into me, you've wasted your time." She turned back to staring at the fireplace. It wasn't lit, but there was still some comfort in it.

Every Christmas they would light a fire—even when it was warm outside—and they would open their gifts. Then after Ralph and her mother-in-law had gone to bed, she would sneak down and give her babies some candy since Beaumonts didn't eat candy.

"I didn't come to talk sense into you. I can't do that. But I think he can." He moved around until he was standing in front of her, holding out a piece of paper.

Celeste stared at it. "What is that?"

"Wes's last letter to me. I got it about three weeks after he died."

Emotion threatened to well and she realized there was something so much worse than rage.

Grief. Never-ending, soul-splitting grief.

"He wrote to you?" He hadn't written to her. He'd been silent those months before his death.

Cal seemed to understand she wasn't going to take the letter from him. He took a step back and sank into the chair opposite her. Those chairs were supposed to be for the man and lady of the house. Instead, for years her mother-in-law had been the one to sit beside Ralph.

Would she have done that to Seraphina if Wes had insisted on marrying her? She rather thought Sera would have had a problem with that.

"We got close when he went to college," Cal admitted. "I think he liked the freedom of being outside of Papillon, though obviously there were things he missed here."

"Sera. Do you understand their relationship? I've been going over and over it in my head. Why choose Harry over Wes? I know Harry's more handsome, but Wes wasn't bad to look at."

"You view marriage as something entirely different than the rest of the world. Or maybe just our little part of it. You married Dad because he could give you a better life. Sera wanted to build a better life with someone she truly loves. She viewed love as the foundation of that life. Your foundation was money."

"You have no idea what it's like to go hungry." She didn't need this judgment from her son. "You were given a car on your sixteenth birthday. My mother took the bus to work every day, and my father worked on cars he could never afford. When he could work. You don't know what it means to not be able to afford medication, to wonder if you would even have a roof over your head. That was my childhood. You think yours was rough."

"I wasn't making a judgment, Mom. I truly wasn't. I haven't walked in your shoes, but you don't understand what it feels like to be in Sera's."

That was the irony. "I don't know about that. We both got pregnant by Beaumont men, and neither of us was married at the time."

Cal's lips curled up in what seemed to be a truly delighted grin. "Everyone knew I wasn't a preemie. I weighed damn near nine pounds." His grin faded. "I know you had it hard. You had to make choices based on how you grew up, on what you valued."

"I know you won't believe me, but I valued you. I valued your sister and your brother."

Cal was silent for a moment. "Yeah, I know."

He didn't believe her. "Cal, I love you."

"I do know that. I know that Wes was sick, and even when he was well, you kept waiting for it to all go to hell with him. I can't understand what it means to potentially lose a child, but I bet Seraphina is feeling that right now."

"Don't you compare the two. Your brother had cancer." A horrible thought struck her. She sat straight up. "Has anyone checked Luc? It could have passed to Luc."

"Sera knows. She always knew Wes had a childhood cancer." Angie stood in the doorway. She'd changed into jeans and her hair was up, her face scrubbed clean like she'd gotten ready for bed before she'd decided to come over. "When she came to me, I made sure she understood that Luc's doctor should know. He's perfectly normal and she knows what to check for."

Celeste could suddenly breathe again. "I'm glad to hear that."

"Mom, I think you should read this letter," Cal said.

"What you and your brother had to say to each other is between the two of you." She didn't want to know what Wes had said about her.

"He didn't leave because of Sera, you know," Cal continued. "He left because Dad told him he was a disappointment. Dear old dad told him Sera couldn't love him because he wasn't a real man. Dad liked to play us off each other."

"I told you not to let him do that." She'd always gone in behind Ralph and tried to make things better.

"It doesn't always work that way," Angie said, taking a seat on the couch. "It's hard to not let it get to you. Read the letter, Mom. I read it. I'm glad I did. Wes died and it wasn't your fault. It wasn't his fault. It wasn't Sera's. He died because sometimes the universe isn't fair. Maybe he died because he'd learned what he needed to and it was time to move on. I don't know, but I do know he wouldn't want us to tear each other apart. I love you, but it's time to let go. Not of Wes. We don't ever have to let go of the love we felt for him. But you have to let go of your fear and your guilt. I need you to because I want to be a part of your life. One day I want my kids to know their opinionated, obnoxious, intelligent grandmother. I can't do that if you put the mother of Wes's child through hell because you have to punish someone."

"She should have . . ." Should have what? Should have married a man she didn't love the way Celeste herself had?

She took the letter from Cal. She owed it to her living children to do as they asked.

Dear Cal,

I've settled in and the surprising thing is, it's not so bad. I like it here. Not Afghanistan, exactly. It's hot and I've already had an encounter with a snake in the la-

trine that will stay with me the rest of my life, but there's a peace I didn't expect to find. Like I'm doing something good for the first time in my life. I know Mom is crazy worried, but I think I'm getting to know who I am without all the crap that comes with being a Beaumont. Like we've talked about. It's good to make something from the bottom up. No one here cares what my family does. They don't give a damn about money or how far back I can trace my ancestry. All that matters is how I do my job, how I take care of my friends. I know everyone expects me to come around and let Dad get me out of here, but I'm staying.

I met someone. She's a translator. Her name is Mila. I've only been close to her a few weeks, but I already know she's the one. I want to bring her home with me when I finally get some leave. We'll see. It could be difficult.

But that brings me to something I need you to do for me. Check in on Sera. I did something I want so badly to take back. She came to see me and things got out of hand. I said some things I had no right to say to her, reacted in a way I definitely shouldn't have. For so long she was an escape for me. I didn't treat her the way she deserved to be treated and I want to make sure she's all right. Tell her I understand. Ask her to forgive me. I scared her the last time we were together. It's why I'm not writing her. I gave up the right, but let her know I would love to hear from her.

Let her know how much I care about her and what a good friend she's been to me.

Tell Mom not to worry. I know she's angry at me for leaving, but she'll see. I'm happy.

I'm free.

Tell her it might be time for her to be free, too. I

think she should divorce Ralph, and damn the conse-quences. We'll all support her. Tell her I love her, too.

And send some snacks, brother. Give Mom and Ang my love.

Wes

Her hands shook as she finished the letter. He was free. Free of pain and crushing responsibility. Free of the con-fines of his name. Tears dripped from her eyes and the world went blurry.

"Mom, it's all right to cry. It doesn't mean you're not strong," Angie whispered. She'd gotten to her knees and her eyes sheened.

"If I start," Celeste managed to gasp.

"Then I'll hold you until you stop." Angie's arms came around her.

"What if I don't?" But she was losing the fight. She could feel all the pain and anger, all the worry and guilt, all the sorrow welling inside her like a tidal wave.

Cal's voice was hoarse as he came to her other side. "Then we never let go. Not ever."

Celeste sobbed, and sometime in the hours of grief, she finally found some peace.

chapter sixteen

❧

Seraphina listened to the message for what felt like the thousandth time:

Hey, Sera. I know you don't want to talk to me right now, but I need you to know that I'm here. I want to help you in any way I can, and if that means leaving you alone for a while, I'll do that, too. Just know that I promise to keep my phone charged in case you need me.

He never kept his phone charged. He forgot about it. He got lost in work and never could remember the little things like charging his phone. He'd been on his own for so long he often didn't think about checking in, didn't understand why people would worry about him.

But he always remembered to bring her coffee when he was making his own. He remembered to come into whatever room she was working in and he would kiss her and tell her how great she was doing.

He remembered the big things. He remembered her.

Luc giggled from where he was playing and suddenly stuffed animals were being thrown in the air.

She had to smile her son's way. He didn't have any idea that the world might implode, and it was her job to make sure that it didn't, to ensure his world was as normal as possible.

He stopped and his head twisted, eyes looking around for something.

"Momma, where Shep?" he asked, leaning against her legs.

Tears sparked but she tried to hold them back. Over the time she'd been with Harry, Luc had gotten so close to the big, loving German shepherd. "He's with Harry, sweetie. You know he's not ours. He's got to be with Harry."

"Harry come here," Luc replied simply.

She shook her head. Maybe it was time to look for a dog of their own. "He's working."

It might be the first time she'd lied to her child.

"Hey, hon. How are you doing?" Her momma walked in, carrying her purse. She'd gotten up early, put on her nicest caftan, tucked her hair in a vibrant scarf, and left. She'd been out most of the morning. Probably plotting with Marcelle on how to fix the situation by calling the spirits of her ancestors or something.

She wasn't sure how the ghost of Pop-Pop Guidry could help unless he'd studied law in the great beyond. Though Aunt Irene as a ghost would probably be a pretty effective scare tactic since she'd been so good at it in life.

"I'm cursing myself for every single choice I've ever made," she admitted.

Her mom put her purse on the table. "Call him."

"I can't do that and you know why." If she called him, she would give in. She would break down, and she couldn't afford a breakdown right now. She had to be strong.

But did Harry make her weak? Or merely lend her another kind of strength, the strength that came from truly loving another person.

"I don't understand it," her mother admitted. "I know I

agreed with you last night, but you'd had a day, and some-times a mother simply must agree with everything her baby says until such time as she can be a bit more reasonable. He made a mistake. He's a man. He's going to make a ton of them. Your father made them, and he was practically a saint."

She glanced up at her mom. It was easy to write off Delphine Dellacourt Guidry as a "character," as they would say in these parts. As she'd gotten older, she'd embraced her kooky side with gleeful abandon, but there had been a time when she was a widow with three children to take care of. There had been a time when her mother had cried herself to sleep every night because she missed the man she'd loved. "Do you wish you hadn't met him?"

Her mom sat down next to her, a sympathetic look on her face. Her mother might not be the psychic she often claimed to be, but she was good at knowing how her daughter felt. "Honey, it's never wrong to love someone. Never."

"I've done exactly what I said I wouldn't. I confused my son." She should have followed her own rules. Never introduce a boyfriend to her son until she was serious about him.

Except she'd been very serious about Harry. Yes, it had happened fast, but she'd been in love with him and worried she wouldn't ever feel that way again. All of her other relationships had been nothing compared to Harry. No one had ever made her feel more herself, stronger, more confident than she did when she was with him.

"It wasn't wrong to bring him in. You had to figure out if he could love your son, and he did," her mother said quietly. "And honestly, at some point you were going to have to tell Celeste. I might not like the woman, but Luc has the right to know where his father came from, who that side of his family is. I know you made the decision for good reasons, but at some point Luc's will has to come into play. I assure you he will want to know. And to answer your question, no. I'm not going to say that in my grief at your father's passing I didn't have moments where I wished I hadn't hurt the way I did, but I never would have taken it back. I got three amazing kids out of that relationship. I got a home I love. And I got him. I got to know him, to adore him, to know what it means to be genuinely loved. That's what the pain means. I loved and that's what we're put on this earth to do, baby girl. We're here to love, and that's why you need to think about forgiving Harry."

Would the need to cry ever abate? She felt like she'd been close to tears every second since that moment she'd known she would have to leave him. "It's not that simple. I think Celeste will use any relationship I have to further her claims. I don't even know what her claims are, but I know she'll twist what Harry and I have. She'll say we moved too fast, that I brought him into Luc's life too quickly."

Her mom nodded. "I know that's what she'll do, but don't you worry about it. Marcelle and I are going to put the whammy on that woman."

Sera groaned. "Don't even start on that."

"It'll work, but if you insist on using the legal process, you should know that Remy's talking to that lawyer in Dallas today," her mom said. "I ran by the restaurant to check in, and your brother's going to set up a phone call with him."

"Good." Talking to Lisa's brother-in-law would settle some of her nerves. At least she would know what kind of position she was in.

There was a knock on the door.

Luc had gone back to rolling around with his stuffed animals. Soon she would have to make his lunch and put him down for a nap. Despite the fact that she should go out to Guidry Place and work on the flooring downstairs, she might lie down with him. She wouldn't sleep, but at least she could hold her baby and remind herself what mattered.

Hadn't Harry mattered?

Her mother stood. "I'll get it. It's probably Sylvie. Marcelle will have talked to her by now and she'll be worried."

So everyone would know soon. She loved Marcelle, but the woman ran the salon, which was a hub for gossip. The only place worse was Guidry's, where the whole town met to eat, drink, and talk about everyone else. Once Sylvie knew, Hallie would know, and they would be over here trying to help. They would be good friends to her like they'd always been, but all she wanted was Harry.

By this time tomorrow she would have a lot of eyes on her, and some of them would be paid by Celeste Beaumont to make reports.

"How dare you show up on my doorstep," she heard her mother say with a vehemence she reserved for the IRS and those who didn't believe in the power of tarot cards. "You know I have a gun."

"It's Louisiana, Delphine," a familiar voice said. "We all have guns. Well, if you're going to shoot me, do it. I don't have all day, and honestly I could use the eternal rest."

She would know that dry, the-world-is-my-never-ending-annoyance voice anywhere. Celeste was here. She was on her porch, and a sudden terror threatened to take over. Was she alone or had she brought the police? Would she walk out there and Armie would explain he didn't want to do it, but he had to take Luc into custody? Would a CPS worker be waiting to haul her little boy away?

"Seraphina, I need to talk to you," Celeste said in a raised voice, as though she knew exactly where Sera was. "I'll be on the porch when you're ready. You seem to have a place to sit out here. I'm prepared to wait however long you need."

She heard heels clicking along the front porch and then a squeaking sound that let her know Celeste had taken a seat on one of the rockers.

Her mom shut the door. "She can wait for all of time. I wish we had sprinklers so I could turn them on and see if that old biddy would melt."

"She's alone?" There didn't seem to be a bunch of county workers waiting outside. She could see through the big window that only Celeste's Benz was in the drive.

"Yes, she's alone. She's got a bunch of files, though," her mom explained. "I could make a homemade flamethrower with a lighter and hairspray and burn them all up. She'll have to have her lawyer write it all again. That might be a good way to deal with this. Kill her with legal fees."

Her momma trying to MacGyver her way out of the situation was a bad idea. "I'll talk to her. It's best to find out what she wants now rather than later. Watch Luc. He needs his lunch soon."

This likely wouldn't take long. Celeste would barrage her with paperwork—none of which she would sign until a lawyer explained it to her—and then she would be on her way.

And maybe she would call Harry and talk to him. It wouldn't be wrong to talk to him and make sure he was all right. He'd been through a lot, too. He'd thought he'd found some family, and now they were lost to him.

He was alone. Did he have to be? Celeste would come after her one way or another. Maybe he was right. Maybe they should face her together.

But not now because she'd sent him away. Now she had to face the enemy alone.

She walked out, unwilling to put this off for another second. She pushed through the screen door and onto the porch. Celeste was wearing her normal designer uniform. Sheath dress, fussy jacket, pearls she could clutch.

That wasn't fair. Everyone needed their armor. Even Celeste.

"What can I do for you?" She wasn't going to take the low road. She was going to act like the woman she wanted to be. Kind. Patient. Reasonable. Strong. "If you need to serve me with papers, I'll take them."

Celeste looked up and for a moment she seemed shocked that Sera was standing there. She looked down at the thick stack of papers in her hand. They were in a manila folder that looked like it had seen better days. "This? No. This isn't legal paperwork. It's medical records. Wesley's records. I kept them. I know. I could have put them on the computer, but it's hard for me to change."

Now it was Sera's turn to be surprised. "Are you worried about Luc?" She found the rocker beside Celeste's and sat down. "Luc is healthy. I promise I don't miss appointments, and I've talked to our pediatrician about the cancer Wes had. We watch him carefully."

"I thought it might be helpful in case anything came up later," Celeste said, her hands clutching those records like they were a lifeboat. "Luc might need them down the line. You should know that high blood pressure runs in my family. I had a grandfather who died of colon cancer. He needs to be careful about that and perhaps screen earlier than normal. I detailed some of it this morning, and I'll send you an e-mail if I remember anything else."

Celeste's voice was perfectly steady, but there were tears streaking down her face.

It was the one thing Sera could never hold out against. She gently put a hand on Celeste's. "Or you could call or come by. This does not have to be a war between us. I wouldn't mind Luc having another grandmother. But that's all you can be. You can't make Luc a replacement for Wes."

Celeste nodded, but her eyes were on the yard. "I know that. Sera, I'm sorry. I have spent a lot of time recently pondering my own hypocrisy. I've been in your position and I blamed you for not making the same choices I did. In many ways, your choices were braver than mine, and I didn't appreciate that mirror I had to look into."

She could rail at this woman. She could demand more than a simple apology, and there were plenty of people who would say she had the right. Having the right and using the right were two different things. In the face of Celeste's emotion, she couldn't find righteousness. She could only find compassion. "I wasn't in your shoes. I don't know what I would have done if I had been."

"Somehow I think you would have found a way to deal with it better than I did."

"I think your kids turned out pretty great. Isn't that what matters at the end? I know Wes loved you."

For the first time, Celeste turned her way. "Did he hurt you that night? Is that why you wouldn't talk to him again? Please understand I'm so sorry I blamed you for Wes leaving. I know why he left now. He wrote a letter to Cal. He said he was so sorry for what he did to you that night. He asked Cal to check in on you, to tell you how sorry he was, but Cal didn't actually get the letter until . . ."

"Until after Wes died," she finished because Celeste couldn't. "And no, he didn't hurt me. He got very angry with me, but we just made a mistake."

"I think he wanted to take responsibility for that. He wanted to let you know how sorry he was," Celeste explained. "I had Cal make a copy of the letter for you. It's here."

She opened the folder and pulled out a single sheet of paper, handing it to Sera.

She took it, and a few moments later, she was crying, too.

"I did love him," she whispered, staring down at his handwriting. "Just not the way he needed."

It was Celeste's hand that came out to cover hers this time. "You loved him the only way you could. We can't make people love us. God knows I tried. I was hoping that when you feel comfortable, I might get to see Luc. Here, of course. I would like to spend time with him."

Sera nodded and so much of her worry fled. Celeste might be wearing her uniform, but it looked like she'd taken off the armor and laid down her weapons. "Of course. You can see him today if you want. We're about to have lunch. It's sandwiches, though. Momma made a ham and we're having leftovers. You don't have to eat."

"I would love to," Celeste said quickly. "My dad used to fry us up bologna for sandwiches. My sister and I would watch him. It was the only thing he could cook, but I think they tasted better because he would talk to us while he did it. He would tell us funny stories." She dabbed her eyes with a tissue. "I think one of the hardest things about all this self-revelation has been the realization that I miss my parents so much. They're all gone. My mother and father and sister. I'm the last one left."

"That's got to be so hard." Sera wasn't going to point out that she had her kids and now Luc. No. It was a different kind of pain, being the last one left, having no one who remembered what it meant to be a child in that particular world. She relied on her brothers, and Celeste hadn't had anyone.

"Well, I made some decisions that kept me apart from

my sister," she admitted quietly. "I want a different life now. I need you to know I've called Quaid and told him to stop everything I asked him to do yesterday. I'm not going to come after you. I promise you that, and I promised my kids. I would like to be a part of Luc's life, but only in a way that enhances it. Not in a way that causes chaos. I've got some thoughts on that, but we can talk later."

Sera was willing to listen. "Okay."

Celeste was silent for a moment and Sera let it lengthen, let them find some comfort between them.

"Sera? Did you read the part in Wes's letter about the young woman? Mila?"

She nodded. "I'm glad he was happy. Do you want to look for her? My brother knows people who could help."

"I know what happened. Cal looked for her after he got that letter," Celeste explained. "She was in the vehicle with Wes. They were heading into a town where there had been some trouble, and she was going to translate for them. She died with the rest of them. I'm going to reach out to her family."

"I'm so sorry to hear that." Sorrow welled inside her again, fresh and purer than the day Wes had died. There was a sweetness to it now, a knowledge that she didn't have to hide anything, that one day if they met again, there would be no anger between them.

Celeste's face was red with emotion, and it made her beautifully human. "Sera, is it wrong for me to hope that maybe she's with him? That she's looking after my boy?"

"I hope she is. I hope he's happy." Sera let her tears flow for the young man she'd cared about, for the father Luc would only know from stories. And she held Luc's grandmother's hand, their fingers intertwined, lending each other strength.

This was how it always should have been. Two women

who loved a man, each in her unique way, sharing their grief, making it easier for the other. If Celeste wanted to, they could make an incredible team in loving that man's son, in helping Luc have the future she was sure Wes would have wanted him to have.

"Everything okay?" her mother asked quietly. She stood at the doorway, Luc in her arms.

She'd definitely been listening. Sera stood, wiping her eyes and smiling at Luc. "It's all good. Luc, baby, come here. I want you to meet someone. This is your other grand-mother."

Luc's smile went wide and he held his arms out because that kid had never met a stranger, never held back on offering his boundless affection.

Celeste stopped, looking at him, her gaze soft. "He has Wesley's eyes. Oh, he's so beautiful."

Her mother handed him over and Luc studied his new grandma, his hands coming up to brush away her tears. He leaned forward and kissed her like he was kissing away a boo-boo.

Celeste held him close and looked Sera's way. "Thank you."

"I'm already Mom-Mom," Delphine declared. "You have to be Mimaw. You look like a Mimaw. Or Granny."

"Grandma will work fine," Celeste said, shaking her head. "Or Luc can call me anything he wants to. Hi, baby. You're so precious."

"He is." Sera relaxed for the first time in what felt like days.

"Well, come on in," her mother said. "I'll make us some sandwiches and I've got sweet tea."

"Thank you, Delphine," Celeste said with a tentative smile. "You know, I was thinking we could have your book club out at Beaumont House."

"Now why would I do that?" Her mother's hands had gone to her hips.

"Because while Ralph wouldn't get the stick out of his backside long enough to enjoy anything, he did put together an amazing collection of wine," Celeste pointed out. "There's over three hundred bottles. They're expensive, and I was never allowed to drink one unless Ralph was trying to impress some politician or businessman. I think the Papillon Literary Society should tear through it."

Delphine had perked up considerably. "Yes, I think you would fit in quite nicely."

Celeste kissed the top of Luc's head. "Here, I'll follow you in a moment, but there's one more thing I need to talk to Sera about."

Delphine took Luc back. "It better be to talk some sense into her about that nephew of yours."

She walked into the house, and Celeste turned Sera's way.

"You have to give Harry another chance," Celeste said. "He loves you. He didn't betray you. Won't you please call him?"

Harry. Sera could now go to Harry with no fear. "I will. In fact, I'll go talk to him now if you don't mind. I know where he's staying."

Celeste agreed, and within moments Sera was on her way to the motel, her car shaking with every mile.

It died as she made it to the parking lot of the hideously titled No Tell Motel. She tried to turn the engine over but got nothing. Frustration welled as she put it in park and set the brake. At least she'd made it there.

But she didn't see his truck. It wasn't sitting outside the room he'd told her he was in.

Had he gone out to grab some food? Or maybe gone to her house? She wouldn't put it past him to sneak in and do some work even though she wasn't talking to him. She knocked on the door in case he'd parked somewhere else, but no one answered.

"You looking for the big guy?" The man who owned the motel had a bag of trash in his hand as he walked out of the room next door. "He checked out. Said he was leaving town. Sad because that dog of his might be my best guest."

Harry was gone? "When did he leave?"

"Not more than ten minutes ago." The man nodded toward the road. "Looked like he was taking the highway toward New Orleans."

"Thanks." She raced back to her car. It was possible she could still catch him if she got him on the phone and asked him to come back.

And that was the minute she realized this time she was the one who'd forgotten her phone. She'd rushed out, eager to see Harry and put things right between them, not bothering to remember that her phone was on the charger and not in her purse.

How had she let that happen? She needed to get to him. If she let him leave, he might not come back, might not let her say all the things she needed to say to him.

She heard the crunch of gravel as a car pulled up beside her. She glanced over and saw a black SUV with white lettering that proclaimed it represented the Papillon Parish Sheriff's Office. The tinted window lowered and Deputy Roxie King sat in the front seat in her crisply pressed uniform, her eyes behind a pair of mirrored aviators.

"Hey, Sera, you all right?" Roxie asked in her no-nonsense manner. She gestured to the back of her vehicle. "He saw you and made me pull over to check on you. I told him you're a grown-ass woman who doesn't need her baby brother making sure she doesn't hang out at hooker motels, but he can be annoying."

She looked in the back, and sure enough, Zep was there, his hands in cuffs.

He grinned her way, holding them up. "Don't worry about this. It's a thing between us. I think it's her way of flirting."

Roxie's expression didn't change but Sera could practically feel the woman's eyes rolling. "He's got a warrant for unpaid parking tickets."

"I told you why I can't pay them," Zep insisted. "Sera needs a lawyer."

"No, I don't. Celeste came by and she's dropping all legal action," Sera explained. They still might be the solution to her problem. "I came to find Harry, but he just left. He was on his way out of town. If he leaves, I won't know where he is, but I can't go after him because my car broke down. I think I still might be able to catch him. He was on the road toward New Orleans."

"Come on, Roxie. This is true love on the line," Zep argued. "You know you can catch him. You can turn the lights on and make this happen. They'll have to name their first child after you and everything. And I'll have money to pay those parking tickets."

The gorgeous deputy's lips curled up slightly. "Well, I wasn't doing anything important anyway."

"Hey, I'm a dangerous criminal." Her brother was frowning.

"Only to beer bottles and hot wings." Roxie opened the door and got out, moving to let Sera in the back. "Let's go find your guy. Hey, you want me to arrest him? I bet he would look good in cuffs."

Zep's eyes flared. "I knew that was why you did it. I make these things look good."

"No," Sera said, sliding in beside him. Unlike her brother, it was her first time in the back of a parish vehicle.

Roxie apparently liked to keep it clean and cozy. "I want to hug him. I want to tell him I love him."

Roxie got into the driver's seat and flipped on her siren and lights.

Sera prayed she found him in time.

Harry stopped his truck and simply stared for a moment.

There was a gator in the middle of the road. A massive gator. He'd been in Papillon for a couple of weeks, and he knew they were in the bayou, but this was his first real look at one on a road, and this bad boy was taking up most of it. He was laid out lengthwise in what looked to be the sunniest part of this particular stretch of road.

Shep barked beside him, his big paws on the dash as though he was ready to go into battle.

If the gator heard all that canine aggression, he didn't show it. The only movement was a slight shift of his big tail. It seemed to be missing the tip, the powerful thing ending in a stump.

He and the gator had something in common.

He glanced down at his phone. He had a couple of texts that stemmed from yesterday's bat signal.

Sam would be able to spend a few days next week shoring up the indoor stairs, while his friend Lena was a master painter, and he'd helped out with her mother's place after it flooded. She'd promised to bring her sister and swore she would work for gumbo. He had called a plaster expert, a roofer, and two sisters who specialized in restoration.

He had a small army ready to knock Guidry Place into shape in record time and they'd all agreed because somehow, someway, in all those jobs he'd done, all the drifting, he'd managed to make a little family for himself.

He would offer it all to Sera. He would show her what he could give her.

But he had to get to New Orleans first because his roofer friend was coming in this afternoon and he needed a ride. He would pick up Jimmy and rush back to hopefully find better lodgings for all of them. His aunt had left a message, but he couldn't listen to it yet.

Of course, he might be sitting here forever. How long did gators nap?

He honked his horn but the gator simply opened and closed his mouth as though yawning and settling in.

What the hell was he supposed to do? The gator was across the entire road, and the sides sloped off at a pretty steep grade, so there was no going around him. The last thing he needed to do was roll his truck. He needed every dime he had to help Sera.

He sat for a little while, staring at his phone and then back at the gator. Shep had stopped barking, curling up on the seat beside him like if the gator got to nap, at least he could do the same.

His phone buzzed again. A text from his aunt.

I'm sending a gift your way. Stay put, my darling boy.

I'll make this right.

What did that mean? Knowing his aunt, it meant she would have Luc Guidry installed in Wes's room at Beaumont House by tomorrow. And what would she send his way?

He wished he hadn't promised Sera he wouldn't call her. It had been the right thing to do. If she said she wanted space, not giving it to her made him every bit as bad as all the other jerks she'd ever dated, but he wanted to call her, to hear her voice.

He wanted to find out if there was any way she could

ever forgive him because there was no way he could forget her.

Shep's head came up two seconds before Harry heard the sirens in the distance.

He sent a small thanks to heaven because the sheriff probably knew how to deal with a gator. He glanced back, and sure enough, a parish vehicle was tearing up the road. The big SUV stopped and the door came open and the deputy swung herself down and opened the passenger door.

Sera slid from the back, her blond hair tumbling around her shoulders.

She was here. She was here and so was a gator. She was running toward the gator, who might swallow her petite form in two quick bites.

He had that door open in no time flat, and shut it before Shep could rush out and try to battle the reptile.

Sera was running his way.

"Baby, there's a gator. I need you to get in the truck." He wasn't about to let her get hurt.

She stopped a few feet from him, looking around to get a glimpse. "Oh, it's no big deal. That's Otis. He's a sweetheart. I need to talk to you."

"Come on, Rox," a deep voice was saying. "She's my sister. Shouldn't I be allowed to watch her get her man?" He looked up as the deputy hauled Zep out of the back by his cuffed hands. "Hey, Harry!"

He was so confused. "Why were you in a squad car? Sera, if my aunt had you arrested . . . Deputy, you can't arrest her. She's done nothing wrong."

Roxie tipped her hat his way. "I wouldn't arrest Sera. She's obviously a saint since she's this one's sister and he's still alive. I would have surely killed him by now."

"Roxie gave me a ride because I went to the motel but

you weren't there," Sera said, looking up at him with big blue eyes. "My car died in that parking lot. I don't think I can resuscitate it. I think it finally passed on."

"But I called you. Why didn't you call me back?" What was she here for? And were they really doing this in front of the deputy, her brother, and a basking gator?

Shep barked from inside the car.

And his dog.

Sera bit her bottom lip. "I forgot my phone. After Celeste came by, I had to see you. I didn't want to talk to you on the phone. I needed to see you in person."

"Celeste came by?"

She nodded. "She wanted to bring me Wes's medical records. She apologized and then she begged me to give you a second chance, but it's not really a second chance. We both made mistakes, but I love you, Harry. I can promise you I won't ever keep a secret from you again. Please don't leave town. If you're still upset, I'll give you time, but I think we should work it out here."

Leaving town? "I wasn't leaving." It was time to come completely clean. He'd meant to spring it on her when everyone was already here so she couldn't turn him down. "I know how much you need to get the house done and keep costs down, so I called in a bunch of favors from my friends in the industry. I need to pick one of them up from the airport. I know I didn't talk to—"

He couldn't finish his sentence because his arms were suddenly full of Seraphina. She threw herself at him, her arms circling his neck, and there was no way he didn't catch her. He held her close, wrapping his arms around her, and her words finally sank in. "You love me?"

Her smile warmed his whole world. "I do. I love you and so do Luc and my mom."

"I don't love you, man, but I approve," Zep yelled.

Harry ignored her brother. All that mattered was her. "I love you, too. I want to stay here in Papillon and build something real with you. You should understand that I'm going to keep asking you to marry me, Seraphina Guidry."

"You should understand that I'm going to say yes," she replied. "But I come with some baggage."

"Yeah, I'm going to want to make your baggage mine, too. I want to adopt Luc, and I'll want to give him siblings."

She held him tight. "I want all those things, too. I want a whole life with you."

He kissed her in the middle of the road, that kiss promising everything he wanted to give her. A life with love and family, a man who would always stand beside her, who would be the best husband, father, and friend he could be.

He kissed her until he heard a mighty snort and realized they couldn't get married if they were the victims of a gator attack. He shoved Sera behind him.

Her arms wound around his waist. "It's okay. He's just done resting. He'll move on now."

"You would almost think that gator knew what he was doing," Zep shouted. "Who would have thought the old guy was such a romantic? Hey, okay. I'm going to jail now, sis. Harry, you treat her right."

Roxie tipped her hat again as she shoved Zep in the back and drove off toward the jail.

He would make an interesting in-law.

He was going to marry her.

"So we're going to pick up a friend in New Orleans?"

"He's a roofer."

Her eyes lit up. "I've been wanting to learn that. Let's go. The road's clear now."

The road was clear and he could see his whole future.

epilogue

Harry smiled down at his aunt as the Rolling Stones' "Wild Horses" began to play. They were in the backyard of Beaumont House, though it had been utterly transformed for Angie's wedding. Twinkle lights made the whole place gauzy and romantic. Not two hours before, Angie had made her vows to Austin and he'd sat with Sera, Luc in his lap as he watched the proceedings.

This dance was the first time he'd had a chance to talk to his aunt in a week. She'd been crazy busy, and Sera had spent more time with Aunt Celeste than he had since there was a lot of woman-only stuff associated with a wedding. But he'd gotten to spend an awful lot of time with his little buddy. He and Luc were settling in nicely to the newly habitable Guidry Place.

"Hey, I thought you looked good walking Angie down the aisle," he said.

Celeste smiled and looked far freer than he'd ever seen her. He could see his mom in her smile. "I was surprised when Angie asked me, but it felt good."

"You're the head of the Beaumont family now," he said. "Even more since you took the CEO job."

So many things had changed in the last few weeks. He and Sera were engaged and had moved into their future bed-and-breakfast. They were still working on the place every day, but it felt so good to be creating a home. Sera was already trying out every recipe she could, and all their friends were complaining they would gain weight because it was all delicious.

His aunt had taken over the CEO position at Beaumont Oil after Cal stepped down. Her first decision was to hire her daughter. The Beaumont women would lead the company into the future.

And Cal was moving to Dallas, where he'd taken a job in marketing. He was looking forward to making his way in the world.

"I finally figured out that the name means nothing. The people are all that matter," Celeste replied. "For so long the Beaumont name felt like a chain around my neck, but you can change the meaning of a word if you try hard enough. It's a different Beaumont family, one I think my son would have loved. And my sister."

"She would be proud of you," he whispered. "She would love the fact that you are finding your real place even after all these years."

She reached up and smoothed back his hair. "You, too. She would love Sera. Speaking of Sera. I wanted you to know what I've done."

The tiniest bit of trepidation flared through him. "What?"

"When Ralph died, I took all of the stock he owned and split it three ways. I kept a third, Cal a third, and Angie a third. We sat down and made a decision. We would like very much to cull a fourth piece of stock from ours. It's Wesley's share, and we're putting it in trust for Luc."

If what she said was true, Luc had just become a wealthy

man. "That's amazing. I think Wes would have wanted that, but Luc might not want to work at Beaumont."

"He doesn't have to. It's his stock to do what he wants with. It's his legacy from his father. Well, from one of his fathers," she said. "Wes would also be happy that Sera found you. You're going to make an amazing daddy to that boy. Watch Delphine. I think she's already planning to bring Luc into those short cons of hers. That woman is a menace."

Yet he'd seen his aunt laughing with Sera's mom. They bickered and laughed and argued over their shared grandson. He'd learned to stay away from the book club because it was more like a drinking club. "I'll do what I can. Sera will be happy Luc has something from Wes."

Celeste winced slightly. "There's a little more to it, and that's why I want you to tell her. He'll need someone to be his proxy at board meetings until he's old enough. I've made Seraphina the guardian of his trust."

That made him stop in his tracks. "What?"

His aunt looked up at him. All around them couples were dancing. "Sera now has the right to vote Luc's shares. She'll be invited to all the meetings, and she's going to need to learn some of the business. It will be up to the two of you to invest what you make off the stock, but I've made sure there's a generous stipend because the trust is going to take some work. The first check is for twenty thousand."

"That's exactly what it's going to take to finish the house and get ready to open the bed-and-breakfast. Someone read my business plan. You know we were going to the bank on Monday," he said, but there was a warmth in his heart.

"Now you don't have to. And it's not a loan. It's payment for all the work you two will do," she assured him. "Unless you just want to let me vote his shares. That would be help-ful."

He shook his head. Sera would want to learn all about her son's inheritance. "I think Sera will insist."

"I do, too. She'll be a breath of fresh air at those stuffy meetings. She, Angie, and I are the only women on the board. We'll have to drag those men into the modern age."

If anyone could do it, those three could. "I look forward to it."

Celeste stepped back, her eyes on something behind him. "Well, I'm going to go and make sure your future brother-in-law stays away from the punch. I swear I would spank that boy but I think he would like it." She winked. "You two have fun, and I expect to see my grandson tomor-row afternoon. Bring Shep, too. I miss him and he makes such a good nanny."

Sera waved as she stepped up to Harry. "She doesn't really leave Luc with Shep, right? It's not like the dog nanny in *Peter Pan*."

She always made him smile. "I don't think so. I think she barely lets Luc's feet touch the ground while she's around. Dance with me."

She moved easily into his arms. "I will admit I like all the babysitting. How about we work on the house tomor-row? Specifically the bedroom."

"The bedroom's done . . ." Ah, that's what she meant. He leaned over and kissed his almost bride. She didn't mind that he wasn't the most graceful dancer. All he could really do was sway. There were plenty of people in his position who taught themselves how to dance, but he hadn't been that great before he'd lost his leg. None of that mattered because there was one place where he moved with perfect harmony. "Yes, we need to work on the bedroom. All afternoon. Come here."

He kissed her again. He had a story to tell her, but for now he let the music flow over him.

He'd roamed the world, but Papillon would be his home.

acknowledgments

As with any book, there are so many people to thank, because while I might write the words there are many people who make those words truly shine. Thanks to Kim and my team of beta readers who remember all the things I forget—Stormy, Riane, and Kori. Liz Berry helped launch this series and continues to support it in amazing ways. Thanks to the women who help me maneuver my way through social media and publicity—Jillian Stein and Jennifer Watson and her team at Social Butterfly. Thanks so much to my agent, Kevan Lyon, and everyone at Marshall-Lyon. And to the team at Berkley, including my editor, Kate Seaver, who is always there for me.

Look for the next Butterfly Bayou novel

Bayou Dreaming

Coming from Berkley in December 2020!

Ready to find
your next great read?

Let us help.

Visit prh.com/nextread